S[illegible]

Book 4 - The Telepathic Clans Saga

BR Kingsolver

Published by B.R. Kingsolver

http://brkingsolver.com/

Cover art by Mia Darien

http://www.miadarien.com/

Previous books in this series

The Succubus Gift
Succubus Unleashed
Succubus Rising

Also look for ***Broken Dolls***, a paranormal mystery with RB Kendrick, private investigator, set in the world of the Telepathic Clans

~~~
~~~

License Notes

~~~

Praise for ***The Succubus Gift***, Book 1 of the Telepathic Clans:

The novel itself is expertly written and an utter joy to read. The characters are all delightful. There were times while I was reading this that I laughed out loud, and other times when I held my breath in anticipation of what might occur. 4.5/5 stars – Night Owl Reviews

Let me just start by saying WOW, because this book completely blew my expectations out of the water and then some. The initial synopsis plot struck me as interesting, but it didn't prepare me for the utterly heart stopping onslaught of sex, violence and paranormal abilities ... a great unique addition to the paranormal/urban fantasy genre and I'd definitely recommend this to fans of the genre! It had everything I could ask for, love, sex, violence, witty banter, supernatural abilities. I am so excited to see what Kingsolver does next! 5/5 HOT steaming cups - Tea and Text
~~~

Praise for **Succubus Unleashed**, Book 2 of the Telepathic Clans:

Succubus Unleashed is a wildly entertaining novel, full of the same dynamic and enchanting characters from The Succubus Gift. The story begins at a very rapid pace and never slows down. 4.5/5 stars – Night Owl Reviews

Fabulous, fabulous, fabulous! BR Kingsolver's second book is everything I would have hoped from reading the first book in the series, The Succubus Gift. 5/5 stars – Wren Doloro

Praise for **Succubus Rising**, Book 3 of the Telepathic Clans:

Must Read - "Succubus Rising" is the third book in the 'Telepathic Clans Saga". The author pens the plot unique, original and picks up from where the first book left off. Filled with action, romance, suspense, emotions, and a touch of humor, this book will hook you in and not let you go. ... Highly recommended for all fantasy, romance fans. – 5/5 My Cozie Corner {Book Reviews}

A story of the heart and the soul in many ways which I enjoyed immensely. Quite simply five out of five pitchforks. The characters make the story, not the story making the characters. The promise of the series continues and that's so very satisfying. – Tera S. @ Succubus.net

Praise for **Broken Dolls**:

I think everyone who enjoys paranormal thrillers will love Broken Dolls. I can't wait to read The Telepathic Clans Saga. It they are anything like this book then I will love them. 5 stars - Reading It All {Book Reviews}

I loved being surprised, I loved this world, and the characters were fantastic even if some of them suck as people. Check this book out, it's a great paranormal read with mystery and humor! It's perfect. 5 Stars - Sunshine & Mountains Book Reviews

~~~
~~~

Contents

Pronunciation Guide to Names

Some of the names in this book have been Anglicized, for others:

Aine: aw-nya – delight or pleasure

Aislinn: awsh-leen – dream or vision

Aoife: eef-ya – beautiful or radiant

Beltane: bel-tane – May Day, the beginning of the summer season, a springtime festival of optimism

Brenna: bran-na – raven, often referring to hair

Caylin: kay-lin – slender, fair

Irina: ee-ree-na – Russian form of Irene

Mairead: mah-rayd – Gaelic form of Margaret

Morrighan: mor-ri-gan – Celtic goddess

Rhiannon: ree-an-on – Welsh for maiden

Samhain: so-ween – The harvest festival, now called Halloween

Seamus: shay-mus – the supplanter

Sean: shawn – Gaelic form of John

Shidhe: shee—An Irish word for the elves, another word for Clan

Sinead: shi-nayd – Irish version of Jeanne

Siobhan: shee-vawn – Variation of Jeanne

Slainte: slayn-cheh – 'Health' in Gaelic, a toast

Tuatha De Danann: - tu-a-tha de dan-an – The people of the Goddess Danu - The original pre-Celtic inhabitants of Ireland

~~~
~~~

A full list and description of the Telepathic Gifts appears at the end of the book

~~~

Forward

This is the fourth book and end of the story about how Brenna O'Donnell and her friends joined the Telepathic Clans. The action begins about two years after the end of *Succubus Rising*. After some internal debate, I decided not to make this book stand alone. It is the culmination of the previous three books in the series (actually, four books if you include RB Kendrick's story in *Broken Dolls*), and I've tried to tie all the plot lines and open questions into a final ending. There are so many of them that to provide back story on all the plot lines and characters would make the book boring for those who read the first books in the series.

That is not to say that this is the end of Brenna or Rebecca, just the end of this part of their story.

In the two years between books, Rebecca got married. Callie, Cindy and Morrighan had babies. Noel and Teresa married, had a baby, and moved to Washington. Siobhan underwent a life change, married, had a baby, and moved to London. Irina lives in New York, filling the role vacated by Siobhan.

~~~ B.R. Kingsolver

~~~
~~~

Chapter 1

A man can sleep around, no questions asked, but if a woman makes nineteen or twenty mistakes, she's a tramp. - Joan Rivers

It was that time of year again, for the April O'Donnell Group annual meeting held in London. Brenna and her closest friends flew in a week early. Four years earlier, at her first annual meeting, Brenna hadn't known what to expect. She arrived in London expecting a week of excruciating boredom, interminable presentations of reports, and having to act like an adult and a lady the entire time.

Since then, Brenna always planned her stay in London to include some holiday time. She, Collin, Rebecca and Irina were looking forward to a week of sightseeing, dining and partying.

After stowing their luggage in their suite at the O'Donnell-owned hotel next to their London regional headquarters, the group went back down to the lounge where Nigel Richardson was awaiting them.

Savoring a good British porter poured from the tap, Brenna looked up and saw her Aunt Morrighan. Her aunt was often confused with being Brenna's older sister. Morrighan walked over to their table, gave Nigel a quick kiss, and then hugged each of the Americans in turn.

"I arrived last night," she said, a slight grin quirking the corners of her mouth. Her eyes went to Collin and then to Nigel. "I was wondering if you have plans tonight," she said hesitantly.

Collin chuckled. "If you're curious as to whether I'll get upset if you take my lady out hunting, then you aren't very familiar with the kind of man who falls in love with a succubus. Do you know the term 'pussy whipped'?"

Morrighan and Nigel laughed. “Yes, we know the term,” Nigel said.

Brenna and Irina, sitting on either side of Collin, both punched him in the shoulder.

“See what I mean?” he laughed.

“Normally, I might decline just to be nice, but after a remark like that? Sure. Where are we going?” Brenna said with a wink. She gave Collin a look out of the corner of her eye. “Of course, he’s being so magnanimous because he thinks he may have a shot at an old girlfriend. Her husband’s out of town.”

To her surprise, Collin colored.

“Oh, my God,” Irina exclaimed. “You dog. Does Pia’s husband know he’s going to get cuckolded?”

“He knows we’re going to see each other, yes,” said Collin.

“Wear your bulletproof vest, boyo,” Rebecca smirked.

“Well, on that note, where and when?” Brenna asked Morrighan. “I’d like to take a quick shower, but it won’t take us long to change.”

“Where’s the baby?” Irina asked.

“Lady O’Byrne is taking care of her,” Morrighan answered. “And although I love her to death, I need some time away. She’s just starting to walk, and I’m going crazy trying to keep up with her.”

The women excused themselves to go change.

After donning a black bra and panties, Brenna wriggled into her black lace dress and pulled on the knee-high stiletto-heeled boots. To complete the outfit, she put on a black and white cameo that Collin had given her for Christmas one year.

Rebecca wore a shining silver sleeveless micro dress with a V-neck down to her naval, an enameled collar necklace and strappy stilettos. Her legs looked about six feet long.

Irina put on a white, low-cut halter sheath that hit her about mid-thigh. She added a choker of small freshwater pearls and six-inch platform heels. Brenna shook her head, not understanding how the tiny blonde could walk in those shoes.

Collin and Nigel were still sitting in the bar when the women came downstairs. They sat down and ordered drinks, smiling and preening at the compliments they received. The bar was about half full, and although it wasn't very noisy, Brenna noticed when the background conversations quieted and then died completely. She and everyone else at the table turned to see what was going on.

Striding toward them was a tall woman with copper-colored hair that reflected the lights as she moved. She wore a skin-tight green one-shoulder minidress, and the only thing more spectacular than her beauty was her bust. Her only jewelry was a short strand of large red beads with matching earrings, almost the same shade as her lipstick.

"Goddess," Irina breathed. She shot a look at Brenna. "Is that the Goddess?"

"Huh?" Brenna said. "Oh, no. Of course not. The Goddess's hair is more of a strawberry blonde."

The men turned and gaped at her, as well as at Rebecca, who was nodding.

"The Goddess also isn't as well endowed," Morrighan said, with a mischievous grin.

"Rhiannon!" Rebecca squealed, jumping up and dashing toward the woman. Morrighan rose as well with a huge smile on her face.

Rhiannon hugged both women, then walked to the bar and the barman pulled her a pint. She came to their table and scooted into the booth next to Nigel, giving him a hip bump to move him over.

Rhiannon Bronwyn Kendrick, or RB as she preferred professionally, was a private investigator with fifteen Gifts, including the Rare Gift of Telekinesis and the Gift of Distance Communication, which enhanced and strengthened a telepath's other Gifts. As a result, she was one of the most powerful telepaths in the world.

Her family included her great-aunt, Lady O'Byrne, and she was the unacknowledged daughter of Hugh O'Neill and granddaughter of Lord Corwin of Clan O'Neill. On her mother's side, she was descended from ancient Welsh Clan Chiefs. Growing up in Wales, outside of any Clan, she nonetheless had been trained at Clan O'Byrne as a teenager, and Lord O'Byrne had paid for her education at Oxford.

Morrighan and Rebecca had first met Rhiannon three years before when she helped them break a human trafficking operation that was selling telepathic women. Brenna had met her briefly a few times, and found her to be impressive. Highly intelligent, Rhiannon had a facility with languages, and was totally down to earth. She acknowledged her beauty, but wasn't impressed or obsessed with it. Normally, she tended toward wearing jeans and formless sweaters, not the devastatingly sexy outfit she wore that night.

Nigel shook his head. "Collin, with this crew I could have stormed Normandy Beach and captured it without a shot fired."

Rhiannon leaned over and kissed his cheek. "You're sweet. Are you staying in tonight?"

"Oh, hell yes. I don't even want to be out with your lot on the prowl. If I were a patriot, I'd call out the Home Guard to prepare for casualties."

"Do you want me to come back?" she asked, her voice dropping into a seductive purr.

He handed her the key to his flat.

She kissed his cheek again and then turned to the women. “What are you hungry for? Fish and chips like all the rest of the tourists?”

“How about that Russian restaurant we went to one time?” Brenna asked Irina. “I liked it.”

Irina perked up immediately. “That’s a great idea.”

So off to the Russian restaurant they went.

The patrons included a number of spectacular Russian beauties, most with older wealthy men. At least three were succubi. But the O’Donnell party attracted every eye in the place as they were led to their table, even though, with the exception of Brenna’s outfit, their dresses weren’t unusually revealing by the standards of the other women. In fact, Brenna was avidly observing some of their outfits, evaluating how they might look on her, and in some cases thinking how she might adapt them to her physique.

“Down, girl,” Rebecca smirked. “If you stare at that blonde any harder, you’ll bore holes through her.”

Looking sheepish, Brenna tried to explain, “I was just trying to imagine how that would look on me.”

“I know what you were doing, but try being more discreet or she’ll think you’re hot for her.”

Brenna felt her face flame.

“Is anyone averse to a real Russian dinner?” Irina asked. Seeing no objections, she said, “You need to pay attention to the alcohol. I’m going to order a carafe of vodka. Speak now or forever hold yourselves. Does anyone have foods you find objectionable or have an allergy to? Okay, put your menus away.”

The waiter came and Irina spent some time ordering in Russian. A couple of times, Rhiannon interjected a comment, also in Russian. The waiter returned with a large bottle of mineral water, a carafe of vodka with five tiny crystal glasses, and a platter of cold meats, salted fish, pickled vegetables, pickled mushrooms and black caviar. Another waiter poured wine and placed a second bottle on ice.

Irina poured vodka into the small glasses, put a small amount of several appetizer items on her plate, then took a bite of salted fish, raised her glass, and toasted, "Good hunting."

Laughing at her toast, everyone followed her lead and tossed back the vodka.

After they had done serious damage to the appetizer plate, they were served soup and five entrées that they shared. At various times, one or the other of the participants would propose a toast, usually after a particularly good story or a pithy comment. Dessert consisted of pastries with sweet farmer's cheese and a hot apple tart served with strong hot tea.

"Irina, there's only one problem with this dinner," Rebecca said, leaning back in her chair and surveying the wreckage. "All I want to do now is take a nap, not go out hunting."

The others greeted this assertion with jeering laughter.

Although Rebecca and Morrighan had become fast friends with Rhiannon, this was the first time Brenna had spent any real social time with the Welsh private detective. Over the past three years, Rhiannon had helped the O'Byrne and O'Donnell Clans break up several operations that were trafficking telepathic girls. Brenna had paid Rhiannon's fees for many of those cases, but Rebecca was the liaison between the two women.

Sitting next to Rhiannon at dinner, Brenna was taken by the pragmatic, down-to-earth quality of the woman, a complete contrast to the beautiful, glamorous exterior.

"It was rather strange," Brenna told her, "to discover

that I have a large family. I grew up feeling completely alone. I mean, we're cousins, and I don't even know you."

Rhiannon chuckled. "Hell, I don't know any of my relatives on my father's side. Except for you, I guess, and Lady O'Byrne. I've never even been to the O'Neill estate."

"That must be hard," Brenna said, "not knowing your father. My dad died when I was young, but at least I always carried the knowledge that he loved me."

Rhiannon's mouth pursed as though she'd taken a bite of something sour. Raising her wine glass, she took a deep drink.

"I know Hugh O'Neill," she said. "I know that he thinks nothing of me, and I don't give a damn about him. The whole bloody O'Neill Clan can burn in hell as far as I'm concerned."

The table became very quiet. Looking around, Rhiannon blushed and said, "Sorry. I guess I need to detoxify a little." She excused herself and went to the washroom. When she came back a few minutes later, she wore a smile and steered the conversation toward the others at the table, asking questions about the Americans' lives.

Throughout dinner, Rebecca was conscious of the attention their table was receiving from the other patrons. While this was common for a party of succubi, there was an uncomfortable edge to the psychic atmosphere.

Rhi, do you notice a bit too much attention being paid to our party? she sent on a spear thread to Rhiannon. The redhead cocked her head, as if listening.

Now that you mention it, there is a buzz. A lot of telepaths in here. I wouldn't have expected so many Russian Clan members here in London.

Turning to look back, as their limo pulled away from the restaurant, Rebecca saw a small group of men standing on the sidewalk watching them. She exchanged a look with

Rhiannon, who pursed her mouth and shrugged.

~~~

Rhiannon took them to an upscale tourist hotel in the West End, not too far from O'Donnell headquarters. She told the succubi the hunting should be good since the hotel's guests were mostly businessmen and wealthy tourists. A bit of Influence and generous tips kept the bell captain and the barman from questioning their presence.

The three succubi quickly attracted men and went upstairs with them. Rebecca and Rhiannon watched them go, then signaled the barman for another round of drinks.

"Are you going to partake of the buffet?" Rhiannon asked.

"No, not really in the mood," Rebecca answered. "I have a date with one of Morrighan's Protectors when we get back to the hotel." Although Rebecca was married, the S-gene she carried caused her sexual energies to become unbalanced. She had to rebalance on a daily basis, using the sexual energy released by her partner when he reached climax. When apart from her husband, she needed to arrange a rebalancing with someone else.

"Are you saving yourself for Nigel?" Rebecca asked Rhiannon.

The redhead laughed. "Something like that. You know my cousin is a succubus, right? I hunted with her at university, but I don't get much pleasure from meaningless sex. I don't have your problem, and I don't get the Glow the succubi do."

"How is it going with Nigel?"

"We're chums. He takes me out to dinner, to the theatre, things like that. A friend of his has an estate with stables north of London, and we go riding sometimes." Rhiannon smiled. "He's an excellent lover."

Rebecca cocked her head. "I don't hear love in there
~~~

anywhere."

"No, not love," Rhiannon said, shaking her head. "I think he would like the relationship to go farther, but I'm afraid he's more enamored with the package than the contents."

"You're incredibly beautiful," Rebecca said.

"Thank you," Rhiannon said, twirling her glass in her hand and staring into it. "You know, sometimes I wonder what it would be like to date a blind man."

~~~

Irina was enjoying the husky Russian who was driving her toward orgasm when the bathroom door opened and two more men stepped into the room. They looked very determined and her Empathy picked up malice radiating from them.

Brenna! she shrieked, sending an image of the unfolding scene.

In a room on another floor of the hotel where the group was hunting, Brenna pushed at the man who was making love to her. "I have to go. Get off."

"Huh? What do you mean?" he answered her in confusion.

She pushed him off using her Telekinesis. Jumping out of bed, she started grabbing her clothes off the floor.

Rebecca, Irina's in trouble, she sent the image from Irina to her sister.

Rebecca answered immediately. *Wait. Don't you jump in there. I don't need both of you in with a bunch of thugs.*

Realizing Rebecca was right, Brenna sent a spear to Irina. *Where are your clothes? Look at them.*

What? Brenna, these guys are trying to kidnap me. They have me wrapped in an air shield.
~~~

Do you want me to teleport you nude?

Oh. Irina tore her eyes from the men surrounding her and located her clothes. As soon as she did, the world shifted abruptly, and she found herself lying on the floor of a different room. Her clothing was lying around her, except for one shoe.

"Are you okay?" Brenna asked, leaning over her.

"What the hell?" a male voice said from the other side of the room. Irina turned to see a naked man standing near the foot of the bed.

Brenna shot him a look, then took control of his mind. He walked to the bed, lay down and went to sleep.

Both women began to dress. **I have her,** Brenna sent to Rebecca.

I figured. Her Protectors are engaged with the men who tried to snatch her, Rebecca answered.

Engaged?

Yeah. They came boiling out of that room, and our guys were waiting for them. Watch yourself. They have guns. This is a mess. We've identified at least a dozen Russian telepaths in this hotel. I've notified Collin that we have a situation here.

"Who in Russia did you piss off?" Brenna asked, pulling her boots on.

Irina's reaction was unexpected. She seemed to be handling things well enough, but at Brenna's question, she froze. Her eyes grew big and she stared at Brenna. "Russia?" She stopped what she was doing and stood in the middle of the room, staring off into space.

"What is Rebecca telling you?" Irina finally said.

"She said there are at least a dozen Russian telepaths inside this hotel," Brenna told her.

"My mom," Irina said. "I wonder if this has something

to do with her. That's the only thing I can think of besides going to that restaurant." She shook her head. "And that doesn't make sense. There were plenty of beautiful women at the restaurant. Russia exports whores, it doesn't import them."

"Well, we can worry about it later. Ready to go?" Brenna wondered again about Irina's mysterious mother. But Irina was correct about the other part. Brenna had done extensive research into the slave trade. The fall of communism had opened the door for thousands of beautiful women to flee depressed economic conditions in Eastern Europe. Many of them ended up being sold into forced prostitution.

Irina looked at her one shoe, then with a wry expression pitched it at the rubbish bin in the corner. "Yeah, I'm ready," she said.

Brenna sent a spear to her Protectors, and they came through the door.

"Let's go, ladies," Donny Doyle said. "This place is getting a little hot."

They stepped out into the hall and discovered Rebecca and Rhiannon with pistols in their hands. Morrighan stood to the side surrounded by four Protectors who Brenna didn't recognize.

"Where do you hide a gun in that outfit?" Irina asked Rhiannon.

"I'd think that was obvious," the redhead said. "I want to know where Rebecca hides hers."

"If you were male, I'd show you," Rebecca said with a smirk. "Everyone ready? Let's go."

Three Protectors opened the door to the stairwell and dived into it. Everyone waited for clearance to follow. Instead, a gunshot exploded and echoed from below, followed by a scream.

Donny shook his head, pursing his lips in displeasure. "I'm sure no one heard that on all twenty-five floors."

A spear thought came to the party from one of the Protectors in the stairwell, and Rebecca cautiously headed down the stairs. The rest followed her. Three floors down, they saw blood smeared on the landing, but no body was evident. All three O'Donnell Protectors looked okay. A Protector held the door open, and they followed him. Checking both ways, Brenna saw another man waving to them from the stairway door at the other end of the hall. Everyone hurried to him and again the party began to descend.

Brenna hesitated and glanced back at Donny and two other Protectors standing near the door from which they had emerged. The door opened and a man stepped through. Immediately, he staggered back. One of the Protectors stepped toward him and kicked him in the head. Brenna sent a spear of mental force toward him, and he screamed as she shattered his shields and captured his mind.

I have him, Donny. Bring him along, she sent. She saw the Protectors grab the man and hustle him toward her, while Donny covered them. It took some time, but cautiously the party worked their way down to the lobby.

"Collin says to hang out here until he can clear the outside," Rebecca said in a low voice.

"Perhaps we can get a drink while we wait," Morrighan said gaily, nodding toward the lounge.

At Rebecca's furrowed brow, Morrighan's Protector lowered his voice and said, "There's no back door to the bar. It would be easy to defend."

"I think that's an excellent idea," Rhiannon said. "Rebecca and I left our drinks when you got in trouble, and at seven quid a piece, I'd like to finish mine."

Rebecca nodded and the women went in and sat down

at a booth. Looking out into the lobby, they saw a swirl of activity. Hotel security was scurrying around and so were others, including two police officers.

Looking at Brenna's captive, Rebecca asked, "What's going on?"

Brenna took a deep breath. "There are fifteen of them all together, some outside. They're only interested in Irina, and they have orders not to hurt her."

Irina sucked on her lip and nodded. "Who sent them?" she said soberly.

Shrugging, Brenna said, "A man named Sergei Gorbachev. He evidently thinks he's your grandfather."

Irina took the news without changing her expression. "My mother's maiden name is Natalia Sergeyevna Gorbacheva. In Russia, the second name is a patronymic and for a woman the surname is feminized."

"I thought you didn't know anything about your mother's family," Rebecca said.

"I don't, but I know her name," Irina said. "I know she and my dad came to the U.S. running from someone." She glanced at Brenna. **May I come in?** she asked. Sliding through Brenna's mind into that of their captive, she sat staring at him for a few minutes. "I think I need to go home and see my parents when we get back to the States," she finally said.

Collin walked into the lounge. Behind him, Protectors filled the lobby.

"Can't you go anywhere without getting in trouble?" he asked. "Come on, let's go."

~~~

Chapter 2

No man will ever put his hand up a woman's skirt looking for a library card. – Joan Rivers (commenting on men being attracted to
~~~

intelligence)

When Irina returned to the States, the first thing she did was call her mother and tell her she was coming home for a visit. Two vans full of Protectors—along with Collin, Brenna, and Rebecca—accompanied her to Ohio.

Irina had been home only twice since discovering the Clan, but she called her parents weekly. She hadn't told them about the Clan, and they still thought she had taken a job with a normal company in New York.

Thirty miles north of Columbus, she directed Collin to pull off on a dirt side-road and asked that the Protectors stay behind. They drove around a bend and past a large copse of trees to where a modest ranch-style house stood. Collin pulled the car next to an SUV and a compact sedan parked on the side of the house.

A short blonde woman looking to be in her late thirties stepped out on the porch and walked toward them. Even from a distance, it was obvious she was a succubus. Irina flew into her arms. They hugged, babbling in Russian and kissing each other's faces. Then Irina broke away and turned to her friends.

"Mama, this is Collin," Irina said, "and Brenna and Rebecca. This is my mother, Natalia Moore."

Natalia ushered them into the house, past an older man with graying hair. In the living room, Irina introduced them to her father, Martin Moore. In spite of living in the U.S. for twenty years, Martin still had an English accent. He glanced at his wife, meeting her eyes.

As Natalia served tea and biscuits, she eyed her daughter's friends.

"You've been keeping things from us, Irisha," Natalia said, using the Russian affectionate name for her daughter. "Your friends are telepaths." Her voice was melodic and soft, and a strong Russian accent still flavored her speech.

"Yes," Irina said, "and you've kept some things from me. I have a lot of news. I'm actually working for a telepath-owned business and I met your mother's twin sister in Ireland. If you don't mind us staying for a couple of days, I'll fill you in on all of it. But the major thing I need to know is, who is Sergei Gorbachev and why did he try to kidnap me?"

Natalia's eyes widened and she gasped. She stared at her daughter for a few moments, then shot a look at her husband. Martin shuffled his feet and turned to his daughter's friends.

"Why don't I show you around the place?" he said, motioning toward the back of the house. Brenna and Rebecca looked to Irina, who nodded. Irina's friends stood and trooped out after her father.

"Mama, I know that Daddy isn't my real father," Irina said softly when she and Natalia were alone.

Natalia took a deep shuddering breath. Biting her lip, she looked out the window, then turned to her daughter. "Sergei Gorbachev is my father, and yours," she said.

Irina thought she was ready for almost anything, but that statement was completely unexpected. Numbly, she stared at her mother.

"I hoped I'd never have to tell you that," Natalia said. She turned from her daughter and stared out the window again. "Where should I start?" she finally said. "My mother was in Moscow and met a man there, a telepath. She got pregnant with me and was trapped there when the Nazis invaded Russia. My father was a high-ranking member of Stalin's NKVD, a very cruel man. In the chaos at the end of the war, she escaped him by hiding with a group of Jewish refugees going to Palestine. She left one war zone for another."

Natalia stood and paced the room. “As I told you, she was killed in the bombing of the King David Hotel in Jerusalem in 1946. It was the headquarters of the British forces occupying Palestine, and Zionist terrorists blew up the hotel. My mother had gone there for an assignation with a British officer. I was only six, almost seven, at the time.”

She pushed her hair back and walked to the window, looking out at her husband and Irina’s friends in the back yard. “The woman who was taking care of me didn’t know what to do with me. She took me to the Russian embassy. In time, my father came and took me back to Moscow.”

“I know the Gorbachev Clan is one of the most powerful telepathic Clans in Russia,” Irina said. “I’ve learned a lot about telepaths since I left home. I had pretty much figured a lot of this out. As I said, I met your aunt, grandmother’s twin sister, in Ireland. She told me about grandmother, and she gave me these.” Irina walked over to her mother and handed her several old black and white photographs. Natalia took them, shuffled through them, and then started crying.

Irina put her hand on Natalia’s shoulder, awkwardly patting her. Among the photographs was one taken the day Mairead O’Conner left Donegal to explore Europe. That was the one Natalia held in front of her.

“I never had any pictures of her. I haven’t seen her face since that day when she left me,” Natalia said.

Irina handed her a handkerchief and led her back to their seats in the living room. She waited for her mother to regain her composure, then asked, “How did it happen?”

Natalia, still staring at the picture in her hand, said, “He came to my bed the first time on my sixteenth birthday. I was a virgin and didn’t understand what was happening. When he passed out, two of his men came into the room and took him away. After that, he sent me to many men through the years. Some were men he wanted to reward; some were men he wanted to use or harm. One of the women in his Clan taught me how to control my ovulation and how to use my telepathic talents. Then, when I grew older, he became cruel. He told me that I wasn't desirable anymore."

She looked up at her daughter. "I met Martin, and we fell in love. I don't know how Sergei found out, but he did. He was furious. He beat me and controlled my mind. I woke up one day and discovered it had been almost two months since I went to sleep. I was pregnant. He said he needed a new woman, a younger woman, and I was going to give her to him."

Straightening and taking a ragged breath, she met Irina's eyes. "It took me another two months to escape, to get away and call Martin. Using my talents and his connections inside the British embassy, we got out of Russia the next day. We came here, and you, my beautiful daughter, were born. As much as I hate my father, I've never regretted having you. I'm sorry, Irina. I hoped I'd never have to tell you this."

Irina sat back in her chair and thought about her mother's story. After a few minutes, she said, "So now that he knows I exist, he's trying to capture me to breed another succubus for him."

Her mother's eyes widened. "Oh, no, Irina. No."

"Oh, yes. He wants to use me the way he did you. The pattern is too clear. Some men become addicted to succubi. It sounds as though he might be one of them. We also know," Irina waved her hand toward her friends, "that the Russian Clans are experimenting with genetic engineering, and they're buying telepathic women."

Irina gazed around the room, trying to find something to grasp out of all the thoughts running around her mind. "I guess I'm going to have to go to Russia," she finally said, her face hard. Natalia gasped. "I'll find him and kill him, and then we'll all be free."

~~~

When Natalia discovered there were a dozen Protectors sitting just outside their property, she insisted that they come for dinner. Conscripting her daughter, Brenna and Rebecca, she set about preparing a feast. It took almost every chair in the house and adding two card tables in the dining room, but everyone had a place.

"Russian mother syndrome," Irina said with a grin. "No visitor goes hungry in a Russian home."

Brenna had been thinking all afternoon about what to do concerning Natalia and Martin's situation.

"Martin, Irina told me that you're a civil engineer. Would you be open to taking a new job?"

Irina froze with her fork halfway to her mouth. **What do you have in mind?** she sent to Brenna.

I think they'd be safer in the valley, don't you? I have a lot of building going on, such as my lab, the school, new housing units. I could use a project manager to oversee it all. The guy doing it now lives in DC, and he's not on-site all the time, Brenna replied.

Irina's smile was all the endorsement that Brenna needed.

"What kind of job?" Martin asked.

Brenna explained what she was doing in West Virginia. "I think you and Natalia would be safer there," she said. "Natalia would have the chance to live among other telepaths, and you would have work in your field."

"And we'd get to see each other all the time," Irina said, looking back and forth between her parents.

Natalia and Martin stared at each other, and Irina held her breath, knowing there was a silent conversation taking place.
~~~

Natalia turned to Brenna. "If you don't mind, I would like to see your valley. Martin can't come for a couple of weeks, but if I like it, then he'll come. Can you wait for a decision until we see it?"

Brenna nodded. "Certainly. You can ride back with us if you wish."

~~~

Although their curiosity was boiling over, it wasn't until they arrived back in West Virginia that Irina told her friends what she had learned from her mother.

"No," Collin said. "Absolutely not. You're not going to Russia. That's the stupidest idea I've heard since Samantha went hunting Gless."

Irina smiled and grabbed him by the ear, drawing his face close to hers and kissing him. "Sweet man, I'm going to let you plan the whole thing. I'm not going to barge into Moscow tomorrow searching for my father. Take your time, and set it up so you're comfortable with it. But go I will. It's up to you to make sure I'm safe and the operation is successful."

Rebecca spoke up, "It could take a year or two to gather the proper intelligence and set up an op to take out a major Clan member someplace like Russia."

Collin barked a laugh. "Not just a major Clan member. Sergei is Clan Chief. Taking him out means taking on the whole Clan."

"That's fine," Irina said, waving her hand as though the difficulty was trifling. "Like I said, I want to be successful when I do this. But I'm not going to spend my whole life looking over my shoulder, afraid he's going to come after me. I'm not going to live in fear the way my parents have." She fixed Collin with her eyes. "But don't think I'm going to forget about it. Plan your operation, and keep me informed."
~~~

~~~

Chapter 3

The life of the dead is placed in the memory of the living. - Marcus Tullius Cicero

Four years before, at the age of 23, Brenna had been named heir of the three Irish Clans. Her grandfathers and great uncle had long dreamed of uniting the clans, and as they neared the end of their lives, they looked to Brenna to make that dream come true.

The dream wasn't shared by everyone. The oldest sons in Clans O'Byrne and O'Neill and their respective sons thought it was a terrible idea. Other people had a problem with Brenna's age or the idea of a woman Clan Chief. Some had a problem with the fact that she was a succubus, or Druid as they were called in Ireland.

The O'Donnell Clan, which was now centered in the United States rather than in its ancestral base in Donegal, embraced Brenna. Her grandfather Seamus was only one hundred and sixty-one years old, and planned to hold his position for at least a few more decades. Clan O'Neill, where Corwin was two hundred, and Clan O'Byrne, where Fergus was one hundred and ninety, knew her ascension was nearing, and so did Brenna. A dread of that day lay in the back of her mind.

On her way home from London, Brenna stopped off to see her grandparents at the O'Byrne estate in County Wicklow. From there, she traveled to see her great-uncle at the O'Neill estate in County Tyrone. After arriving home in the States, she went to visit her Aunt Callie at the family estate in West Virginia.

Callista O'Donnell Wilkins was Chief Executive Officer of the O'Donnell Group, the Clan's business interests. With their long lives, telepaths need to 'die' and
~~~

switch their identities to avoid suspicion. In a previous 'life', she had been a professor of genetics at two prestigious universities. Her major research, for obvious reasons never published, concerned mapping the telepathic genome. She had collected genetic samples from hundreds of thousands of telepaths. Even those Clans unfriendly to O'Donnell had participated, wanting the results of her research.

"Callie, I've been looking at the genetic profiles in your database," Brenna said. "Something isn't jiving with Hugh O'Neill."

"We aren't perfect," Callie said, sitting down at her computer. "Look at what happened with your baby sample." The genetic swab taken when Brenna was a baby was never entered in the database. When it was analyzed, the results were so fantastic it had been discarded as a contaminated sample.

"You know this manifestation, Talent, Gift, whatever you want to call it, that I have? The one where I see auras and can tell what Gifts a person has?" Brenna asked.

Callie nodded.

"When I look at Hugh, I see twelve Gifts, including the O'Neill Gift and the O'Byrne Gift. Neither of those shows on the analysis you have on file."

Callie called up Hugh's record. "Yes, the database shows seven Gifts, and not particularly strong ones. I think that's why Corwin was reluctant to have Hugh inherit. He doesn't think Hugh's strong enough to protect the Clan, or to command the respect to lead it."

"Where did you get that sample?"

"Hugh gave it to me. Remember, I started this project in the 1970s, and the tools and knowledge we had then were fairly primitive. Let's see," Callie said, clicking to another screen on the computer, "1984 is when this sample was catalogued. Why?"

"Call up Finnian's record," Brenna said. Finnian was Hugh's son and had tried to assassinate Brenna shortly after Corwin named her heir to O'Neill. Corwin had exiled him as a result of that attempt.

"They're identical," Callie said, her brow furrowed. "Either Finnian's a clone, or one of these isn't accurate. A father and son wouldn't be identical."

"Yeah. I haven't seen Finnian since my Talent manifested," Brenna said, pointing to the screen. "But I know that the Gifts I see when I look at Hugh are definitely different than what is listed there."

"It shows the Lindstrom Gift on these profiles. And these are the Gifts that everyone thinks Hugh has. He's a Construct Artist," Callie said.

"His mother, Corwin's wife, was from the Lindstrom Clan," Brenna said. "The daughter of the Clan Chief. She could have embedded a nine-level construct for him. It's a fairly common way for those with the O'Neill Gift to mask their abilities."

"She died around the time Hugh reached puberty," Callie mused. "Hugh would have been tested at puberty, as we've always done with children. If you're right, then he's been masking his abilities all his life."

"If I'm wrong, it would be the first time," Brenna said. "I wonder why Hugh's doing that."

~~~

Brenna was working in her office in Washington when she received a call from Hugh O'Neill. "Brenna, Father's dying and he's asking for you."

"Right now?"

"As soon as possible. I don't think he'll last out the night."
~~~

Brenna swore as she disconnected. The moment she'd dreaded had come, and no matter how many times she had run scenarios through her mind, she wasn't sure what to do.

Rebecca was draped across a chair next to the window, trying to decipher a book in Gaelic from Fergus O'Byrne's library. "What's up?"

"That was Hugh. Corwin's dying."

With a sigh, Rebecca said, "It never rains but it pours. I've been expecting this."

"In Ireland, it just rains all the time," Brenna said.

"True."

"Do you know where Rhiannon is?"

"No. Why?"

"Can you contact her?"

"Probably. If I can use your Gift." Rebecca was referring to Brenna's Gift for Distance Communication. Rebecca had manifested a Lost Gift, inelegantly called the Soul Thief Gift. One of its elements was that she could use another telepath's Gifts if she was in the person's mind.

Brenna opened her mind and invited her sister in. Rebecca found the Gift's trigger and reached out through the bond she had with Rhiannon.

*Rhiannon. Where are you?*

*Rebecca? <confusion> In Monaco. Where are you?*

*In Washington. I need to come see you.*

*How are you ... how can you reach this far?*

*I'm using Brenna's Gift. I'll explain later. Are you alone? Can you visualize a landing spot? We need to teleport in.*

A blank space of carpet was transmitted from Rhiannon into Brenna's mind. A few seconds later, that spot, thousands of miles away, had two women standing on it.

Rhiannon Kendrick stared at them with her mouth open. She was dressed in a black off-the-shoulder evening dress with silver trim, with her copper-colored hair in a French twist. Brenna thought that she'd never seen anyone look so beautiful and elegant.

"That's a beautiful dress," Brenna said.

"Thank you. And to what do I owe the honor of this unexpected visit?"

"Are you on a case? What are you doing in Monaco?" Brenna asked.

"I'm on holiday. Just spending a bit of time at the casinos refilling the coffers and having a good time."

"So, you don't have any pressing engagements? Are you here with anyone?"

"I'm alone and I don't have a date tonight. Brenna, what the bloody hell is this about?"

"The world, my world, is going to hell in a hand basket. I need your help, and I need it now. Corwin is dying. I need you to come to O'Neill with me. I need more than Rebecca to keep me alive."

"Well, if that's all. Give me a moment to change."

"No, we don't have time for that, and that dress is perfect. You can change later. Rebecca, help her pack a bag."

Rhiannon frowned. "Perfect for what?"

Brenna turned away, not answering, and sent a spear thought to Jeremy, her transition manager in County Tyrone at the O'Neill estate. In less than ten minutes, Brenna took the other two women by their arms and teleported to O'Neill.

They appeared back in reality in an empty room. Looking around, they saw Jeremy and his wife Maggie standing in the doorway.

"Just leave your bag here," Jeremy said. "I'll take you to Corwin."

Do you ever get used to that? Rhiannon sent to Rebecca. **I'm completely disoriented.**

It makes my stomach all flip-floppy, Rebecca replied. **But the disorientation isn't from the teleportation. It comes from being in close proximity to Brenna.**

Do you know what I'm doing here? Rhiannon asked. **I mean the real reason.**

No, I don't. She's like you. She just does things. When she gets going, she's moving too fast in her head to explain anything, and no one has a chance to catch up until the roller coaster comes to a stop.

Jeremy led them down a hall and through the main parlor of the O'Neill manor house. Halfway through the room, Brenna stopped and gestured to a painting hanging over the massive fireplace. They all looked up, and Rhiannon gasped.

"Delilah O'Neill. Mean as a junkyard dog, sweeter than sugar, prettier than a sunset," Brenna said. "That's what Seamus told me once about our great-grandmother."

The woman in the portrait was dressed in a nineteenth century evening dress, black with red trim. Her copper-colored hair was in an elaborate up-do, and her face was a mirror image of Rhiannon's.

"Holy Goddess," Rhiannon breathed.

"We were told the picture was painted around 1830," Rebecca said. "You haven't been time traveling, have you?"

"It seems to run in the family," Jeremy said. "Brenna and her mother are carbon copies. I guess the Goddess likes to reuse the most beautiful faces."

Brenna reached out and took Rhiannon's arm. "Come on. We have an appointment, and we can't afford to be late."

"Where are we going?" Rhiannon asked. She looked around and found that they were completely ringed with O'Donnell Protectors.

"To meet your grandfather," Brenna said.

Rhiannon stopped so suddenly that Brenna was almost jerked off her feet.

"No," Rhiannon said, shaking her head. "Just because he's dying doesn't mean I want to meet the old bastard."

"I don't have time for this," Brenna growled.

Rhiannon drifted off the floor and Brenna pulled her along. Rhiannon tried to fight, but discovered that Brenna had covered her with an O'Neill super mental shield so strong and tight that she couldn't access her Gifts. Rhiannon was one of the strongest telepaths in the world, fully mature and at the height of her power, but Brenna had overwhelmed her as though she was a little girl. For one of the few times in her life, Rhiannon experienced fear of another telepath.

"Brenna, what are you doing?" Rebecca asked, clearly alarmed. "That's not right. You can't just bully someone like that!"

"Don't fuck with me," Brenna responded. "He's dying. I can feel him. We don't have much time."

Brenna broke into a trot, hauling a terrified Rhiannon behind her. Rebecca shot a look at Jeremy, who shrugged.

When they reached Corwin's quarters, his son Hugh met them. "He's been asking for you," Hugh said. "I think he's almost gone."

Then he saw Rhiannon. "Who is that? What's going on?"

Brenna didn't answer, pushing past him and through the door to Corwin's bedroom. She sat Rhiannon back on her feet, and taking her hand, pulled her toward the old man lying in the bed.

Corwin's hair had turned completely white. His breathing was labored and shallow. Multiple strokes had stolen his strength and ability to speak.

Uncle? I've brought someone to meet you, Brenna sent to Corwin, including Rhiannon in her transmission.

The old man opened his eyes, then they opened so wide Brenna thought they might pop out of his head.

Mother? Have you come to take me home? Corwin sent.

No, Uncle. This isn't Delilah. This is Rhiannon, your granddaughter.

He stared at Rhiannon in horror for a full minute, then tears began to spill down his cheeks and he sent, **Oh, dear Goddess. What have I done? I shall surely burn in hell for what I've done.**

He looked back and forth from Brenna to Rhiannon. **What should I do?**

Acknowledge your blood, Uncle, Brenna sent. **Give Rhiannon her birthright.**

"Rhiannon, my beautiful granddaughter. Please forgive me," Corwin said aloud. Hugh jerked as though he'd been slapped.

The old man reached out, taking Rhiannon's hand and also grabbing Brenna's elbow. His eyes rolled back in his head, and his breath rattled in his throat. He lay still.

When a telepath dies, at the moment when the soul leaves the body, his or her memories can pass to another telepath in physical contact. Long before, Corwin had told Brenna that he planned to pass his Death Gift on to her. Brenna had dreaded that moment, and hoped she could engineer the passing of the O'Neill legacy to Corwin's granddaughter, where Brenna believed it properly should go.

She hadn't found anything in her research or from talking to other telepaths that a Death Gift could be passed to more than one person. With the old man holding her arm in his death grip, she discovered that she should have asked the question.

The others in the room saw Corwin breathe his last, his hands touching each of the young women standing in front of him. Brenna and Rhiannon stood stock still as if frozen. They stood that way, eyes unfocused, for almost half an hour, and then both slumped to the floor, senseless.

~~~

Memories and knowledge flowed into Brenna, overwhelming her. It was worse than when she was a little girl, before her mother taught her to shield, when the thoughts of everyone around her invaded her mind. She couldn't figure out who all the people were, or where they stopped and she began.

Thoughts and memories, men and women, children and aged crones, a flood of people were in her head. Some of the memories were beautiful. Others were horrifying. Memories of war, torture, and death. Memories of giving birth to a child, of being in love, of betrayal and humiliation. All the things a person might have done when they were alive now crowded her mind. Memories of sunny summer meadows in mountains she had never walked through mingled with memories of making love to men and women she had never met. Memories of being a man and making love to a woman. Terrifying memories of an axe descending, splitting her skull, the pain and darkness bursting through her mind. A sword piercing the child in her arms, continuing through and into her chest.

Over and over, the memory of dying. All of them had died. A mother held her child in her arms as it died, and received its young memories. A wife had held her husband,
~~~

and discovered he had been faithless. A man held his father's hand and discovered that in spite of his hard, unbending ways, he had loved his son and been proud of him.

It was too much for one mind to hold. She was going mad.

But every one of those people had done this and the majority had survived and emerged from the experience sane. Not all. Some had succumbed to madness, and those memories were there, too.

Attempting to restore some kind of order, she began categorizing, cataloging, and finding a place to store all the memories. Telepaths have extremely well-ordered minds, unlike the fragmented disorder, the chaos, in the mind of a norm. Fearing for her sanity, she worked to restore the order she was used to.

But there was so much of it. Centuries of memories, hundreds of people. Sometimes she would find memories of the same event as remembered by two different people. It was so confusing that her frustration grew and grew. Even trying to figure out how to store it, and where, was so much work that she despaired she would ever get it under control.

Corwin had the O'Neill Gift. Those with the Gift had seventeen mental levels as opposed to the nine levels of those without it. Figuring out where Corwin had stored a piece of information helped her to construct a model to use. It struck her that Rhiannon only had nine levels. The confusion and chaos must be worse for her.

Guilt hit like a hammer. Brenna had been so terrified of Corwin's Death Gift that she'd attempted to force Rhiannon to take it instead. Forcing another telepath, someone weaker than you, was a major breach of the rules her society lived by.

That hadn't been her original intent when she brought

Rhiannon to O'Neill. She just wanted to force Corwin to acknowledge his granddaughter. She wanted to bring some reconciliation between the two. She knew how much pain Rhiannon carried from the denial by her father and grandfather. If Brenna was going to be Lady of O'Neill, she planned to bring Rhiannon into the Clan and give her a place of honor. When Corwin acknowledged her, it fulfilled her wildest hopes. And then a wild idea had blossomed inside her. Rhiannon was the rightful heir. Brenna might be able to dodge the responsibility she had no desire to assume.

Her half-formed idea went awry when Corwin grabbed them both. Now she and Rhiannon shared a bond she had never imagined, two millennia of memories and knowledge. And if Brenna was terrified of what that meant, at least she had agreed to it. Rhiannon had been given no choice. But there was even more to it than that.

Worst of all, when Corwin's mind had flowed into them, their own minds had merged and she had absorbed Rhiannon's. Everything Rhiannon had ever done, ever felt. She knew every thought, feeling and hope another living being had ever experienced. Each of them knew every pain, fear, and joy of the other. They knew each other's motivations, insecurities, and hopes.

Even though Brenna and Collin had merged their souls, they didn't rummage around in each other's minds. They still had their privacy. Even as close as she and Rebecca were, there were things they didn't share. What she had done to Rhiannon, and to herself, was almost unfathomable. It was the ultimate breach of privacy. It was a crime so appalling that other telepaths might consider it grounds for a mind wipe.

Finally, her mind cleared. Order was restored. She opened her eyes and saw that it was light outside, a bright sunny day.

Rebecca?

You're finally awake, Rebecca answered her.

I did a bad thing.

Yes, you did. I think I know why you did it, but good intentions don't make it right.

I know. I think she's going to hate me, and I wouldn't blame her.

Ask her yourself. She just woke up, too.

Brenna reached out and contacted Rhiannon's mind. It wasn't difficult. It was like looking in a mirror.

Rhiannon?

You bitch! You forced me! I should slap you silly for that. What the hell were you thinking?

I'm sorry. I'm so sorry. I didn't mean for this to happen.

Yeah, I know. Hell, I know everything about you. But guess what? You failed. He acknowledged me as his granddaughter, but he didn't name me his heir. You're stuck with it.

We're also stuck with each other.

Yeah, we are. At least you're not a monster. I can think of a lot of people I wouldn't want in my head, but you're not so bad.

You forgive me?

Hell, no. I'm going to hold this over you for the rest of your life. You owe me.

But you don't hate me?

No, I don't hate you. I'm hungry.

A feeling of well-being settled over them, a feeling of warmth, safety and comfort that Brenna had felt before, and a presence entered her and Rhiannon's minds.

*The triumvirate is complete. The Power and the

Shadow I foresaw, but I had not hoped there would be a Pathfinder. Three shall lead my people out of the apocalypse and into a new world. Brenna, Rebecca, Rhiannon. Know that you carry my blessing. *

The presence withdrew.

**Was ... that ...* * Rhiannon asked.

**Yes, that was the Goddess,* * Brenna answered.

Brenna struggled out of bed and found Rebecca sitting in a chair watching her.

"Pathfinder?" Rebecca asked.

"You heard my conversation with Rhiannon?"

"I didn't hear that. I heard the Goddess speak to us. I guess She forgives you, even if Rhiannon won't. Do I need to order her taken to the dungeon so she doesn't kill you?"

"No, I think we're okay. But we're hungry."

Rebecca chuckled. "I'll bet you are. You've been out for thirty-six hours. I'll order you breakfast and tell Rhi to come here and have breakfast with you."

"Thank you. I'm going to take a shower."

Breakfast and Rhiannon arrived at about the same time. Rebecca served them in a small dining room off Brenna's bedroom, then left them alone.

~~~

Chapter 4

Yeah, I read history. But it doesn't make you nice. Hitler read history, too. - Joan Rivers

That afternoon Brenna met with those she trusted most, Rhiannon, Rebecca, Jeremy and Thomas O'Neill. They used a private parlor in Corwin's suite of rooms. While she had been wrestling with Corwin's memories, Rebecca had flown her protection team in from the States, so Donny
~~~

Doyle sat in as well.

Jeremy was one of Brenna's oldest friends in the O'Donnell Clan. At one time, he had been the third-ranked Protector there and head of Brenna's security team. Thomas O'Neill was Corwin's nephew. Around a hundred years old, he had been the security chief for the past twenty years and, according to Jeremy, was well respected.

"Corwin's death has not been announced," Thomas said. "We wanted to wait until you were conscious. Other than those in this room, only Hugh, the healer, and Daria, Corwin's companion, know."

"We should announce it tonight," Brenna said. "I'm sure there are rumors already, and we can't keep a lid on something like this very long."

"Fergus and Seamus have been informed," Rebecca said. "Seamus has five hundred Protectors flying into Belfast tonight. They'll arrive here sometime before dawn."

"Where's Finnian?" Brenna asked.

"In Scotland, as far as we know," Jeremy answered. "He has a fair amount of support there."

"How is Hugh taking this?" Rebecca asked.

"He seems to be fine. I think he's been waiting for his father to die for a long time. He went hunting today," Thomas said.

"Thomas," Brenna said, "I want you to stay on as security chief here."

The older man nodded, and Brenna saw his shoulders relax a bit.

"Jeremy is going to assume the position as my steward, with complete authority to speak in my name. You'll report to him. I just can't be here all the time, and the situation at O'Byrne is going to be problematic once they hear I've taken control here."

Brenna regarded Thomas, reading his aura. "I can't put someone in your position without trusting him," she began. "There is a lot about me that you don't know. I'll have Collin contact you and transmit my profile to you." Thomas nodded again. "But there are things you need to know now, things that we have kept secret. Perhaps Corwin told you some of them, but in case he hasn't ..." Her voice trailed off.

"Brenna has twenty-seven Gifts," Rebecca said. Thomas's head jerked toward her, and he stared, his mouth hanging open.

"Yes," Rebecca said, "there are more than twenty-five. We've identified twenty-eight in total. Goddess knows what else she has up her sleeve to surprise us."

"The one that's pertinent to this discussion," Brenna said, "is one we've dubbed the Truthsayer Gift. I'm not sure what all of its manifestations are, but I see auras. It seems those auras are true reflections of the person's soul. I can also see how many Gifts a person has, and what they are."

She leaned forward and looked directly into Thomas's eyes. "We know how many Gifts Corwin and Hugh told us that Hugh has, and we have a DNA sample that he gave Callie for her database. Neither of those things matches what I see when I look at him. I see twelve Gifts, including the O'Neill Gift, the O'Byrne and the Krasevec. Are you aware of that?"

Thomas chewed the inside of his cheek, then sat back in his chair and looked up at the ceiling.

After a minute, he looked back at her. "No, I wasn't aware. I'm sure Corwin was. Hell, how can a parent not know what Gifts their child has? Hugh and I are near the same age, but I was away when he hit puberty. I was always under the impression he only had seven."

"I also see a soul that shows signs of deviousness, as

though he's living a lie," Brenna continued. "And I know he's committed murder. I don't think what people see is really who Hugh is. I don't trust him."

Thomas glanced around, realizing that everyone was watching him. He took a deep breath.

"All right, I've always suspected that Hugh didn't show the world who, or what, he really is. For one thing, he can control Finnian when he wants to, but he rarely wants to. Sometimes I think his leniency is covering another agenda. But hell, he was the heir. It's not my job to question Corwin or his son."

"It is now," Brenna said.

Thomas nodded. "I guess it is." He was silent a moment, his eyes unfocused. "All right. I'll put five men I know I can trust to watching him."

~~~

Wearing an evening dress in O'Neill colors, Brenna followed half of her security team through the halls of the O'Neill manor house while the other half followed her. Built in the eighteenth century, over a hundred years before the O'Donnell manor in West Virginia, it was a fortified stone building in an older tradition. Not quite a castle, which would have been frowned upon by the English conquerors, it nonetheless could withstand quite a siege.

The quarried stone walls and floors seemed to press against her, their physical weight heightened by the weight of their years. The place was a maze, and Rebecca had taken the maps given to her by Thomas and assigned a team to verify them. That included the hidden passages and doorways, along with the tunnels and dungeons under the house.

It didn't matter. Corwin's grandfather had built the house, and Brenna knew the place as well as she knew her own bedroom in West Virginia. She looked down a cross
~~~

passage and remembered that was where Conan O'Neill had seduced a serving wench, and where Dolan O'Conner had tripped and skinned his knee when he was seven years old.

She would be expected to move into Corwin's rooms. A third world village would probably consider the suite comfortably roomy. Her college dorm room was smaller than any of the closets.

Her entourage trooped down a staircase wide enough to draw lane stripes on. Portraits of old men dressed in old-fashioned clothes watched her pass. She assumed that Rebecca knew who they all were, and when they lived. They continued through a series of large rooms, decorated for a movie set in the nineteenth century, with more people on the walls watching her. Only in the main parlor, the one presided over by Delilah O'Neill, were the portraits on the walls of women. She determined to ask Rebecca who they were.

Eventually, she was shown into a large banquet hall for entertaining two or three hundred of her closest friends. Hugh O'Neill was awaiting her.

"Are you ready for this, lassie?" he asked.

"I think so," Brenna said. "You'll have to be more formal with me in public after this, you know."

"Aye, I'll be the picture of propriety," he chuckled. There was a glint in his eye that made her uneasy.

When Brenna looked at Hugh, nothing stayed stable. His aura was alive, streaks of color shooting through it. Hugh was nervous, but the streaks changed color. She'd never seen anyone with an aura that looked anything like it.

He held out his arm and she took it. They walked out into the grand ballroom, and he escorted her to the low stage at the front. The room was packed. A microphone was hooked to speakers outside in the large quadrangle where even more people waited. It was also hooked to communication lines leading to all of O'Neill's facilities across Northern Ireland, Scotland, and their trade office in Paris.

Hugh left her on the stage and stepped off to the side. She looked out on the faces before her, and realized that she knew all of them. Corwin's memories in her mind told her who each of them were. She knew details about their lives. She might be a stranger to them, but to her they felt like family.

"Corwin, Lord O'Neill, is dead," she announced. "He has passed and the mantle of Clan Chief, confirmed by the Council, has passed to me. I am Brenna Aoife O'Donnell, daughter of Jack Brian O'Donnell and Maureen O'Neill O'Byrne O'Donnell, grandniece of Corwin and granddaughter of Caylin Mairead O'Neill O'Byrne. I claim the high seat of O'Neill."

Hugh, Thomas, and a number of others knelt. Like a wave, those behind them knelt, until almost everyone was kneeling.

What the hell? Brenna sent to Thomas.

It's traditional. Remember, it's been a hundred fifty years since this has happened here. Just go with the flow.

An old woman who did not kneel attracted Brenna's attention.

"Donegal whore!" the woman shouted. "I'll be damned if I kneel to an O'Donnell!"

A ball of fire flamed in her hand and she threw it at Brenna. It only traveled about two feet before it hit an air shield and splashed throughout the tight bubble that encased her. The flames engulfed her, and she screamed a hideous, tortured scream. Everyone stared at her in horror as her blackened corpse slumped.

Good God! Wasn't there another way to stop her?

Brenna sent to Rebecca.

Wasn't me. That was Rhiannon.

Brenna looked at the copper-headed woman. Dressed in blue jeans and a sweater, Rhiannon leaned against the wall halfway to the back of the hall. Her arms crossed under her breasts and her legs crossed at the ankles, she looked as though she was bored and about to fall asleep.

Any other way of stopping it would have splashed it across the hall, Rhiannon sent. **Too many people in here, too many innocents. I'm good, but not good enough to catch a fireball in mid-air. I constructed the air shield around her before she created it.**

"Butcher!" a man shouted from the back of the room. The hall started to devolve into chaos.

Shaken, Brenna shouted, "That wasn't me! Our Protectors are here not just to protect me. They protect all of you. They protect the Clan. They couldn't let someone loose a fireball in a room with innocents." As the room quieted, she looked down at a young boy kneeling in front of her, his eyes wide. She allowed her voice to drop to a normal volume. "They couldn't allow a fireball loose in a room with children."

And then a ripple of movement from the back of the room became two lines of women dressed in white robes. They walked toward her on each side of the hall, making their way to the front. People melted away in front of them. The line on Brenna's right was led by Morrighan. Brenna realized that all the women walking toward the front were Druids.

Morrighan and the other women formed a half circle at the front of the room, standing in front of Brenna, and turned to face the hall. All of them had their Glamor turned up full, to that Goddess-like glow the Druids used when they presided over the Clans' holy rituals.

Morrighan raised her arms into the air.

"Hear me, Clans of Ireland! This woman is the blessed of the Goddess! The Druids declare their support for Brenna O'Donnell and support her claim to the Seats of the Irish Clans. Once, the Tuatha de Danaan were one people. Under Lady Brenna, we shall be one people again. Hear me, Clans of Ireland! The Druids bless this woman's claim!"

What the hell? Brenna sent to Rebecca and Rhiannon.

Is that the only question you're capable of asking this evening? Didn't you know? Rhiannon sent back. **Morrighan is the High Priestess, the head Druid. Don't you Americans know anything? Brenna, reach into Corwin's memories.**

Brenna looked for Morrighan in Corwin's memories. The woman she found there was nothing like the fun-loving succubus that Brenna knew. A flash of her own memory surfaced. Morrighan conducting the ceremonies of Beltane at the O'Byrne estate.

That's a helluva lot of firepower standing in front of you. Rebecca sent.

Brenna counted twenty-seven Druids standing there. Rebecca was right. It was enough firepower to take out a Roman legion.

~~~

It was more than an hour later when Brenna was able to break free. People wanted to talk to her. Some seemed only to want to touch her. Parents brought their children to meet her. Surrounded by Druids, she made her way out to the quadrangle, and the scene inside was duplicated for another hour and a half. Brenna had never been comfortable in crowds and at times, she felt as though she was on the verge of being crushed.
~~~

Not everyone was welcoming, and using Corwin's memories, she was able to match the negative auras with identities. She marked those whose auras showed the most hostility and sent their names to Rebecca, Jeremy and Thomas.

But finally, tired and emotionally drained, she and her security team made their way through the manor back to the room she shared with Rebecca. Over the following week, she would be working with the household staff to convert Corwin's suite to her own. But for tonight, she wanted only the room she had always occupied at the O'Neill manor and a bed that felt somewhat familiar.

"What are you doing here?" Brenna asked Morrighan.

"When Rebecca contacted us and told us Corwin had died, I started contacting Druids across Ireland. I knew things up here might get nasty. We still have influence in this country, and I hoped we'd be able to calm things. We couldn't all come, but I think we had enough here to make an impression."

"You were certainly a welcome sight," Brenna said. "Thank you."

Reaching the room, one of her Protectors opened the door and stood aside so she could enter. She was startled when Rhiannon jumped in front of her.

"Has this room been vetted since she was last here?" Rhiannon asked.

"No," Donny said. "It should be all right. We were here just a couple of hours ago."

"Did you leave a guard here?" Rhiannon pressed.

"No, we didn't." He shot Brenna a guilty look. "You're right." Donny waved toward the door, and three Protectors swept into the room, electronic scans in their hands. A couple of minutes later, an O'Neill Protector came down the hall with a dog, and they also entered the room.

Donny stood in the doorway overseeing their search. Rhiannon stood behind him, craning her neck to look around him.

"You're going to have to treat this as a hostile setting," Jeremy told Donny. "You can't relax here like you do at O'Donnell."

Red-faced, Donny nodded.

The dog stopped in the middle of the bedroom and whined at the ceiling, then started to bark. Everyone's attention went to the animal, and then to the light fixture in the middle of the ceiling above him.

One of the Protectors, looking back over his shoulder at the dog, opened the door from the bedroom to the bathroom.

A massive explosion sent fire roiling through the bedroom and sitting room and out into the hall. Donny and Rhiannon were blown out of the doorway and across the hall, the team leader landing on top of her. Everyone in the hallway was knocked off their feet.

Someone threw an air shield over the doorway, containing the fire and smoke in the suite. The hall was already full of smoke and everyone was coughing.

Brenna crawled to where Donny and Rhiannon lay. Both were unconscious. Donny's clothing was burned away from his body, and the revealed skin was black with open red wounds. She peeled his pants away from his leg and found normal skin on the back of his calf. Placing her hand there, she began pouring healing energy into him even as she cast her mind into his body to diagnose his injuries.

The healers from her security team and Morrighan's found their way to them and began adding their efforts to hers. Then Rebecca was beside her, gently lifting Donny's body off Rhiannon and pulling the woman out from under him.

Rhiannon's hair was singed almost to her scalp in the front, her face and left hand burned bright red, but she mostly had been shielded from the blast by Donny's body.

"Can you take him and I'll see to her?" Brenna asked the healers.

"Keep feeding him energy," one replied. "He's going to need everything we can give him."

Morrighan crawled up.

"I can feed you," she said to the healer.

The healer nodded, and Brenna turned to Rhiannon. She sent her mind into her cousin's body. Quickly, she determined that the woman's injuries weren't serious, though she did have a concussion. Her burns were superficial. Brenna began to heal the bruising in Rhiannon's brain.

Additional Protectors, both O'Neill and O'Donnell, poured into the hallway, adding to the chaos of the scene.

"Get a fire hose through the window into that room!" someone shouted in an Irish accent. "Clear out the wounded, and clear the hall. Get this damn scene under control!"

~~~

Hours later, Brenna sat on the bed in Corwin's bedroom. After some debate, it had been decided to move her there as the safest place in the house. It had taken a small army of housekeepers to clean his clothes and personal effects out and change all the linens and towels. But that was after the Protectors declared it safe. Rebecca took a bedroom next to Brenna's in the suite, and Corwin's grieving companion was moved into a room in another wing.

A second bedroom, which had been used by Corwin's valet, was given to Rhiannon, and she was resting there
~~~

with a healer monitoring her. Rebecca and Morrighan sat with Brenna, sharing a glass of whiskey before going to bed.

"Donny is stable," Rebecca reported, running her fingers through her hair. "The healers tell me that he's looking at a long recovery and rehabilitation. The four Protectors that were in the room are dead."

She looked at the ceiling and took a long shuddering breath. "He's blind. They say there isn't anything they can do for that." Her voice broke at the end and she bit her lip, forcing back tears.

"Exactly what happened?" Brenna asked.

Rebecca squared her shoulders and assumed a straight-backed military posture. "Jeremy said there was a thermite bomb inside the ceiling. The light fixture was removed. They planted the bomb, then replaced the fixture. The trigger was wired to the bathroom door. When the door was opened, it went off. I think they wanted to make sure you were in the room, and they expected that you, or I, would be the one to open that door."

"Any idea who 'they' were?"

"No, though Finnian and his followers are the obvious suspects. Suspiciously, though, as soon as people found out that you had survived, Hugh and several hundred Protectors pulled out."

"Huh? Pulled out?" Brenna shook her head. "What the hell is going on?"

"They took a convoy of lorries and other vehicles and left."

"Where did they go?"

"Took the road to Derry. Not all of them arrived, but Hugh commandeered several aircraft there and flew out. To where, we're not sure."

In all their planning, they had always considered

Finnian to be the dangerous one. His father, Hugh, was dismissed as weak and uninterested in the succession.

"If they didn't all arrive in Derry, I guess we have some insurgents to worry about," Brenna said.

"So we assume."

"Hugh has the O'Neill Gift," Brenna said. "He's been hiding behind his shields, and possibly a construct, for years."

"Yeah, that's what I'm thinking, too," Rebecca said. "He wasn't strong enough to take out Corwin, so he bided his time. I wonder if he was the brains behind Finnian's rebellion."

"I want to screen everyone," Brenna said. "I want to meet everyone in the Clan. Until I approve people, no one should be considered safe."

Rebecca nodded. "That's going to take a long time. There are over thirty thousand people in the O'Neill Clan."

"Better that than leaving a snake in our midst."

"Can you read the aura of someone who's wearing a construct?" Morrighan asked from her chair across the room.

"Yes. A construct masks the mind. What I see is the soul. No one can mask what's in their soul." Brenna took a deep breath. "What's the word from O'Byrne? Has there been any trouble there?"

"A couple of minor incidents," Morrighan said. "Jared and Devlin think Andrew left the country. No one has seen him since Corwin's death was announced." Andrew O'Byrne was the oldest of Lord O'Byrne's surviving children. Unstable and a sadistic bully, he was generally disliked by those who knew him, and hated by his siblings. His was the only voice raised in opposition when Brenna was named the O'Byrne heir.

"So, at this point, our intelligence is that Andrew,

Finnian and Hugh are all out of the country, but we don't know for sure. Sounds more like guesswork than intelligence."

"That's basically it," Rebecca said. She downed her whiskey. "I'm going to bed, unless my lady has further need of my services."

"No, and thanks. Morrighan, have they found a bed for you?"

"Yes, although it's a bit tight. They've cleared the entire wing where your old room was. Fire damage to several rooms, especially on the floor above, and smoke damage throughout. But I usually don't have any difficulty finding a place to sleep." Morrighan winked at Brenna and made her way out.

~~~

Chapter 5

Progress is impossible without change, and those who cannot change their minds cannot change anything. - George Bernard Shaw

During the next week, Brenna spent ten hours a day screening a constant stream of people. First the Protectors, then the rest of the adults living on or around the O'Neill estate. Those people whose auras didn't look right were told to drop their shields and submit to a scan. If they didn't, Brenna smashed through their shields.

Seventy-three of the Protectors had their Gifts burned out and then they were exiled. Twenty-three were spies for Finnian, the rest for Hugh. Another two hundred sixty people were exiled for treason, and forty people were remanded to the Protectors for previously undetected crimes.

When she was finished with those people who lived close, she toured the Clan's facilities throughout the rest of Northern Ireland. For the time being, it would have to be
~~~

enough. Finnian was rumored to be in Scotland, and her security team didn't want her traveling there.

Hugh had also surfaced in Scotland. Three days after he left the O'Neill estate in Tyrone, Hugh walked into the Clan's Glasgow shipyard and announced his open rebellion. The majority of the fifteen hundred workers there had pledged him their support.

As soon as the healers had given their permission, Brenna teleported Rhiannon to the O'Byrne estate in Wicklow to complete her recovery. She was well known and respected in Wicklow and had many friends there. It seemed a safer place for someone who had been prescribed rest and quiet.

The healers told Brenna that Donny was stable, but needed better care than they could provide at the small infirmary on the estate. They recommended transporting him by helicopter to a Clan hospital in Derry. Checking with healers she knew and trusted in West Virginia, she decided the facilities in the States were a better option.

Brenna teleported Donny directly to the burn ward at St. Brigid's, the O'Donnell hospital in Charleston, West Virginia. The doctors and nurses put him in a special burn bed. He was dosed to the gills with painkillers and neural blocked by the healers. Brenna stood looking down at him, tears running down her cheeks. He had protected her for four years, giving scant regard to his own safety. More than that, he was a close friend, Collin's cousin, and a frequent guest for dinner when she and Collin entertained.

Donny told her telepathically, **It's not so bad being blind as a telepath. I can use other people's eyes.**

I'll find out who did this, and they'll pay, Brenna answered.

That I don't doubt, knowing you. Has Clarice arrived yet? Clarice was his long-time lover. She had driven to the hospital from the O'Donnell estate.

Yes, she got here a few minutes ago.

Donnie took a deep breath. **Do I look really bad?**

Brenna projected an image to him. He was nude, covered head to toe in white cream. Gross fluids leaked through cracks in the cream.

Can you convince her not to come in? he asked.

Yes, I'll have the doctors tell her the risk of infection is too high and you're too weak. I'll tell her she can visit you telepathically until you're ready to receive visitors.

Thanks, Brenna. He drifted off to sleep.

Collin had arrived in Tyrone with the first five hundred O'Donnell Protectors. Another five hundred Protectors bolstered security in Donegal, the traditional O'Donnell homeland, and five hundred more were sent to Wicklow. After Hugh's treason was discovered, a thousand Protectors were dispatched to Edinburgh to bolster O'Donnell's hold on eastern Scotland.

For Brenna, having Collin there provided all the rest and calm that she needed. It seemed as though it had been months since she'd shared a bed with him, and she relished having him there, both personally and professionally.

Collin calmly took over coordination of the security forces. Brenna teleported to Wicklow and returned with Jared Wilkins, Brenna's and Rebecca's cousin, and Devlin O'Conner, O'Byrne's head of security. Almost immediately, Collin convened a council of war.

"We've received word that about three hundred workers at the Glasgow shipyards have abandoned Hugh," Thomas O'Neill was saying as Brenna entered the room. "We've recruited about thirty, all former Protectors, to stay inside as intelligence assets. All told, it appears Hugh has about a thousand Protectors, and of course, the other five thousand people who have declared for him have Clan training. We're rounding up as many as we can identify and find."

Beginning at puberty, when a person's Gifts manifested, the Irish Clans trained all of their children in basic Protector skills, as well as in their Gifts. Brenna knew that O'Donnell required at least five Gifts for a person applying to the Protectors, including Aerokinesis, but most people didn't qualify. Many young people worked as Protectors after college for thirty to fifty years, then retired and pursued other endeavors. It was a great way to see the world and extend their educations.

"How many Protectors does O'Neill have?" Brenna asked.

"About three thousand, after the defections to Hugh and Finnian," Thomas said.

"And O'Byrne?" she asked, turning to Devlin.

"About two thousand," he answered.

She looked at Collin, raising one eyebrow in question.

"We have three thousand normally stationed in the British Isles," he said. "We've added two thousand more in the past two weeks."

"Jesus," she breathed. "How many do we have total?"

Collin sent her a spear thread, **We don't normally let those numbers out.**

Collin, the people sitting here are 'we'. These are my people now.

Collin looked around, then said, "I've just been reminded that essentially we're all the same Clan now. O'Donnell currently has about fifteen thousand Protectors spread across the globe."

"That's almost a quarter of the Clan," Brenna said.

"No," Collin said. "The Clan is over eighty thousand, with another thirty thousand people affiliated with us."

Brenna blinked at him, attempting to assimilate that.

While she had held the title of Vice Chairman of the Board of O'Donnell Group for the past four years, most of her time was spent with the Clan's business side. She left security and Clan organization issues to Rebecca. "What do you mean by affiliates?" she finally asked.

"People that we consider as friends, that we can call on if need be, and to whom we extend our protection if they need it," Devlin answered. "RB and her family fall into that category at O'Byrne," Devlin answered her.

"RB is Clan now," Rebecca said. "Brenna, the three Clans have about two hundred thousand members and affiliates. If you add in our allies, you, Lord O'Byrne, and Seamus are responsible for over three hundred and fifty thousand people."

"And we're going to protect them with twenty thousand Protectors? That doesn't seem like enough," Brenna said.

"If we called a general mobilization, we could quadruple that," Collin said. "That would include all of the retirees under a hundred twenty years old, and probably a lot of older ones. That means people like Jeremy who officially aren't Protectors any longer."

"And we've got five thousand renegades in Scotland and Northern Ireland," Brenna said. "What are we going to do about them?"

"We can't just stage a frontal assault," Thomas said. "The shipyards are right on the River Clyde in Glasgow. Any kind of military operation would be much too public. We need to draw Hugh out and overwhelm him."

"And he knows that and has no reason to come out and fight on our ground," Collin said. "For now, he has the upper hand."

"Blockade it," Rebecca suggested. "No one in, no one out. Surround him and bombard the people inside with propaganda. Let them know they're trapped and their families are under our control."

"That would assume we controlled Glasgow," Thomas said, "which we don't."

"How many Protectors would it require to take the city?" Brenna asked.

"To totally control the city? Probably between three and five thousand," Devlin answered.

"The majority of the people who work at the shipyards live in Dunallen, a small town on the outskirts of Glasgow," Thomas said. "It's an O'Neill town. The government and constabulary are all telepaths. We can take control of it and the workers' families."

Brenna was silent for several minutes, then looked at Collin. "Do it. Shut off the shipyards and evacuate all of their families to Edinburgh. Mobilize all the retirees in the British Isles from all three Clans. I've checked with Fergus, and he's given me the authority, subject to Devlin's veto on any plans that might make O'Byrne less secure. Set up internment camps for the mutineers' families. I'm not going to play their damned game. I want peace restored and I want it done as soon as we possibly can."

"You can order a mobilization of O'Neill," Collin said. "You don't have the authority to mobilize O'Donnell without Seamus's approval."

"That's what I was just doing. A three-way with Seamus and Fergus. Do it," she said, rising to her feet. "I want to see a plan to cut off Hugh's rebellion by this time tomorrow. And don't forget Finnian and Andrew. Find them. I want them shut down, too."

Immediately, all communications in or out of the shipyard were cut off. Customers and suppliers were notified that routine maintenance originally scheduled for two months hence had been moved up, and the production lines would be idle for a month.

~~~

Chapter 6

We are made wise not by the recollection of our past, but by the responsibility for our future. - George Bernard Shaw

That night when they were alone, Collin told Brenna, "I think there's a critical piece of knowledge you haven't been told about the O'Donnell Clan. The statistics Callie has compiled about how Gifts are distributed don't accurately reflect the Irish Clans, and especially not O'Donnell."

"Statistics? I don't understand what you mean," Brenna said.

"Worldwide, about fifty percent of all telepaths have only one Gift. Remember that statistic? Another twenty-five percent have only two Gifts?"

"Yes, that's what I was told."

"Well, that doesn't apply to the Irish Clans. When Seamus immigrated to the States, the people who went with him were among the strongest telepaths who were sworn to him. They were a small group, and that's why we're so aware of the need to avoid inbreeding. In the O'Donnell Clan in the U.S., only about ten percent have a single Gift. About seventy-five percent have five or more. That's why we can field such a large Protector force."

"You said those statistics don't reflect the reality in all the Irish Clans."

"That's correct. Telepaths in Ireland also are much stronger than those in the rest of Europe. From what we know about Africa, it's rare to find people with as many as five Gifts. Look at Carlos. He's strong enough to be a Clan Chief in South America, but he isn't strong enough to be
~~~

considered for the O'Donnell Protector force," Collin said, referring to Rebecca's husband.

"Do the other Clans know that?" Brenna asked.

"They know that O'Donnell Protectors are elite," Collin answered. "There are strong telepaths among our enemies, but on average a hundred of ours will kick ass on five hundred of theirs."

"And what good does that do us in a civil war?"

"I'm hoping we don't have a war," he answered.

~~~

The following day, word came that an O'Neill factory in Dumfries, Scotland, had been damaged by a car bomb. Over forty people were killed and a couple of hundred were injured. An hour later, another car bomb went off at an O'Byrne facility in Wales, with an even greater loss of life.

In notes left at the scenes, Finnian claimed responsibility for the Scottish blast, and Andrew took responsibility for the Welsh explosion. The lists of demands contained in the notes were almost identical. Collin's experts determined that the bombs were of identical manufacture. It didn't take a genius to figure out that Finnian and Andrew were working together.

Security at all three Clans' facilities in the British Isles was boosted to levels normally seen at military bases. It was difficult to conceal such measures in the large cities, such as London. It was even more difficult to deal with the English and Scottish police who swarmed over the bombed sites. And then there was the press, who broadcast news of the bombings and speculated that the IRA, or maybe Al-Qaeda or the Mafia, were responsible.

The police were frankly baffled as to who would want to bomb those particular targets. Neither of the sites was the type of place normal terrorists would strike. O'Neill and O'Byrne corporate representatives were besieged by both
~~~

the police and the press seeking answers.

"We can't have too much of this," Collin said to a meeting of Brenna's security officers. "It brings too much attention to the Clans."

"That may be what they hope," Rebecca said. "But they can't expect that we'll meet those ridiculous demands."

"They're delusional," Thomas said. "Hugh might have some hope that he could succeed Brenna if she stepped down, but the Clans would never accept those two fools."

"Perhaps they're hoping we'll offer something to buy them off," Brenna said. "Hugh may be hoping I'll give him Scotland."

"That's possible," Collin conceded. "He's obviously been building a base of support in Scotland for years."

"Hugh was the O'Neill in Scotland for the past twenty or thirty years," Thomas said. "Corwin rarely traveled, and I doubt the younger people there have ever met him."

"Have we heard anything from him?" Brenna asked.

"Yes, he's said that he would allow you to exit gracefully," Thomas said. "We've shut down two printers in Belfast that were printing up a manifesto to distribute. In it, Hugh says that O'Neill has never been subservient to O'Donnell, and it isn't going to start now. It's a call for rebellion."

"That probably has some appeal," Brenna said.

"Yes, it might," Thomas acknowledged, "but the bombing in Dumfries throws a spanner into his argument. He can't be happy with Finnian. No one in the Clan wanted this to come to bloodshed, and those spilling our own blood won't be very popular."

"The statement you put out after the bombings has been very well received, especially in Scotland," Jeremy said, referring to a statement drafted by Brenna's advisors and posted in all O'Neill and O'Byrne facilities. It was also posted on the Clans' websites.

"Any support Andrew might have in Wales has evaporated," Devlin said, "and your support in Dublin and Wicklow has grown. No one wants to get blown up, and Andrew made a mistake by claiming responsibility. Those who know him think even less of him now."

Jared spoke up. "Andrew made a major strategic mistake. If he'd waited until Lord O'Byrne stepped down, his actions could be interpreted as a strike against you. But by throwing in with Finnian and striking now, it's rebellion against his father. Everyone likes Fergus, and in spite of his kindly country lord demeanor, he's tough as nails. There's a manuscript in the O'Byrne library that your mother wrote about the campaign he led in Italy during the Silent War. Very interesting reading."

"Yes, Andrew is a fool," Devlin said. "Lord O'Byrne is mad as hell. He's issued a kill-on-sight order against Andrew."

~~~

Additional incidents involving snipers firing on Protectors and small explosive devices on roads to the estates in Wicklow and Tyrone occurred over the next week. They were more in the line of nuisance attacks, but there were no more large events that drew the press.

By the end of the week, Protectors were staged around the village of Dunallen and the roundup of the mutineers' families began. The blockade of the shipyard was put in place at the same time. Anyone wanting to leave the yard was taken into custody and shipped to Ireland. The families were shipped to warehouses that had been prepared to house them in Edinburgh.

A majority of the five thousand telepaths living in the Glasgow area resided in Dunallen. That included shipyard workers and their families, as well as merchants and those
~~~

who worked for other businesses in the Glasgow area. The town's administration and constabulary were all O'Neill Clan members. All of the realty agents in the town were telepaths, and all home sales and rentals were only advertised locally.

Rebecca was on hand to observe the operation as Brenna's representative. The new Clan Chief was very concerned that none of the people involved were abused or mistreated in any way. Before her life with the Clans, Rebecca would have marveled at the quiet efficiency involved in evacuating most of a town. There was no shouting or arguing, no violence. Protectors drove lorries into a neighborhood, broadcast their orders telepathically, and people left their homes and boarded the trucks. The Protectors encountered only a few instances of resistance, and the troublemakers were surrounded with air shields and carted off.

The names of all the mutineers inside the shipyard were known, and the locations of their family members were known, too. By the end of the third day, less than two thousand inhabitants remained in Dunallen. The number of workers remaining inside the shipyard had also shrunk. When the roundup started, three hundred people simply walked out to the Protectors surrounding the yard and asked to join their families. All of these workers were told to drop their shields and submit to interrogation. Two hundred were allowed to join their families in Edinburgh, the rest were escorted to a ship for transport to Ireland.

Two of the workers abandoning the yard resisted. One used Neural Disruption against the Protectors and was shot dead. The other was subdued and transported.

Attacks by insurgents outside the yard began the evening of the second day after the blockade began. These were hit-and-run attacks against Protectors and occurred at multiple locations all over the area. Interrogated captives revealed that some of the insurgents were loyal to Finnian, others to Hugh. It was unclear whether the two forces were coordinating with each other.

A car bomb was stopped half a block away from the main O'Neill offices in the Glasgow city center. Unfortunately, the driver managed to detonate the bomb, taking out a block of the city that had nothing to do with the Clan.

Rebecca had taken part in numerous small operations and tactical battles, but she'd never been in the middle of such a large operation before. She moved around the area, checking in with the evacuation forces, then traveling to the shipyard, and occasionally checking in with the operation's headquarters at the town hall. Brenna checked with her every hour wanting to know what was going on.

Finally, Rebecca told her sister, **Look, you're driving me nuts. I'll call you when I have something to report. Okay?**

I'm worried. I need to know that you're all right, Brenna responded.

I understand that. But you're a distraction. Just cool your jets and I'll stay in touch.

Brenna reluctantly agreed, but Rebecca found out later that she just switched her constant badgering to Padraig O'Malley, the operation commander.

The fourth morning, about two hours before sunrise, Hugh's forces counter-attacked out of the shipyard. Seven hundred rebel Protectors hit the Clan forces at three points. With heavy equipment and air shields as cover, the rebels used telepathic and conventional weapons to drive their advance.

One group contained a large number of electrokinetics. Drawing on the massive electrical capacity of the shipyard, they drove a hole through the blockaders' line. A second group flooded the area outside the main gate with fire. Even an air shield couldn't protect a person from the heat of the flames and fireballs if he was exposed long enough. The air inside an air shield could heat up beyond what a person could survive. The blockading Protectors were forced to retreat.

The third group used a combination of Neural Disruption, Empathic Projection and Dominance to clear a path to the River Clyde. Reaching the docks, they commandeered two ships and sailed away downriver to the sea.

The offensive was preceded by an attack on Clan headquarters in the town hall. Between fifty and one hundred fighters shut down all electric power to the hall and used a combination of conventional and telepathic weapons to breach the main entrance doors.

Clan Protectors on the roof and inside the building held off the attack until help could arrive, but while the loyal commanders were distracted, the breakouts from the shipyard occurred.

Rebecca missed all the action, being asleep in a spare bedroom in the Dunallen Mayor's home. Carrying a take-out cup of coffee, she arrived at the town hall at sunrise. Workers were fitting heavy metal panels to close off the gaping hole where the main entrance doors had been blown off their hinges. The area around the building looked like a war zone, with scorch marks, two burned out cars, and a lot of debris.

Shaking her head, she entered the building through a side door and encountered the Mayor and Padraig speaking to five representatives of the Scottish national police. Although no bodies were present, Rebecca could see at least three large smears of blood on the floor. The building foyer was a shambles.

"Something happened here," the lead policeman was

saying. "You can't bloody tell me you have things under control. Just look at this place."

"Shit. We don't have time for this," Rebecca said, and took control of the man's mind. Then she moved into the minds of the other four policemen and controlled them, too. The Mayor and Padraig turned to stare at her.

"What in the hell are you doing talking to them?" Rebecca asked. "You can't explain something like this."

"We have police and press all over the place, and at the shipyard, too," Padraig said, his bearing stiff. He hadn't said anything during the past three days, but he'd made it obvious enough that he resented a young girl looking over his shoulder.

"Bloody hell," Rebecca said. "Call your O'Donnell commanders and tell them to implement damage control around the shipyard. Find some people with more than half a brain who can *think* and assign at least one to every press crew you can find. Block off all entrances to the battle zones and blur the minds of anyone who approaches. This is Containment 101. Don't you people in Ireland prepare for this kind of crap?"

She held up her hand to forestall any answers and pulled out her phone to call Brenna.

"Sis? We have a major clusterfuck in Glasgow. I need at least one, preferably several, containment teams here ASAP."

"What's happening there?" Brenna answered. "We're getting reports of a major battle."

"Call me," Rebecca said and hung up. Immediately, she heard Brenna's voice in her head.

What the hell's going on?

We had at least two battles. We have Scottish police and press. The people on the ground here are bloody incompetents. They were trying to* talk *to the Goddamn* *police!

She showed Brenna the scene in the town hall.

**I need people here who know how to deal with a public problem. I need them now, and I don't care how they get here,* * Rebecca sent.

**I'll call Nigel and Callie,* * Brenna sent and then broke the connection.

"Okay," Rebecca said, turning to Padraig, "what's our status?"

Red faced, he gathered himself and said, "We had an attack here that we fought off. There was a three-pronged breakout at the shipyard. Heavy casualties. Hugh's forces captured two ships and took them to sea. Hugh has several hundred men loose in the Glasgow area."

"Wonderful," Rebecca said. She gestured toward the police, still standing in the middle of the room and staring into space. "What are they doing here?"

"There was a police helicopter that witnessed the battle at the shipyard and reported it. These men showed up a few minutes ago wanting to know what's going on," the mayor said.

"Why are they here and not at the shipyard?" Rebecca asked.

"They showed up and some idiots let them into town," Padraig said.

"Idiot is right. Find out who it was and ship them to Ireland. I wouldn't bet that they weren't working for Hugh."

The looks on the Mayor's and Padraig's faces showed sudden shock.

Rebecca ran her hand through her hair and thought furiously.

"So, what's our story? The town hall was hit with a

meteor? An industrial accident at the yard? Alien invasion? I know there were containment plans included with this battle plan. Haul them out and let's figure out what we're going to plant in these guy's minds."

Fifteen minutes later, Rebecca received a spear thought from Brenna.

Visualize a landing spot for me.

What? You can't come here. It's a Goddamn war zone.

I'm not staying long. I need to bring you some help.

Rebecca looked around and then sent the image of a large clear space in a nearby hallway. Almost immediately, Brenna appeared holding Collin with one hand and a slender woman in a Protector uniform with the other. Rebecca recognized Shia MacDonald, one of the Clan's strongest distance communicators.

Brenna looked around. "This is a mess," she said.

Then she noticed the Scottish police. "Collin, what are we going to do with them?"

"We've been discussing that," Rebecca said. "I don't know how to explain this."

"Don't try," Collin said. "When you have a disaster this big, go for the big lie. Implant in their minds that nothing happened here. They came out, found everything normal, had tea with the mayor, talked about football, and went home again."

"What about the press and the helicopters?" Rebecca asked.

"Same thing. Wipe out everything everyone saw." He looked at the mayor. "Have your people at the news organizations and the police stations crash all the computer systems, wipe out everyone's memories of this morning, wipe all the recordings. Don't worry about inconsistencies or lost time."

"And the helicopters?" Rebecca prompted.

"How many distance communicators do you have?" Collin asked Padraig.

"About fifteen or sixteen," the operations commander answered.

"Set them up in shifts around the clock," Collin said. "If any helicopters or small planes fly over, take over the pilots' and passengers' minds, and send them into the bay."

"Collin, they're innocents!" Brenna protested.

"No, they're threats," he said, his face hard. "Treat them like enemy combatants. They could destroy us all. The last thing we need is global attention to a telepathic war."

He looked at Shia. "Do you have any problem with that?"

She shook her head, her face totally expressionless. "No. I was in Ecuador. I doubt anything we do here will match that horror."

He reached out and squeezed her shoulder. "We'll do our damnedest to avoid that."

Collin pulled Brenna to him and kissed her, then said, "Get out of here. Tell Nigel to get me those containment teams and to monitor everything coming out of this area."

"Okay," Brenna said. "Padraig, do we know if Hugh is still in the shipyard? Some communications we monitored indicated that he may be on one of those ships they stole."

"We don't know," Padraig said. "We know he was still in the yard yesterday."

Brenna nodded and disappeared.

~~~

Chapter 7

I learned long ago, never to wrestle with a pig. You get dirty, and
~~~

besides, the pig likes it. - George Bernard Shaw

Collin immediately took charge. After assessing the situation, he called Shia to him and had her link him to Brenna.

**I need about half a dozen of your Druids,* he told her.

I'll talk to Morrighan. What do you need Druids for?

I can't believe we allowed the shipyard to maintain electrical power. I want to cut it all off. And never put Padraig in charge of a major operation again. The man is a good soldier, but he lacks any kind of imagination.

Of all electrokinetics, the Druids were the most adept. Their ability to detect and manipulate electricity went far beyond that of any other telepaths.

Aren't we closing the barn door a little bit late? Brenna asked.

Perhaps, but I doubt that all of their electrokinetics broke out last night. Most, if not all, of the welders and electricians employed at the shipyard are electrokinetics. Besides, if we want a siege to be successful, we cut off all of their resources. No lights, no refrigeration, no electricity to draw on as a weapon. I've already given orders to cut off their fresh water.

Gotcha,* Brenna sent. *I'll get you some Druids. Anything else?

Magnetokinetics, cryokinetics. People who are strong in Empathic Projection. Hugh was very creative in putting the force together that stole the ships.

**Sounds as though you need more than a half-dozen Druids,* Brenna sent.

The more the merrier. You know as well as I do what a Druid can do.

By that evening, Brenna had teleported twenty-five Druids to Glasgow.

~~~

"Hi, handsome," a familiar voice said from the door to Collin's office. He looked up and saw Irina standing there in a seductive pose with a sultry, come-hither look on her face.

"Well, hello," he answered with a smile. "What are you doing in Glasgow?"

"I heard you were holding a succubi convention, and I came to chastise you for not inviting me."

He chuckled. "I asked for Irish Druids to augment my forces here. I hadn't thought of it as a party."

She walked in and sat across the desk from him.

"I was bored in London, so I thought I'd come up here and see if you could use me. And if you don't want my body, maybe you can use my talents."

"Actually, I probably can."

He spent the next half hour filling her in on the situation. Over the past three years, she had received extensive training in espionage and covert activities. When he finished, she leaned back in her chair, chewing her lip and staring off into space. After a few minutes, she turned her gaze back to him.

"You don't know where the rebels who broke out of the shipyard are located?"

He shook his head. "There have been a few quick strikes against our forces, but for the most part, no, we don't. We don't think they've left the area. They're out there, and if we move on the shipyard, they'll be at our backs."

"It would help if you could get someone inside," Irina said. "Someone who might help to locate them."
~~~

"Yes, it would," he acknowledged. "Do you have an idea on how to do that?"

"I could get captured," she said.

Of all the things she might have said, that was completely unexpected. "I'm sorry. I guess I wasn't paying attention. What did you say?"

"You could send me out with one of your electric detection teams and let me get captured," she said. "Send us to one of the hot spots, where those guerilla raids have taken place, and try to draw out some of Hugh's forces. Let them capture me." She smiled. "The chances of Irish Clansmen hurting a Druid are very low, and I can control a bunch of men better than anyone else could. And since Brenna and I are linked, she'd be able to track me, no matter where they might take me. With some luck, they're going to be in contact with Hugh's other forces, maybe even Hugh himself. You'd have a spy inside and they wouldn't even know it." She batted her eyes and pushed her chest out. "How could anyone see me as a threat?"

Rebecca,* Collin sent, *Can you come to my office? I have a succubus with a martyr complex pitching a plan to me that I'd like you to hear.

On my way. I thought she was in Tyrone. The exasperation in Rebecca's mental voice was evident.

When Rebecca arrived, she greeted Irina and hugged her. Then she looked around and asked, "Where is she?"

"You're holding her," Collin said.

"Huh? When you said a succubus with a martyr complex, I thought you meant Brenna."

"It's obviously contagious," Collin said. "Irina, could you please explain your hare-brained scheme to Rebecca?"

After explaining her plan again, Irina said, "I understand that it carries an element of risk, and the assumptions may be wishful thinking, but if it does work, it significantly hurts Hugh's capabilities."

"I thought you weren't paying attention when Siobhan and I were trying to train you in covert operations tactics," Rebecca said.

"I multitask," Irina said with a wry grin. "Just because I'm reading a fashion magazine doesn't mean I'm not listening." She looked up at the ceiling and took a deep breath. "On July 21st, two years ago, we discussed various methods of insertion for covert operatives. Among those methods were several variations on creating captive or hostage situations that are more advantageous to us than to the captors."

She turned her attention back to Collin and Rebecca. "It just seems to make sense in this situation. They know all their own people. We're not going to get anyone from O'Neill or O'Donnell inside that they trust."

Rebecca stared at her, mouth agape.

"Do you know who trained Siobhan O'Conner in covert operations?" Collin asked.

Both women shook their heads.

"Maureen O'Donnell. Brenna's mother. It was before my time, but Seamus and Rory have told me she was the best operative the Clan ever had. But Maureen could take more chances than other people could. In addition to being a succubus, she was a Dominant with the O'Neill Gift and air shielding. She was almost invulnerable as well as being lethal."

"So I have to be a little more cautious and subtle," Irina said.

"Yeah," Rebecca said. "But, Collin, I think it would work. As she says, Brenna can track her, so we can pull her out if things get too sticky."

"You forget that these Irish fighters are far more familiar with Druids and their capabilities than other people. They all grew up around Druids."

"Yes," Irina said, "but intellectually understanding what a Druid can do and fitting that into their own experiences are two different things. Mostly they'll just avoid having sex with me. They won't think of other things I can do. I mean, how dangerous can a tiny little thing like me be?"

~~~

Most of the tactical groups Collin sent out with the Irish Druids had sixty to ninety Protectors. It was decided to send only fifteen men with Irina to make them a more attractive target. Rebecca, who was linked to the diminutive young succubus, would follow at a discrete distance.

"What's the maximum distance you can track her?" Collin asked.

"About half a mile," Rebecca said. "I'll need a car available in case they escape that way, but I can follow them fine if they stay on foot."

Collin didn't say anything. He was a strong telepath, but his own range was half of hers, and she still hadn't fully matured. He'd become so used to Brenna and Rebecca's occasional matter-of-fact revelations concerning their abilities that he wasn't even surprised anymore. He was just happy that he was on the same side as Seamus O'Donnell's granddaughters.

The area chosen for the operation was north of the shipyard where a major set of underground electrical cables ran. The team drove to a neighborhood four blocks north of the yard and then set out on foot, with Irina tracing the cables through her electrokinetic ability.

Druids felt electricity without thinking about it. It was a constant background hum to them in an urban setting. Rebecca, who was also an electrokinetic but not a succubus, had to reach out and search for an electrical
~~~

source. Irina simply needed to separate all the cables into individual sources in her mind.

Collin's plan for the succubi was to follow the cables until all connections and subsidiary cables had branched off. At the point where there was no more branching, and the cables left ran only into the shipyard, Irina would block the current. Using utility company maps, the team would then call in a team with a backhoe to dig up the street and physically cut the cable or cables.

The team was less than a hundred yards from the fence surrounding the shipyard when Irina stopped, pointing at a spot in the street near a manhole. "Here," she said to the Protectors.

She walked across the street, then came back. "Yeah, there aren't any more branches. Only one cable running straight into the shipyard."

Several men pried up the manhole and one of them dropped into the hole with an electric torch.

"We don't even have to dig," he shouted up from the hole. "There's a large tunnel going right into the yard. Electrical, water and sewer lines, the whole works. We might even be able to send assault troops through here."

"Shut it down," the team leader said to Irina.

Almost immediately all the lights in that section of the shipyard went dark. The lights in the houses and businesses around and behind them stayed on.

The team leader smiled. "Nice job."

"Mmmmm," Irina replied. "I've never held this much electricity before. Kinda makes me feel ... horny."

He laughed.

Is there anything that* doesn't *make you feel horny? Rebecca asked.

I mean this makes me feel* really *horny, Irina told

her.

The streetlights dimmed and a bolt of electrical energy splashed across the air shield covering Irina and the team leader. A large fireball followed.

Retreat! the team leader sent. **Let the electrical line go. Execute the plan!**

A larger force was ready to come into the area and cut off the electricity into the shipyard if Irina's plan worked. The important thing now was to get everyone out without injury.

The Protectors withdrew in good order. Irina lagged behind the team, as though she was having trouble keeping up with the larger men. When they were less than half a block away from the attack site, she stumbled and fell to the ground. Her team rounded the corner of a building and disappeared, apparently unaware she was no longer with them.

Several men swarmed her. One of them grabbed her and pulled her off the ground.

"Uh-oh. Shouldn't have done that," Irina said as the enormous reservoir of electricity she held discharged through him. A sound like a thunderclap accompanied the release of the electricity. She found herself sitting on the ground, dazed and looking at six still bodies lying in a circle around her.

Are you okay? Rebecca asked. She had been hitchhiking in Irina's mind.

I think so. The lights are back on.

You were still holding the electricity from the line?

Yeah. I forgot to let it go.

Shit. No wonder you fried everyone. You just channeled the power from a 400-volt main industrial line into them.

A number of men ran up to her, some wearing Protector uniforms. That confused Irina at first, then their leader pointed a pistol at her face and she realized they were rebels.

"What happened here?" he asked in an Irish brogue.

"We were running after you attacked us," Irina said. "I couldn't keep up and then I tripped. Someone covered me in an air shield and then these guys showed up." She waved her hand at the bodies. "Then there was an explosion. I guess the air shield protected me."

He looked skeptical.

"Killed by electrical shock," one of the other men said.

"Not Neural Disruption?" the leader asked.

"I don't think so," the other man said. "There are electrical burns."

Another man approached and reported that Irina's team had escaped.

"Come along, lassie," the leader said. "Stand up and walk in front of me. I'll have this pistol pointed at your head the whole time. You know what will happen if I twitch, don't you?"

Irina nodded.

"Then be a good girl. It sure would be a pity for such a lovely lass as yourself to lose her head."

They walked several blocks, winding their way through the streets and heading north from the shipyard. Turning a corner, Irina saw a white van with the back doors open.

**They're putting me in a van,* Irina sent to Rebecca.

**That's okay. I'm in the car already,* Rebecca sent.

I won't be able to see where we're going.

Look around. Can you see any street signs?

**Yeah,* Irina said, and gave Rebecca the names of the

cross streets.

I have you located. You may not be able to see where you're going, but you'll be able to tell if the van turns right or left. Just tell me that, and I'll be able to track you.

Rebecca looked at the GPS map on the tablet in her lap, and marked Irina's location with a stylus. She told her driver, "Head for this location, and I'll give you directions from there. We'll have to play it by ear and hope we stay close."

~~~

They drove for twenty minutes, making a lot of turns, and the leader held his pistol to Irina's head the whole time. When they stopped, another man tied a blindfold over her eyes and she was hustled out of the van. She could tell when they took her inside a building.

We've stopped, she sent to Rebecca.

We're still in range, Rebecca sent. **We're going to drive around and try to triangulate your exact position. Let me know if I start to fade out.**

"Take off your shirt," a man's voice said.

"Pervert," Irina told him. "Men are all alike. You want to see my boobs? Fine." She unbuttoned her shirt and took it off.

The barrel of a pistol pressed against her temple.

"Be very still," the voice said, "and raise your hands straight up."

She did as she was told, and a cold, round rod was pressed against her spine. Someone wrapped wide tape several times around her torso and the rod. Then the blindfold was taken off.

"You can put your shirt back on," the rebel leader said. He still held the pistol.

Another man stepped into her line of vision. He held
~~~

up a small plastic box.

"Do you see the button I'm holding with my thumb?" he asked her.

Irina nodded.

"This is a dead-man's switch. It's wired to set off the detonator on the stick of dynamite we just taped to you. Anything happens to me, and you'll die a very messy death. Do you understand me, lass?"

Numbly, Irina nodded.

"I'm truly sorry to have to do this," the leader said, "but you have to understand I can't have a Druid here without some means to control her. I don't want to hurt you, and if you're a good girl, we'll eventually set you free. The detonator has a range of about 75 feet. If you get farther than that from Walter, it will be the same as if he took his thumb off the switch."

"So, I don't have to go to the loo with him?" she asked.

"No, and he doesn't have to go with you," the leader chuckled. "Would you like something to eat or drink?"

"Yes, that would be nice. Thank you."

To her surprise, they led her out of the room and through a large, rambling house to the kitchen.

She was finishing her sandwich when Rebecca contacted her again.

I'm pretty sure I know where you are. We drove by a large house with all the curtains drawn and saw a white van parked in the driveway. What can you tell us about the inside?

Irina told her about the dynamite and went on to describe what she had seen inside the house. **I've seen a couple of dozen men, and I can hear people moving around upstairs. I've also seen several laptop computers, and* *everyone seems to have a cell phone. As far as I can tell, they're communicating with people outside.**

You mean using the cell phones? Rebecca asked.

The phones, but I also saw someone talking to a computer screen. And they're also getting and sending emails.

You said they're using laptops? What are they hooked to?

A wireless network, I guess. None of the ones I've seen has a cable.

Hold on, Rebecca sent and went quiet.

The rebel leader came into the dining room and sat down across from Irina.

"I need to ask you some questions, lass."

"My name's Irina. And yours?"

"Brian. What were you doing out there? You can't tell me that Lady O'Donnell is sending wee lassies such as you out on patrol."

"I'm an electrokinetic," she started out.

He barked out a laugh. "You're a damned bit more than that. Batting your eyes at me with the face of an angel and the body ...," he trailed off. "Lass, I've known Druids all my life, but you're in a class by yourself."

He questioned her for over an hour, and Irina did her best to answer him honestly but without revealing any information that she figured he didn't already have. During the interrogation, Rebecca contacted her, and then simply stayed in her mind.

Eventually, Irina asked to go to the bathroom and Walter led her to one on the second floor.

Once she was alone, Rebecca sent, **We know where you are, and Collin has set up a monitoring station. They're transmitting without encryption, and we've already* *connected to their wireless network. The question now is how to get you out of there in one piece.**

I don't think they have any intention to hurt me, Irina told her. **They're afraid of me, or at least their leader is. That's why they taped the dynamite to me. If I can get hold of that switch, then I can zap all of them and just walk out.**

Don't do anything stupid, Rebecca sent. **Just be patient.**

Oh, I don't mind spending the night.

What are you planning? Rebecca asked, catching a suspiciously gay tone in Irina's mental voice.

Well, I've been dribbling pheromones at a low level since I got here. They're already starting to act a bit distracted. I'll gradually increase the dose. When they give me a place to sleep, the guy with the switch is going to be cooped up in a closed room with me.

Be damned careful.

Oh, I will be. I have a constant reminder of my situation taped to my back.

~~~

Things worked out better than Irina dared hope. They put her in a small room in the attic, away from all the activity in the house. There was a small bed, and a chair that her guardian sat in next to the door.

A young protector came to the room to relieve Walter just as she was ready to undress for bed. As covertly as she could, she watched them transfer the switch. The first man slid a small slide switch on the side of the box to another position and handed it to the new man. He in turn put his thumb on the big red button and then moved the slide switch back to its original location.

They lied to me, Irina told Rebecca. **I'll bet that if I'm more than seventy-five feet away from the box, it*
~~~

*doesn't go off when it loses connection with the detonator.** She sent an image of the scene she'd just witnessed.

Collin agrees with you, Rebecca sent a few moments later. **If it worked the way they told you, it would have gone off when they turned it off. Be careful, girlfriend.**

Walter left, and the young man sat down in the chair.

Irina turned up the release of her pheromones, and turning to face him, took off her blouse.

"I'm Irina. What's your name?"

"Harold."

"Is there a way to dim the light?" Irina asked, taking off her bra. The duct tape was irritating her skin, and she wanted to nothing more than to rid herself of it so she could scratch.

"No, there isn't," he said.

She leaned down and skimmed her jeans down to her ankles. His eyes followed her breasts. She stood up straight and his eyes rose, never losing sight of his targets. Then he realized what she'd done, and she saw his eyes dart lower, to the neatly trimmed blonde hair between her legs.

She kicked off her pants, stood, and neatly folded her clothes. Turning away from him, she bent over at the waist, leaned across the bed, and put the clothes in a pile on the far end. She began projecting her Glamor at a low level before she turned around.

"Well, I guess I can sleep with the light on," she said, yawning. She pulled back the covers and crawled into the bed, covering herself only with the sheet.

"Good night, Harold," she said, smiling at him.

"Good night, Irina," he whispered.

She closed her eyes and slowed her breathing to a steady pace. The dynamite made the pose wildly uncomfortable, but she lay on her back, inhaling deeply and pushing her chest up as she did. A bit of stimulation directed to her nipples contracted them to points. Harold's breathing became louder and more ragged, indicating that he was anything but relaxed. Figuring that men like women who smile, she didn't even try to control her facial muscles.

A soft knock at the door brought Harold to his feet. He answered it, and she heard Walter whisper, "Is everything all right?"

"Yes, she's asleep."

"We'll have someone relieve you in three hours," Walter said. "You'll be okay that long? You're not sleepy?"

"No, I'm fine."

"Call someone if you need to. Remember that in this small a space, that dynamite will kill you, too."

"I know. Believe me, I won't fall asleep," Harold said, a bit of exasperation shading his tone. He closed the door and sat down again.

Rebecca, Irina sent, **I have about three hours. What time is it?**

Just past midnight, Rebecca answered.

Time to go to work, Irina said, kicking up her Glam a bit more and restlessly rolling onto her side, facing Harold. As she did so, the sheet slipped down, uncovering one of her breasts. She released more pheromones and watched him through her eyelashes as he squirmed in his chair.

Over the next hour, Harold became more and more restless as Irina saturated the room with pheromones. She was beginning to wonder what it would take to arouse him when finally he rose to his feet and approached the bed. He stood looking down at her, practically panting, the bulge in his pants prominently displayed.

She opened her eyes, blinking and feigning sleepiness.

“Is everything okay?” she asked, making an abortive effort to sit up, which caused the sheet to fall to her waist.

“Yes, everything’s fine,” he whispered. “You’re beautiful.”

“Thank you,” she said with what she hoped was a sleepy-looking smile. “You’ve all been so nice to me here, but I’m still scared. I feel so alone. I just want someone to hold me and tell me everything’s going to be all right.” She punctuated her speech with a large pheromone burst and pull of her Influence.

Harold took a deep breath, which proved his undoing. She watched his eyes dilate and his breath quicken even more.

Giving him another burst, she said, “Could you hold me? Can you do that and still hold on to the switch?”

He sat beside her on the bed and reached out to her. She flowed into his arms, holding him and pushing her breasts against his chest.

“Thank you. Goddess, Harold, I’m so afraid. Hold me, please hold me.”

He looked down at her face, and she kissed him. He returned the kiss and she gave him a massive dose of pheromones. With a moan, he found her breast with his free hand. In response, she slid her hand down to his lap and stroked his erection through his pants.

During the awkward fumbling to get his cock out of his pants, she managed to move the slide switch on the dead man’s box to the off position. Irina pulled his pants down around his knees, pushed him back onto the bed, and mounted him.

“Oh, Goddess, Harold, you don’t know what this means to me. You’re the most incredible gentleman, to comfort me like this,” she said, leaning forward and kissing him as she began to ride him.

It was over quickly. When he spent in her, she drained him and watched his eyelids flutter and close. She took the box from his hand carefully, replacing his thumb with hers. She thought it was turned off, but she wasn't taking any chances.

She searched his pockets and found a large folding knife. As she cut the tape, her hands shook so much that she nicked herself a couple of times, but the adrenaline was flowing strongly through her system and she didn't feel it.

Beginning to dress, she sent, **Rebecca? I'm free. Send in the cavalry.**

Are you someplace safe? Someplace out of the way?

Don't shoot anything into the attic and I'll be okay.

Hang on.

Irina looked at the box in her hand and suddenly had a thought.

Rebecca, wait! If our people assault the house, some of them might get hurt. Are you physically here?

I'm about half a block away. Why?

There's a dormer window in my room. I was thinking that there might be a way to lower me to the ground.

Not a bad idea. I think I can arrange a ride for you.

Irina took the dynamite and taped it to the door of the room. Then she moved the chair in front of the door and tipped it up, gently setting one leg down on the red button on the box. Holding her breath, she moved the slide switch into the on position.

Rebecca? Irina sent, and followed her hail with an image of what she'd set up.

Got it, Rebecca replied. **Give us one more minute, then go to the window.**

Irina counted the seconds. She was at one hundred fifty-six when she heard Collin's mental voice in her head.

Go to the window and open it, he sent.

She couldn't reach the latch. Cursing, she searched the room. She found a small stool in the closet and dragged it to the window. Standing on her tiptoes, she was able to open the latch and push the window open.

Okay, Collin sent. **I see it. Can you crawl onto the windowsill?**

Silently thanking Rebecca and Brenna for harassing her into a regular exercise routine, she managed to pull herself up and knelt on the sill. Staring out into the night, she couldn't see anyone. The residential neighborhood was quiet.

Time for a flying lesson, Collin sent. **Put your hands together over your head, and when I lift you, hold your legs together.**

That's the first time a man ever told me that, she responded with a giggle.

She did as he said, and felt herself enveloped in an invisible force that lifted her into the air. Her heart in her throat, she felt a moment of disorientation and fear of falling. The next moment, she was flying through the air like Superman. She took a sharp right turn, and followed the street, gradually dropping and slowing until she slipped under the branches of a tree and found herself in Collin's arms.

"Wow! That was great!" she said, throwing her arms around his neck and giving him a kiss that rocked him back on his heels. "You are a wonderful man!"

He set her on her feet. Whirling around, she looked back the way she'd come. She could barely see the open, lighted window in the attic of a three-story house halfway up the street.

"Now that you're safe, we can go in and take them out," he said grimly.

"Do you want to risk your men?" Irina asked.

"Not really. Why?"

"Just toss some tear gas through the window and stand back. We can dig the survivors out of the wreckage if you want prisoners." She sent him an image of the trap she'd prepared.

He seized her arms and leaned down close to her face. "Did they hurt you?" His voice was fierce.

"No, they were actually fairly nice. Other than taping a stick of dynamite to my back. That kind of pissed me off."

He stared at her. "Remind me never to piss you off."

"I'm a succubus, sweetie," she said, with a predatory smile that caused him to shiver. "Don't mess with me or mine. Morrighan calls us the protectors of the Clan. Hugh started this. They blinded one of my lovers. Tried to kill my best friends. Do you really think I give a damn about whether they all go to hell now or later?"

He straightened and she could tell he was sending orders to the Protectors who must be hiding in the darkness all around them.

Seconds later, she heard several muffled explosions and saw several glowing, smoking canisters fly toward the house. One went in the open window in the attic, the rest broke windows on the first and second stories.

They waited. Less than two minutes later, the top of the house exploded. The roof collapsed, and then so did the rest of the house.

~~~

Chapter 8

You see things; and you say 'Why?' But I dream things that never were; and I say 'Why not?' - George Bernard Shaw

Collin had more than two hundred Protectors staged to
~~~

assault the house where Irina was held. When the house collapsed, they scooped up Hugh's fighters that managed to crawl out of the wreckage.

As the emergency personnel showed up on the scene, the Protectors took control and directed the ambulances to the small hospital in Dunallen. Memories were implanted and the police and fire services believed that the house was unoccupied at the time of the "gas explosion."

Between the hacking of Hugh's computer network and the interrogations of the survivors, Collin was able to build a complete picture of Hugh's operation. Over the following three days, Collin's troops spread out and surrounded all of the safe houses and hiding places of Hugh's forces in the Glasgow area. When they could, they quietly captured rebel fighters on their way in or out of such places.

A major force moved quietly toward the town of Ayr, south of Glasgow on the coast facing Northern Ireland. All indications were that Hugh was running his rebellion from an estate outside the town.

Collin's strategy concerning the shipyard was working. Since cutting the utilities, over two hundred workers had come out and given themselves up. They told the Protectors that food was becoming a problem with no refrigeration. The more immediate problem was sanitation. With no working toilets, almost all of the few women inside came out.

Rebecca joined the force heading to Ayr. As she scrambled into a van filled with Protectors, she heard someone call her name. Turning, she saw Rhiannon running toward her.

"What are you doing here?" Rebecca asked.

"I flew in from Dublin. I heard that you've located Hugh O'Neill."

"We think so," Rebecca said cautiously.

Rhiannon looked into the van. "Teddy," she said to a man sitting there, "catch the next ride." She punctuated the order by gesturing with her thumb.

He blinked. "Who are you?"

"I'm Corwin O'Neill's granddaughter. Out, or I'll tell the world about what your mum used to do on Wednesday afternoons."

Teddy's eyes grew wide, and he scrambled out of the van.

"That's a good boy," Rhiannon said with a wink. "I'll bring you some of those cookies you like when I get back." She crawled into the van and took his seat.

What was that about? Rebecca asked as she got into the van.

Teddy's mum used to get together with Corwin on Wednesdays when Teddy's da was in Derry on business. Corwin bought him off with cookies.

You're shameless. Do you know that?

I didn't ask for Corwin's death gift, but knowledge isn't any good unless you use it.

But ... blackmail?

Rhiannon turned a beatific smile toward her, one that reminded Rebecca of the visions she'd seen of the Goddess.

Rebecca, I'm a licensed private investigator. I'm not your run-of-the-mill blackmailer. I'm a professional.

I'll remember that.

They rode for an hour in silence, and then Rhiannon sent a spear thread into Rebecca's mind, **You're one of those people who can't be blackmailed.**

Why do you say that? Rebecca asked.

Did Brenna explain what happened when we shared Corwin's death gift?

**Not in detail, no. But I was there, and I'm linked to*

*both of you. I could feel the chaos.**

Rhiannon laughed out loud.

Chaos? You have no idea. Rebecca, when we shared Corwin's mind, we also shared each other's.

Rebecca turned to her, mouth gaping.

You called me shameless, but I'm really not. My skeletons are legion. Most people are that way. People don't understand blackmail. You can only blackmail someone if you can find something they're ashamed of. You have no shame.

You've been in Brenna's mind and you think that?

You're not the girl you used to be. The woman you are is shameless. You made a conscious decision to dump shame in the toilet and flush it. Instead of feeling shame, you just get angry at people who try to shame you.

Rebecca thought about that for several minutes. **Is that what Brenna thinks?**

It doesn't matter what Brenna thinks, or what I think. Tell me one thing that you're ashamed of.

To Rhiannon's surprise, Rebecca blushed. **I forgot to brush my teeth this morning. It's been bothering me all day.**

Rhiannon erupted with laughter so loudly that the men in the front seat of the van turned to look at her.

"Oh, Goddess, I forgot how much I enjoy you," Rhiannon managed to sputter.

~~~

The force driving down to Ayr from Glasgow numbered almost five hundred Protectors. They were joined by another three hundred that flew in from Edinburgh and two hundred that arrived in Ayr harbor by ship out of Glasgow. Collin had no intentions of letting Hugh or any of his adherents escape.
~~~

The shipboard troops disembarked and quietly took control of the harbor. Half of those who came in by plane took the airport, and the rest fanned out and cut off all the roads out of town. Masquerading as Scottish National Police, one hundred Protectors took up stations in the city.

The force Rebecca and Rhiannon rode with donned battle gear and surrounded the estate where Hugh had his headquarters. At noon, the Clans' Protectors moved on the rebels throughout the Glasgow region, in concert with the opening attack in Ayr.

The response from Hugh's forces at the Ayr estate was immediate and violent. Heavy machine guns opened fire. Fireballs were launched at the attackers. Despair and futility were broadcast using Empathic Projection.

The Clan forces responded in kind with rifles, submachine guns and fireballs. With both sides protected by air shields, it was a lot of noise and flash without much damage.

A telepath's power comes from his or her own physical and mental energy. Part of Collin's plan depended on getting close enough that the six Druids, augmented by Rebecca and some others, could begin to use their Energy Draining Gifts to drain energy away from the defenders and feed it to the attackers.

"We need to get closer," Rebecca said. "I can't do anything from this distance."

She turned to the Druids crouched with them behind a stone wall. The closest one shook her head. "I can't either."

"Well, hell," Rhiannon said. "I can do something. We don't have time for this."

She stood, and began walking forward, covered by her air shield. The front door of the manor house suddenly crashed inward, the thick wood shattering. The next thing Rebecca noticed was the machine guns, one by one, going silent.

A fireball splashed off Rhiannon's air shield. Bullets ricocheted off of it. She continued to walk, and the sounds of battle diminished. The Clan forces held their fire, staring at her in awe. The entire battlefield fell silent.

Rhiannon stumbled, caught herself, then sank to her knees.

Rebecca, I can't hold my shield, she sent, then fell on her face.

Rebecca raced from her cover and, reaching her friend, extended her air shield to cover them both.

"What the hell?" Rebecca said to no one in particular.

"She expended too much energy. She's exhausted herself," a redheaded Druid who had followed her said. "She needs an energy infusion."

The Druid put her hands on Rhiannon's back and Rebecca could feel the energy flowing.

"Be careful. Don't exhaust yourself," Rebecca said.

"No danger of that," the Druid said with a smile. "I took five lads last night to prepare for today."

"I've never seen anyone pass out like that," Rebecca said. "I've seen people tired after a battle, but not like that."

"You've never seen anyone release that much power before," the Druid said. "Hell, I'm fifty years older than you are, and I've never seen that much power released either."

Rhiannon stirred and they turned her on her back.

"What the hell did she do?" Rebecca asked.

"Listen," the Druid said.

"I don't hear anything." Indeed, total silence had fallen on the battlefield.

"Exactly," the Druid said. "She killed them all with a massive blast of Neural Disruption."

"But we're still three hundred yards from the house," Rebecca protested.

"I'm aware of that," the Druid answered.

"Holy Goddess," Rebecca breathed.

Another Druid reached them and extended her hand to touch the fallen woman. Rhiannon's eyelids fluttered and then she opened her eyes, looking at Rebecca.

"Well, I'm not dead," Rhiannon said, "because you're no angel."

She turned her head and smiled at the redheaded Druid. "But you might be."

The redhead laughed. "Nay, not in this life. I'm just Emily. That was a pretty impressive display."

"Stupid," Rhiannon said. "I got angry."

"You have the Krasevec Gift," the other Druid said, referring to what was commonly called Distance Communication. It enhanced a telepath's other Gifts. "But that was still impressive."

"She's an impressive woman," Rebecca said.

"How many ...?" Emily asked, her eyes flicking to Rebecca.

"Fifteen Gifts," Rebecca answered.

"Goddess," the other Druid breathed.

Rhiannon struggled to a sitting position. "Hell, what are we sitting here for? Let's go see what a mass murder looks like."

"There might still be ..." Rebecca started, but the look on Rhiannon's face stopped her.

"No, I can't feel anyone," Rhiannon said. The Druids helped her to her feet.

Protectors swarmed around them, weapons at the ready and air shields deployed. They walked toward the manor house, passing the machine gun emplacements and dozens of bodies on the way. When they reached the house, Rebecca motioned to the shattered double doors.

"I shaped an air shield as a battering ram," Rhiannon said. "I was going to tear the house down with air and Telekinesis, but then I realized I didn't have to go to all that trouble."

"How strong is Brenna going to be?" Rebecca murmured.

"Stronger than me already. Stronger than Seamus O'Donnell, stronger than Niall," Rhiannon said, referring to the legendary High King from whom the telepathic aristocracy, O'Neill, O'Donnell, O'Conner, O'Byrne, and all the rest, traced their heritage.

"Niall is in your memories?"

"Yes, he was in my and Corwin's direct lineage. He's the only one in my memories who had all four Rare Gifts. Except Brenna, of course."

They walked through the house. Bodies of people lay everywhere, twisted into grotesque positions, along with a few dogs and a cat. Rebecca saw a mouse lying in a corner. The Protectors silently fanned out to the upper floors. The silence was eerie, but no one seemed in the mood to break it.

The task force leader approached Rebecca.

My men report three hundred seventy-two bodies in the house and surrounding area. We haven't found anyone who survived.

Rebecca nodded. *I didn't expect survivors. I should say that she didn't expect any survivors.*

She's Lord O'Neill's granddaughter?

Yes.

She has the power of a Clan Chief. She's a worthy heir.

She didn't want it, so he chose Brenna instead.

He nodded.

"I need to go to the airport," Rhiannon said.

"What? Which airport?"

"The Ayr airport. I need to go to Belfast."

"Why?" Rebecca asked.

"Because that's where Hugh is."

A hundred men were detailed to take care of the bodies, and the rest of the force gathered to leave. As Rhiannon approached the van, the task force leader stepped toward her and took her elbow.

"My Lady," he said, bowing his head in respect, and helped her into the van.

"What was that about?" Rhiannon asked Rebecca.

"An acknowledgement of your heritage," Rebecca answered. "A gesture of respect to Corwin's granddaughter."

Rhiannon stared at her. "You're joking, right?"

"No, I'm not joking. That kind of display of power is what they expect of the aristocracy. You've probably carved a permanent place in O'Neill family lore today."

"I'm not an aristocrat."

Rebecca shrugged. "When I first came to the Clan, I didn't understand the difference between the great families and the people who follow them," Rebecca said. "I thought people who had ten, twelve, fifteen Gifts were fairly normal, because those were the people I knew. But the Clans are still a tribal, feudal society for a reason. We're not all equal. They follow us not because we have a certain name, but because they look to us for protection and stability."

She shook her hair back out of her face.

"The Clan didn't know I was an O'Donnell, but they

suspected I was a bastard of a Clan aristocrat because of my strength. Was Kendrick a Clan in Wales?"

"Yes, though it was destroyed and scattered by the English long ago. The name is derived from the Old Welsh word *cynwrig*, which meant clan chief."

"Well, take some genes from the old Welsh Clan aristocracy, put them in a womb with genes from the O'Neill direct line, shake and stir for nine months, and the result is you," Rebecca said.

"I'm just a commoner," Rhiannon said. "The hair and the boobs draw more attention than I'm comfortable with. I never wanted to be famous or an aristocrat."

"If you hold Brenna's memories, you know that you can tell people from here to Sunday that you're not special. They'll just nod politely and assign you an unwarranted reputation for humility. But hell, who am I to interfere with your fun? If you want to pretend that you're not special, I won't say a thing."

~~~

Brenna was at the O'Neill estate in Tyrone, following battle reports and worrying. Over a dozen clashes were being fought in the Glasgow area as Collin's forces attacked the rebels. The expected battle in Ayr had started, and then unexpectedly she received word that it was over.

A spear thread from Rhiannon to Brenna interrupted a conversation she was having with Collin.

Brenna, I need a plane at Ayr airport. The tone of Rhiannon's thought was as cold and bleak as winter on a Scottish moor.

A plane? Brenna asked. **Where do you need to go?**

Belfast. Hugh is in Belfast. He went there to meet with Finnian.

Do you know where?
~~~

Yes, at a pub Finnian owns. I got the information from the mind of one of Hugh's men.

What happened in Ayr? Brenna asked.

I killed them. I killed them all, but Hugh wasn't there. I need to get to Belfast.

Okay, go to the airport, Brenna told her and broke the connection. Immediately, she contacted Rebecca.

What the hell happened in Ayr?

Rhiannon went berserker. Goddess, Brenna, she killed almost four hundred men in a couple of minutes. From hundreds of yards away. Now she's just staring out the window. She told us to take her to the airport.

She evidently took control of someone's mind before she killed him. She just told me that Hugh is in Belfast meeting Finnian. She wants a plane so she can go there and kill him.

Oh, Goddess. Are you going to let her?

No. I know she hates him, but I'm not going to let her spend the rest of her life tagged as a patricide. I'll go and do it. Stall her.

You're going to do it? Brenna, don't be foolish. Wait until we can get there. You need someone to watch your back.

There isn't time. But don't worry, I won't walk in there alone.

Brenna broke the connection and contacted Collin.

~~~

Chapter 9

A journey is a person in itself; no two are alike. And all plans, safeguards, policing, and coercion are fruitless. We find that after years of struggle that we do not take a trip; a trip takes us. - John Steinbeck
~~~

Several black vans and a limousine with the door open waited near a private hangar at Belfast airport. Brenna stood next to the limo dressed in a black Protector's uniform. The past weeks were taking their toll, and she felt tired. It hadn't seemed so bad when Collin was in Tyrone with her, but he'd been in Scotland for the past two weeks. She missed him terribly. At least when he was with her, they could retire to their bed and ignore the world, at least for a short time.

Brenna didn't even have time to take lovers when he was away. As if she could get away with it. As Lady O'Neill, she was supposed to refrain from being too blatant about her succubus nature. She wondered how he was rebalancing his energies, and with whom. He couldn't go more than a day or two without sex or he'd go crazy. He and Rebecca had the same problem, but they usually didn't seek each other out for relief.

Waiting for him, thinking about him, imagining his body, his hands on hers, she grew more and more agitated. An uncomfortable warmth built between her legs.

Collin's plane finally landed and taxied to the hanger. He climbed down the steps and when he reached her, she threw her arms around his neck and kissed him.

"I missed you!" she said, pulling him into the car. It immediately lurched into motion.

Brenna pulled off her boots and started unbuckling her belt. "Take your pants off," she ordered.

"Do we have time for this?" Collin asked.

"Half an hour. More than enough time for a quickie. Get your pants off, Doyle."

He pushed his pants down to his knees and she swung around and straddled him. She let out a deep sigh as she sank down onto his erection. Life was never so good as when Collin was inside her, their minds and their souls merging into a cosmic state of bliss and the Goddess's joy of the world. Reveling in having him again, she sat for a moment gazing at his face and the love for her that she saw in his eyes.

Leaning forward, she kissed him and began to ride him, hard and fast. Working him with the special muscles in her vagina, she brought him quickly to his climax. Feeling his seed spill into her, she relished his life energy flowing into her mind and body, triggering her to a shuddering orgasm. Then she touched the place in her mind that sent thc energy flowing back into him. She watched his aura start to glow, and that special smile that made her feel so special spread across his face.

Reluctant to break the moment, she slid off him and began to dress.

"I don't know about you," Collin said with a smile, leaning over and softly stroking her cheek, "but I feel a whole lot better."

"Not me. I didn't feel a thing," Brenna said. "Did you get it in?"

She couldn't keep a straight face and started giggling like a teenager.

"I'll take that as a challenge," he said, "when this is over."

"Oh, good. A determined man on a mission is so exciting." She leaned over and kissed him again, and then reached for her boots.

"I missed you," he said.

"Oh, God, I missed you so bad," she responded. "I sat there waiting for your plane to land, and it seemed to take forever. I was thinking of you, and I got so horny. Then I thought that it would be a good idea to make sure your energies were balanced before we walked into this mess with Hugh and Finnian."

“Sounds like a good story to me. A commander should always be aware of the welfare of her troops,” he said with a grin.

The limo rolled to a stop. Looking out the window, Brenna saw men getting out of the van parked behind them.

“Time to go back to work,” she said, reaching for the door handle.

Collin reached out and grabbed her braid, pulled her back to him and kissed her.

“Be careful, Brenna.”

“You, too.”

“I’m glad to see that you’re wearing protective clothing,” he said. The Protector’s uniforms were made of a bullet-resistant fabric, and their jackets were bulletproof.

“I’m wearing that damned corset, too,” Brenna said. After she had been shot two years before, Seamus had ordered some of the bulletproof fabric sent to Brenna’s dressmaker. The result had been half a dozen bustier corsets. Rebecca and Collin usually had to force her to wear one when she went out in public.

Collin hadn’t checked on the team Brenna had with her, and was surprised to see Thomas O’Neill approach them. He had assumed the O’Neill Director of Security didn’t usually involve himself in field operations.

“We’re staging around the pub,” Thomas said. “When you give the signal, we’ll move in through the three doors, with a reserve force left outside.”

“I’m surprised to see you here,” Collin said.

“This could be a dangerous game,” Thomas said. “I have two men with the O’Neill shielding Gift in addition to me. We’ll be covering everyone to deflect any Neural Disruption attacks. It’s the only offensive Gift Finnian has, and of course, Hugh has it, too.”

"How did we miss that Finnian was using this pub as a base?" Collin asked.

"It's been closed since he was exiled four years ago. We've checked it a couple of times since Hugh rebelled, but didn't see any sign of activity." Thomas ran his hand through his gray hair. "Of course, that makes it a perfect meeting place. It's been checked out, so we'd be unlikely to think of it now."

"How many men do we have?"

"Fifty," Brenna answered. "We know from Rhiannon that Hugh has five men with him. He could have picked up a few more when he landed in Belfast, but a large force might attract attention. We've had the pub under observation for about two hours, and only a few men have gone in. None have come out."

"Hugh just went inside," Thomas said. "We'll send thirty in with twenty outside."

The distinct sound of a gunshot sounded from inside the pub. An extended volley of gunfire followed, including that of automatic weapons. It sounded like a small war had broken out. Then there was silence, followed by a couple more shots, and then silence again. Everyone had ducked for cover outside, but the shooting was all inside the building.

Thomas looked at Brenna and Collin. Brenna nodded, and Collin said, "Let's go."

The Clan Protectors, including Collin and Thomas, rushed for the doors, smashing them in and diving inside. More gunfire erupted.

As soon as they disappeared inside the building, Brenna caught a hint of movement by the front door. She couldn't see anyone, but she had the impression that something was moving away from the building.

An adept with the O'Neill Gift has mental shields so

strong that they can completely block any telepath except one with the O'Donnell Gift of Domination. The shields of someone with the O'Neill Gift can block even Neural Disruption energy. The telepath can become virtually invisible, both to telepaths and to normal humans. But to pull off that trick, the telepath needs to stay completely still. Any movement can betray the person's presence.

Brenna realized what she was seeing, and moved in the direction of the escaping telepath. She sent a message to the Protectors outside the pub.

Hugh has his O'Neill shields locked down and he's escaping out the front door. Look for a distortion, like a heat wave, that's moving away from the pub.

Protectors moved to intercept a man they couldn't see.

"Hugh," she called, "I can see you. I've alerted my force, and they're cutting off your line of escape. You're surrounded."

He became visible as he whirled around to face her.

"What the bloody hell are you doing here?" he snarled.

"I'm here to tell you that your rebellion is over. We've smashed your forces in Scotland and taken the estate at Ayr. The shipyard will surrender by the end of the week. It's over, Hugh."

"Rebellion? I'm just defending what's rightfully mine."

"The time to contest that was when Corwin was alive. I've been entrusted with Clan O'Neill, and I'm going to hold it," Brenna said.

"You bitch! Damn Maureen to hell! I got rid of her, and her damned daughter shows up to hound me."

He loosed a blast of Neural Disruption at her, which she deflected with her own O'Neill shield. Then he pulled a pistol and fired, simultaneously hurling a fireball. Both hit her air shield.

With both of them protected by O'Neill shields and air shields, they were virtually invulnerable. He started to turn, but Brenna seized his air shield using Telekinesis, freezing him in place.

She sent a stream of fire to bathe his shield, hoping to heat the air inside to a level he couldn't tolerate. He expanded the air shield, pushing the fire farther away from him.

Hugh laughed. "It seems we have a stalemate. I can't hurt you, and you can't hurt me. So, until next time, I'll say goodbye."

"That's where you're wrong, Hugh. You're not going anywhere."

He hit her with an empathic projection of fear and loathing that made her want to retch. She locked her shields down tighter and filtered him out. He responded with a stronger burst of Neural Projection, but she blocked it also.

"What do you mean you got rid of my mother?"

He sneered at her. "Women think they're smart, but they're just good at manipulation. I drove Jack and Maureen to the airport. I gave her a box of chocolates as a going away present. The dumb cow carried her own death onto that airplane."

Hugh's face grew red, his expression twisted with rage. "I was the heir. Then Maureen bewitched my father. What a slut! Fucking her own damned uncle. Turning him against me and charming him into taking away my birthright. She was an abomination, a demon, just like you are."

"That's not true," Brenna said. "I have his memories. He despaired of you because you refused to take any responsibility. Your whole life, all you've done is be a playboy. And there was a prophesy, from Delilah, that he would be succeeded by a black-haired Druid who would unite the Clans. He thought my mother was the fulfillment of the prophesy."

"You lie!" he screamed. "My grandmother was another abomination. She fucked her own son! She took Corwin's virginity and groomed him to be her lap dog. He wasn't a real man. She controlled him."

Brenna shook her head. "That's not true either. Where did you get these weird ideas?"

She had continued to bathe his air shield with fire, and she could see sweat pouring off his face. The inside of his shield was becoming uncomfortably hot.

He hit her with Empathic Projection again, filled with all the rage and bitterness of his life and an incredible loathing of Druids, attempting to get inside her shields. Then he abruptly dissolved his air shield, and dashed away. Brenna had been holding his air shield with her Telekinesis, and his action took her off guard.

She invoked her O'Donnell Gift, forming the mental projectile that could breach any mental shields, and launched it at him. He screamed, stumbled, and fell to the ground.

In the brief instant while she drove through the shields protecting the seventeen levels of his mind, Brenna saw those thoughts and memories that lay on the surface of each level. And then her Gift shattered Hugh's soul. His body shook, and the rattle of his final breath leaving his body announced his death.

~~~

Collin led Brenna into the pub. "Are you sure you want to see this?" he asked.

It was a scene from a nightmare, bodies in every room, blood pooled on the floor and splattered on the walls and furniture. The Protectors had captured three of Hugh's men, but they were the only survivors. Finnian's body was in the
~~~

main room, a bullet hole in his forehead. The expression on his face, however, suggested that the bullet came after he'd been disabled with Neural Disruption.

"How many?" Brenna asked.

"According to Hugh's men, two of the bodies are theirs. The other twenty-seven are Finnian's. It was a massacre. Finnian wanted to talk, to negotiate an alliance. Hugh's men opened fire with submachine guns and Neural Disruption as soon as they were inside. Hugh lost one man then. The other one died fighting us."

Brenna shook her head, walking behind the bar and blowing dust off the bottles there.

"Need a drink?" she asked, opening a bottle of whiskey and taking a long drink straight from the bottle.

Collin nodded and she brought it to him. It got passed around, and then another one was opened and passed. Even though the men with them were professionals, several had thrown up when they had seen the carnage.

"Do I own this pub now?" Brenna asked Thomas.

"Probably."

"I'll pay a bonus to whoever draws the short straws and has to clean it up," she said.

"Bloody slaughterhouse," one of the men said. "I've never seen anything this bad."

"Gives you an idea of who we've been fighting," Collin said. "He killed his own son."

"I've known Hugh all my life," another man said. "I never would have believed him capable of this."

"No one knew Hugh," Brenna said. "His whole life, his personality, was a sham. He was playacting a role. The amount of hatred and bitterness that formed him was incredible." She turned to Thomas. "He was mildly schizophrenic. He had delusions and heard voices. It wasn't too bad, and so he could hide it. He was a true O'Neill. He had the Gift. He wasn't completely divorced from reality, but he inhabited a slightly different reality from the rest of us. If anyone had ever done a brain scan, they would have found it, but without symptoms, no one had any reason to look."

"Goddess protect us," Thomas said. "Imagine the damage if he had become Clan Chief."

As they walked to their cars, Brenna sent a spear thought to Rebecca, **You can tell the pilot that he can take off now. Has RB chewed holes in the furniture yet?**

Damn near, Rebecca replied. **She's pissed. If there wasn't an ocean between here and Ireland, she'd have commandeered a car and been gone hours ago. Did you find Hugh?**

Hugh's dead, and so is Finnian.

Brenna broke the connection, dreading the coming confrontation with Rhiannon.

~~~

Thomas O'Neill stood outside the gates of the O'Neill Shipyard in Glasgow holding a bullhorn. The sun was just rising over the city to his east. The sky lit gold and red, and Thomas hoped it was a sign of a glorious morning ahead, and not one drenched in blood. Inside the yard, a crowd had gathered, recognizing the long-time Director of Security and Corwin's nephew.

"I have an announcement," he spoke into the bullhorn. "Last night, Finnian O'Neill was murdered by his father in Belfast. Hugh O'Neill died while attempting to escape during his apprehension by the Protectors.

"Lord Corwin named Lady Brenna O'Donnell as his heir. She has been confirmed by the Council, and blessed by the Conclave of Druids. The rebellion is over. We will give you one hour to open the gates and surrender. After
~~~

that, we will break down the gates and come in."

He repeated the announcement using a mental broadcast.

Forty minutes later, a group of men came out and opened the gates. They put their hands above their heads and stood aside to let the Protectors outside enter the yard.

~~~

About the time Thomas was making the announcement of Hugh's and Finnian's deaths, Brenna sat alone in a conference room at O'Neill Industries' headquarters building in Belfast. She was waiting for Rhiannon and Rebecca, who had just entered the elevator on the first floor.

When the women walked through the door, Brenna gestured Rhiannon to a chair and said, "Rebecca, can you please wait outside?"

Rebecca hesitated, looked at an obviously agitated Rhiannon, then nodded and closed the door behind her.

"He should have been mine," Rhiannon shouted, pacing the office. "You stole him from me."

"No, he shouldn't have been," Brenna replied, keeping her voice calm and level. "He was rebelling against me. This wasn't personal, Rhiannon. And if it was, then I had the greater right."

"Right? What right? He ruined my life. He fathered me and abandoned me. Kept me from my birthright. What right of yours is greater than that?"

"He killed my parents."

Rhiannon stopped and stared at Brenna.

"He told me at the pub, after he killed Finnian."

Rhiannon's demeanor changed. "Oh, God, Brenna. I'm so sorry."

"Nothing for you to be sorry about. But I didn't want
~~~

you to kill him out of hate and spend the rest of your life regretting it."

"I wouldn't have regretted it."

"Maybe not. But it would have marked your soul. You would have always been that woman who killed her father. Your mother loved him once, and he gave her you. Would you want her to think of his murder every time she looks at you? Would you want to cause her that much pain?"

Rhiannon closed her eyes, standing still and swaying in the middle of the room. Then she took two stiff steps toward the chair Brenna had offered and sank into it.

"No," she whispered, "I wouldn't want that. Damn you. You know exactly what makes me tick."

"Two of us are in that basket," Brenna said.

"Yeah, I guess we are." She raised her eyes to Brenna's. "He killed them? He planted the bomb?"

Brenna told her what Hugh had said, and what she had seen in his mind when she killed him.

"Hugh had a mental disorder," Brenna said. "He was sane enough to know other people would see it that way, but crazy enough to believe that he was sane and everyone else was crazy. He spent a lifetime listening to voices and had a major persecution complex. He hated succubi, Druids. He thought that his grandmother was conspiring against him, conspiring to turn O'Neill into a Clan controlled by the Druids, who would then enslave all the men."

Brenna stood and went to the sideboard. "Would you like a drink?"

Rhiannon nodded and Brenna poured two glasses of whiskey.

"When he saw you as a little girl, he recognized pictures he'd seen of Delilah as a child. He thought she had come back to keep him from his rightful place as Clan

Chief. He didn't know much about genetics. He thought you were a succubus and that if Corwin ever saw you, you would seduce him and control him, and Corwin would be unable to resist. Then he would toss Hugh aside and name you the heir."

Brenna handed Rhiannon the glass. "Slainte."

They touched glasses and drank the shots.

~~~

The following week was quite busy for Brenna. The dislocations in Scotland would take far longer to fix than the short rebellion that caused them. Collin, Thomas and Devlin were overhauling the Protector force at O'Neill, which had been hard hit by the rebellion. The town of Dunallen needed extensive rebuilding.

She was told that it would take at least two weeks to restore production at the shipyard, but a thorough review was needed and management had to be replaced. The top five executives of the shipbuilding operation had declared for Hugh, and her retribution was swift, severe, and public. Mind wipe and exile was the verdict, as she held them responsible for hundreds of deaths. Another four hundred rebels were slated for the same fate.

Sitting in the large conference room used for meetings of the Clan Council, Brenna listened to members of the Council. Some argued that most of the rebels were good people. Perhaps they were misguided or misled by Hugh, but such an extreme sentence wasn't warranted and they could be rehabilitated.

"What is the normal sentence for premeditated murder?" she asked after letting them discuss the issue for almost an hour. Her question was met with silence. "Should I slap their wrists and tell them they were bad little boys? What do I tell the mothers and wives and husbands and children of the people they killed? What kind of message should I send to those who might decide to rebel or try to
~~~

assassinate me in the future?"

She looked around the room. Every eye was on her. "Yes, wiping four hundred people is horrendous," she continued. "Exiling over a thousand people, telling them never again to set foot in the British Isles on pain of death, is going to be a wrenching dislocation in O'Neill's social and business affairs."

Her voice rose to an angry shout. "It's not my damn fault! They took it on themselves to do this! They made a conscious decision to kill people to get something they wanted." She got herself under control and continued in a more normal tone, "They haven't left me any choice. If we wish to disband the Clan, each of us wander off into the world to do as we will, to live without laws, then the choice is there for us to do that. Clan O'Neill has survived for thousands of years. The laws and the traditions are well established and proven over time."

She looked around at the Council. "Corwin told me to guide this Clan into the twenty-first and twenty-second centuries. He didn't tell me to dismantle what he and the other Clan Chiefs so painstakingly built and nurtured. He told me to protect it. To protect you. I hold this seat by your choice. You can replace me at any time. I have promised always to listen and seriously weigh your advice. In the end, for better or worse, I make the decisions. Your choices are to vote me out, leave, or learn to love me."

Looking around the room, she saw people nod. Some in agreement, some in resignation. One man sitting near her, Corwin's memories told her his name was Dermot O'Conner, jokingly said, "Were you always this hard a bitch or is that Corwin's memories speaking?"

Brenna smiled at him, batted her eyes, and said, "When Corwin touched my soul, he said I would hate him forever for naming me, but that I had the stones to do the job." She paused, then thrust her chest forward and wiggled her shoulders. "I told him no, but I have the tits to do the job."

The Council erupted in laughter, the tension broken. As the Council broke up and the members were leaving, Dermot approached her and drew her aside.

"That was well done, lass," he said. "Many that argued for leniency were simply testing you. Your answer to them was spot on. It's what they wanted to hear, what they needed to hear."

"What you needed to hear, Dermot?" Brenna asked.

"Yes. But what has spoken louder to me these past few weeks is Seamus O'Donnell's absence. He hasn't set foot in Ireland since you inherited the Clan. It tells me two things. One, that you're not a puppet, and two, that he trusts you. He has faith and confidence in your judgment."

"We needed help from O'Donnell to put down the rebellion. I have O'Donnell Protectors building a barracks next to the manor house."

"That is true, but Corwin might have asked Seamus for help, and expected he'd get it. The two Clans have been allied for four hundred years. That's not what I mean. You walked in here today with no one to back you up. No one from O'Donnell. You might have been walking into the lion's den, and you brought not a single bodyguard."

"This was a meeting of the Council of Clan O'Neill," Brenna replied. "Someday the Clans will be united, but that hasn't happened yet. None of you brought a bodyguard. If I have to worry about my Council, then I need to find some new councilors. I don't expect the Council will always agree with me, but I do expect that we'll treat each other with civility."

He stepped away from her and bowed. "Welcome to Clan O'Neill, my Lady. I think we're very lucky to have you join us."

~~~

Chapter 10

Management is doing things right; leadership is doing the right things.
- Peter Drucker

"You need to name an heir," Morrighan said. They were having dinner alone on the terrace overlooking the gardens at O'Byrne. Having the Teleportation Gift did have its advantages, and Brenna had needed some quiet time.

"Huh?" Brenna stared at her aunt for a moment and then shook her head. "Why do I need to do that?"

"Because it's traditional and it makes people feel secure. Especially with people plotting your death, the people you're leading want to know their future. I'm sure no one is thinking about that tonight, but give it a few days and it will be a major source of speculation."

Brenna drew a deep breath and sat down on the bed. "I haven't thought of that. It would have to be someone who is acceptable to all three Clans, wouldn't it?"

"Yes, if you plan on keeping the Clans united after you're gone. Brenna, someday you'll have children and you can change the heir, but right now, you're going to have to name someone for the next forty or fifty years."

Brenna thought of all the people she knew, in all three Clans. No one came to mind.

"What should I consider in looking for someone?" she finally asked.

"Power," Morrighan said. "Power above all else. The Clan Chief is a protector. But he or she also has to have enough power to hold their position. Power also has to be coupled with kindness and mercy and true empathy. The person has to be altruistic. They have to be able to put their
~~~

personal needs and desires aside for the good of others. That's not an easy thing to do."

Morrighan looked away, then took a deep breath. "Fergus, Corwin, and Seamus each have fifteen Gifts, including at least one of the rare ones. They all have the Krasevec Gift. That kind of power isn't common. As strong as Rebecca is, she wouldn't do."

Brenna shook her head. "She wouldn't do for other reasons. She'll die when I do."

"Yes," Morrighan nodded, "your Shadow."

"I guess I can have Callie do a search for the strongest telepaths in her database," Brenna said, looking at her hands twisting together in her lap.

"No, you can't."

Brenna's head snapped up at the commanding tone in Morrighan's voice.

"It has to be someone who is loyal to you. Someone who loves you. Someone who won't stick a knife in your back at the first chance. It has to be someone who doesn't want it, who would do almost anything to protect you and make sure they *don't* inherit."

"I can't think of anyone with that much power," Brenna said.

"I can. But you have to make the choice, and I'm not going to put any thoughts in your head."

~~~

The following morning, she had breakfast with her grandparents in a sitting room off their suite. A large bay window gave them a view of the grounds outside and the mountains in the distance.

"This is a lovely room," Brenna remarked.

"I'm glad you like it," Caylin said. "We've had breakfast here almost every morning for a hundred years. It
~~~

helps to ground us, set a calming mood for the day."

"Yes, I can see that. I need to ask you about something. Last night, Morrighan mentioned that I need to name an heir. I thought about it all night, and I can't think of someone who would be acceptable to all three Clans. I'm wondering if you had given any thought to the matter."

Her grandparents looked at each other, and Brenna knew they had discussed this issue between them.

"What are your plans for children?" Caylin asked.

"Fifteen, twenty years," Brenna replied. "I know that I want kids, and I know who I want the fathers to be, but I'm not ready for that now. I also know that Samantha, Seamus and Cindy's daughter, will be very important in my life, but she's just a baby. Morrighan said that I could change my heir in the future when I have children, but she also said I need to name someone now."

"Yes, the people you lead will expect you to do that," Fergus said. "The trick is to find someone who is qualified, powerful enough, and has links to all three Clans. And that person has to be loyal to you."

"Links to all three Clans," Brenna said. "I can't think of anyone."

"The link could be through you. You have relatives in all three Clans," Fergus said.

"So, you think it should be one of my relatives?" Brenna asked.

"Brenna," Fergus said, "our society is feudal, and that has persisted out of necessity. The ruling families have conducted an informal breeding program for thousands of years."

He chuckled at the expression on her face and held up his hand to forestall what she might say.

"Please, let me finish. The strongest of us have ruled the Clans. We tend to marry other strong telepaths and so our children inherit more Gifts than is normal. Seamus, Corwin and I all have fifteen Gifts. Your parents each had fifteen. Your half-sister has fifteen. Callie has thirteen. Your Collin has twelve. Most of the people you know and those who are related to you are very strong telepaths. But remember that half of all telepaths have only one Gift."

"So, you're saying that the chances of someone who is not a relative being qualified are rather small," Brenna said.

"Not impossible," Caylin said. "Keep in mind that the person would have to be extraordinary to overcome the Clans' traditions. Power isn't everything, of course, but you'll tend to find that power and intelligence are closely linked. Again, just a by-product of our breeding practices."

"Okay, so who do you have in mind?" Brenna said, raising one eyebrow and quirking her mouth into a half-grin. "It's obvious that you have discussed this."

Fergus told her. Someone she hadn't considered.

"I wonder if that's who Morrighan had in mind. She said she didn't want to influence my decision."

"No, she wouldn't," Fergus said. "I have no such qualms. You don't have to take our suggestion, but I'm not bashful about telling people what I think they should do. I also know that Seamus would have no problem with such a selection."

Brenna stared out the window for a while and then said, "I think I need to go back up to O'Neill and talk to a couple of people there."

~~~

"You've lost your fucking mind! How can you even consider such an insane idea?"

"It's not insane. Everyone agrees with me. Seamus, Fergus, Morrighan, they all think you're the proper person. Besides, Rhiannon, it's a ceremonial title. Rebecca says that I won't die until I'm very old."
~~~

"And how does she know that? She told me once she doesn't put much credence in precognitive visions."

"I think she feels it was a vision sent by the Goddess on Samhain."

"If it's ceremonial, then it doesn't matter who you name. Name anyone else."

"Don't you think the people of the Clans deserve better than that? Shouldn't the heir be someone qualified and capable of leading them? Do you think they deserve an heir like Hugh? Someone who could do an incredible amount of damage even if he never inherited?"

"Is this going to be a circular argument that I have no chance of winning?"

"The only way I won't name you is if you absolutely tell me that you won't take it. I have no desire to embarrass either one of us. Tell me that you feel no sense of obligation or responsibility to Clan O'Byrne, and I'll find someone else."

"You don't play fair. Choose Morrighan."

"I can't sell Morrighan to Clan O'Neill or to Clan O'Donnell. Not enough power. Besides, she will argue that as the High Priestess she already has a job. You know that Seamus and Fergus were hoping you'd press a claim to O'Neill."

Rhiannon gave her a sour look. "I'm not a business woman. I don't have any interest at all in sitting behind a desk and telling people what to do. I'm terrible with math and money. I'm not going to get sucked in to running a major corporation like you did."

"Agreed."

"Bitch. Quit being so damned agreeable."

Brenna laughed.

"What do you mean by ceremonial? Do I have to show

up and smile pretty for ribbon cuttings and crap like that?"

"There's an annual meeting of O'Donnell in London in April every year. I assume O'Neill and O'Byrne do the same thing. If they don't, they will be now. It's boring as turds, but it's important, and I'd expect you to be there. O'Donnell throws a formal ball at winter solstice. It's a great party, and I'd like you to attend. And yes, you have to dress up, but after seeing you in that gown in Monaco, you can't bullshit me that you don't like to wear nice things. I attend Beltane at O'Byrne. Morrighan and Rebecca always throw a big bash at Samhain. Otherwise, act as my surrogate occasionally if I think it's important."

"Are you going to pay me, or do I do it for the prestige?"

"Five percent of the stock in O'Neill, with five percent of O'Byrne when I inherit. Five percent of O'Donnell if you're still my heir when I take the seat there. Non-revocable."

Rhiannon sighed, "You really don't play fair. I'd have to be a complete idiot to turn that down. Shit. I also have to be a complete idiot to take it. Damn you."

She abruptly changed the topic. "What's a Pathfinder?"

Brenna called mentally, **Rebecca, can you please come in?**

Rebecca opened the door cautiously and stuck her head into the room.

"Is it safe? I don't see any blood anywhere."

Rhiannon shot her a look. "No, and all the walls and furniture are intact."

"Rhiannon wants to know what a Pathfinder is," Brenna said.

"Oh. Well, I've been researching that," Rebecca said, stepping into the room and closing the door behind her.

"There isn't anything definitive, but some of the old Gaelic texts mention it. Of course, they're talking about something that was handed down in oral histories, and I'm not sure the people who wrote it down understood it. It would help if I read Gaelic better. I wish Siobhan was here."

"I read, and speak, Gaelic quite fluently," Rhiannon said. "Where are the books?"

"Some are here, but O'Neill has the most extensive library. Do you want to look at them? I'm actually surprised that Corwin didn't have anything in his memories."

"All he had was a vague knowledge of the term."

"I'm starving," Brenna announced. "Let's go get some dinner first, then I'll take you to whatever library you want to start with."

Within a week, Rhiannon had been confirmed as Brenna's heir at O'Neill.

~~~

Meanwhile, Rhiannon and Rebecca disappeared into the O'Neill library, emerging only for meals and sleep. Four days of that were followed by them informing Brenna that they were going to O'Byrne. Rhiannon had been in contact with Fergus, and he thought there might be some information in the library there.

The O'Byrne library, with its dark wood and heavy furniture, was an amazingly light room due to floor-to-ceiling bay windows on one wall. The women were sitting on a sunny padded bench in the alcove created by one of those windows, overlooking the garden and small lake beyond. Books and scrolls were scattered around them.

"I've probably spent hundreds of hours in this room over the years," Rhiannon said, "but we're looking through books and letters and stuff I never imagined existed."

"Yeah, I've got my work cut out for me," Rebecca
~~~

said. "O'Neill actually has a librarian, but the library at O'Donnell had been neglected for fifteen years until I got there, and this one hasn't seen much care for at least ten years longer than that."

"Maybe you can talk Brenna into hiring a librarian," Rhiannon suggested.

Rebecca looked at her in horror.

"What's wrong? What did I say?" Rhiannon asked.

"It's *my* library," Rebecca said. "I'm not letting someone else come in here and screw things up."

"I'm sorry. Goddess, I didn't mean to tread on sacred ground."

"Go stick your nose into something else. If you want to play heir, find your own niche. The libraries are *mine*."

Rhiannon laughed. "I consider myself warned."

Rebecca gave her a sheepish smile. "Sorry. I didn't mean to come on so strong. Maureen was the librarian here and at O'Donnell. My dream growing up was to be a librarian. To have such a treasure trove of rare books and manuscripts ..." Her voice trailed off as she looked around.

"In Brenna's memories," Rhiannon said, hesitating and watching Rebecca's reaction.

"Yes?"

"You found information on two unknown Gifts?"

"We call them Lost Gifts. They were known centuries ago, but they seem to have disappeared. The one I have seems to have been passed down in the O'Donnell bloodline, because Callie has it, too. She just never knew that she had it. We found a description of it in a medieval Italian text. They called the person who had it a Soul Thief, but that's only part of its manifestation. It allows me to use someone else's Gifts, if they give me access to their mind."

"Do you mean you could use my Telekinesis or

Distance Communication Gifts?"

"Yes, if you let me. I can't use them unless you give me access to the levels in your mind where the Gifts are located. But I can see the triggers, whereas you probably can't see the triggers in my mind for Gifts you don't have. Brenna lets me use her to talk to Carlos sometimes, and I use her Animal Communication Gift to talk to my horse."

"Or if you controlled someone's mind," Rhiannon said.

"Yes. Although that's rather rude."

Rhiannon laughed. "What about Brenna's new Gifts? I mean, I have her memories, and I think I understand what they are, but ..."

Rebecca put down her book. "Just ask. What doesn't make any sense?"

"The other day, she touched my hair. Wound a lock around her finger. It was very odd. Was she trying to memorize something about it?"

"She was analyzing its resonance," Rebecca said. "She's fascinated with the idea of being a redhead. It's some kind of fetish with her. She does that with almost every redhead she meets. You have her memories of being Samantha, right? I think it's the idea of being free. Not being the heir, the Lady." Rebecca thought for a moment. "It wouldn't surprise me if, in the future, she just disappears sometimes. Takes a holiday to get away from everything. And I think she'll disguise herself as a redhead."

Rhiannon compared what Rebecca said with Brenna's memories. "I think you might be right. I can't find a memory of her planning anything like that, but when I bump that idea up against what I know, it makes sense."

~~~
~~~

Chapter 11

Never be bullied into silence. Never allow yourself to be made a victim. Accept no one's definition of your life; define yourself. - Harvey Fierstein

On a rare evening when they were all in the same place, Brenna and Collin sat with Rebecca, Morrighan and Rhiannon on the terrace at O'Byrne, having drinks and watching the late summer sun sink behind the Wicklow Mountains.

"It kind of feels good to get back to normal," Brenna said.

"We have a normal?" Rebecca asked.

"Well, I keep hoping. I'm thinking of bringing our horses over to Ireland."

Collin leaned over and kissed her on the cheek. "It may take some time, but we'll get there."

As twilight deepened into night, Collin's phone rang. Brenna and Rebecca immediately recognized the faint voice on the other end.

"Hang on," Collin said to the phone, "Irina, slow down. I can't make any sense of what you're saying."

He held the phone away from his ear so the others could hear her better.

"I'll kill the son of a bitch and the fucking horse he rode in on. I'm not going to put up with this shit, Collin." Irina's voice was loud and shrill. "I'm not waiting any longer. Either you put up or shut up. If you're not going to help me, I'll do it myself."

"Irina, what are you talking about?" Collin asked when Irina took a breath.

"My fucking grandfather," Irina answered.

Collin's phone chirped, and he said, "Hang on, Irina. I

have a call on the other line."

"Don't try to put me off, you bastard," Irina hissed.

"Just let me check the other call, Irina. I'll be right back to you." He punched a button on his phone. "Darren, what's going on?" Darren was the head of Irina's security team. Collin listened for a while, then said, "Okay, Darren. I'll be there in the morning."

He switched back to Irina. "I just talked to Darren. You know, it would help if you'd frame what you're talking about before you start yelling at me."

He held the phone out at arm's reach. The group heard a stream of profanity that proved Irina had been paying attention over the years to Rebecca's creative use of language. When she wound down, Collin brought the phone back to his face and said, "I'll be there at ten o'clock, okay? We'll sit down and figure out what we need to do."

"Bring a Goddamned nuke with you," Irina replied and broke the connection.

"What's going on?" Rebecca asked. "Is there a shortage of high heels in the shops in London?"

"There was another kidnapping attempt in London," Collin said with a sigh. "Darren said Irina was on a date and a large group of Russians took over the restaurant and tried to capture her. There was a battle between the Russians and her security force. There are containment issues."

"Is she alright?" Brenna asked.

"Oh, yeah, she's unharmed. But as you heard, she's angry as a wet hen. Darren said she rose to the edge and killed seven men before he could talk her down. Even the three people they captured are burned out or crippled."

Eyes wide, Rebecca asked, "Collateral damage? Any innocents hurt?"

"Thankfully, no. The words Darren used to describe her were 'surgically precise and ruthlessly lethal'."

"She looks like a little doll," Rhiannon said. "I always have difficulty remembering she's an adult."

Rebecca nodded. "She cultivates that, but her ability to focus is incredible. She's a succubus in every sense of the word. She scares me more than Brenna does."

"Really?" Rhiannon asked and glanced at Brenna, who nodded.

"She's one of the few people I'm truly afraid of," Brenna said. "When she rises to the killing edge, she has a hair trigger. She's been prey too many times in her short life, and both her sense of self preservation and her sense of outrage are very finely honed."

"Don't piss her off," Rebecca said. "She'll kill you before she thinks about it and be sorry for it afterward."

"She has the same Gifts I do. I'm twenty years older than she is, but she's already more powerful than I am," Morrighan said. "I don't know why. There's something in her mental makeup that allows her to focus her power better than any Druid I've ever seen."

"I don't think she understands she has limits," Rebecca said. "When she does something, she puts everything she has into it."

"It's because it's all or nothing with her," Brenna said, turning to Collin. "I'm going with you to London. This crap has to stop, and it's time we put Gorbachev on notice that this is unacceptable. If we have to replay Leningrad, then that's what we need to do."

"I didn't plan on taking an entourage," Collin said.

Rhiannon smiled at him. "No extra charge."

His eyes widened slightly. "You're going, too?"

When her smile didn't change, he sighed. "I'll go make

arrangements."

Walking away, he waited until he turned a corner on his way down to the command center and pulled out his cell phone.

"Seamus? It's Collin. I need some help."

"Do you know what time it is in West Virginia?" the Lord of the O'Donnell Clan growled.

"Sorry. I'm surrounded by females and I need some backup in London at ten a.m. local time."

~~~

Collin flew into London with the four women and took a helicopter to O'Donnell regional headquarters in the West End. Nigel showed them to a conference room, and then Brenna contacted Seamus. A few seconds later, Seamus O'Donnell appeared with his daughter Callista.

"I hope you have coffee," he growled.

Rebecca jumped up and strode to the sideboard to pour him and Callie a cup.

"I didn't know you were coming, too," Collin said to Callie, who looked as though she was still half-asleep.

"You give me entirely too much credit," Seamus said, taking the coffee from Rebecca and bending down to kiss her on the forehead. "When you said you needed backup to deal with a gaggle of women, I figured I should bring someone they might listen to."

He looked around the room and his eyes came to rest on Rhiannon. He stared down his hawk nose at her until she began to squirm a little in her seat. The Lord of Clan O'Donnell was a legend, but he and Rhiannon had never met before. She had always been intimidated by his reputation, but was surprised at how intimidating he was in person. Almost seven feet tall and wide as the doorway, with gray hair to his shoulders and a gray beard, he looked like an ancient Irish warrior king.
~~~

"You must be Rhiannon," he said, his voice low and gentle, startling everyone. "My dear, you are the spitting image of your great-grandmother." He bowed and extended his hand. "I have heard very good things about you. It's a pleasure."

Flustered, Rhiannon shook his hand, and became even more nervous when he didn't let go. Taking a sip of his coffee, he continued to regard her.

"Fifteen Gifts, including one of the Rare Gifts," he said. "The Krasevec Gift also, is that right?"

Rhiannon nodded.

"You come highly recommended, my dear. Your great-uncle is quite enamored with you."

"I owe a great deal to Lord O'Byrne," Rhiannon said. "He has always treated me as one of the family."

"And so you are," Seamus responded. "I should like an opportunity to speak with you later. Will you make some time for an old man?"

"Of course." Rhiannon shot a panicked look at Rebecca.

It's okay,* Rebecca sent. *He's really a big teddy bear. Mostly.

Oh, yeah, that makes me soooo much more comfortable.

"I'm Callie," Seamus's daughter pushed between them and extended her hand. "Father, you're making her nervous. Go sit down and drink your coffee."

Rhiannon didn't feel much more comfortable meeting Callista O'Donnell Wilkins, who was also a legend in her own right, but the smile Callie gave her was bright, cheerful and welcoming.

"So, what's going on?" Seamus asked.

Collin filled him in on what had been happening,

including a recap of the kidnapping attempt the previous spring and the visit to Irina's parents. He had barely finished when the conference room door opened and Irina entered like a whirlwind.

"I'm telling you, Collin, I'm not putting up with this shit any longer. If a girl can't even go out and get laid without worrying about ...." Irina noticed Seamus and Callie. A bright smile blossomed on her face and in a seamless transition, she said, "Seamus, it's so good to see you. No one told me you were coming." She walked over and gave him a hug and a kiss on the cheek.

"Callie, what a pleasant surprise." She repeated the hug and kiss with Callie, who returned the hug with a chuckle.

"I know you, Irina," Callie said. "Don't go spreading blarney on me. If you're upset, let's hear it."

"It's been very disturbing," Irina said very earnestly. Callie and Rebecca burst out laughing.

"Yeah, I sort of picked that up last night," Collin said. "Why don't you sit down, and let's figure out what to do about it."

"It's very simple," Irina said, taking a seat. "Give me a protector team and we'll go to Russia and I'll kill the bastard. Then we can all live happily ever after."

"Have you ever been to Russia?" Seamus asked.

"Well, no. But I'm fluent in the language and I know everything about Russia."

"Then you're not prepared," Rhiannon said. Everyone turned to look at her. She blushed and looked down at the coffee cup she was holding in her lap.

"Please continue," Seamus said with a soft smile.

Taking a deep breath, Rhiannon said, "Just having the language and knowledge of the customs isn't enough. You've never been anywhere remotely like Russia. The people look like us, but they don't think like us. The culture is truly something between east and west. Not a blend, not a hybrid, but unique unto itself. I don't know what it was like prior to the Revolution. I don't know if the Soviet system changed the way people think, but I do know what it's like now."

"How much time have you spent there?" Collin asked.

"I've been there a half-dozen times, including eight months undercover for Interpol. I was fluent in the language the first time I went, and it was a shock. People picked me out as a foreigner immediately. It wasn't my accent. It was something about the way I carried myself or maybe the expressions on my face. I don't know. I do know that after living there for some time, I can pass."

Collin nodded. "Irina, we have three hundred operatives in Russia, another two hundred in Ukraine, and about fifty more in other parts of the former Soviet Union. All are fluent in Russian. There are five Russian Clans, and Gorbachev is the largest with about fifteen thousand members. Their strongholds are Stavropol, Rostov and Krasnodar in southern Russia, and they also control Moscow. The other Clans are centered in Ukraine, Belarus, St. Petersburg, and the fifth Clan holds territory from Yekaterinburg to Kazakhstan."

"I know all that," Irina said. "I don't need a history lesson."

"I'm just making sure everyone here has the same information," Collin said. "Are you aware that the five Clans are all enemies? There's a mini-cold war going on in the former Soviet Union. Gorbachev controls the FSB, Federal Security Bureau, and is allied with the Kremlin. The Romanov Clan, also called the Russian Mafia by the western media, controls St. Petersburg. But things aren't very neat and clean geographically."

"There were eight Clans in the Soviet Union before the

Silent War," Seamus said. "Three were destroyed, and their members were either absorbed by the survivors or they escaped to the west. What Collin is trying to tell you is that independent telepaths are almost non-existent in Russia. If you're not extremely discreet, you'll stick out like a sore thumb."

"But on the other hand," Rhiannon said, "if we play our cards right, we should fly under everyone's radar. Beautiful women are sixpence a dozen. The Clans there are completely run by men. No one will pay a couple of women any mind if we keep our heads down."

"We?" Callie asked, one eyebrow raised.

Rhiannon shrugged. "I speak fluent Russian and I know the country. I'm of some use in a fight. I figured I'd tag along with her."

"And I'm going," Rebecca said.

"You're not going anywhere," Callie said. "You don't know the language or the customs. You'd be a liability."

"I'm going with Brenna," Rebecca said, crossing her arms across her chest and glaring at Callie.

"Brenna isn't going. She doesn't know the language, and besides, she's Clan Chief at O'Neill. Her adventuring days are over," Collin said.

"Ya gavaryu po Russki," Brenna said and then turned to Rebecca, "but Collin's right. I can't go any more than Seamus can." Everyone stared at her.

"I didn't know Corwin knew Russian," Seamus said with a slight smile.

"He didn't," Rhiannon said, "but I do." She glanced at Seamus. "Grandfather wasn't very discriminating about who he grabbed onto there at the end."

Brenna blushed. "I guess I neglected to tell you that Corwin shared his Death Gift."

“For the Goddess’s sake!” Seamus exploded, sitting bolt upright. He looked from Rhiannon to Brenna. “What in the hell happened?”

The two women exchanged a look but didn’t answer. Seamus closed his eyes and took a deep breath. “We need to talk after this meeting. Alone.”

In the ensuing silence, Irina said, “Can we get back to *my* stupid grandfather? Collin, I’m not going to spend the rest of my life in a cage. I understand the risks. I’ve been researching the Russian Clans using every spare minute I can. What I need is a plan to get me face to face with him.”

Pursing his mouth, Collin opened a portfolio and leaned forward. “We can provide you with security. We can both cover you and provide you with a small assault force in limited circumstances. What we can’t do is tell you where Sergei Gorbachev is. No one has seen him in almost a year. Rumor is that he’s in Moscow, but he has a villa on the Black Sea coast south of Krasnodar. All we can do is facilitate a search.”

He turned to Rhiannon. “If you are willing to be a team player, and curb your impulses to fly off on your own, I’ll put you in charge of the operation. But if you are going to follow the pattern you’ve used on your cases in the past, I’ll have you restrained and held until Irina and her team are in Russia.”

Instantly, he regretted speaking so frankly. The look in her eyes caused his blood to run cold and he was tempted to throw up an air shield around himself. Not that it would do him any good. If she tipped to the killing edge, only Brenna might be able to save him. Then she closed her eyes. When she opened them, she had herself back under control.

“You would put me in charge?” she asked. “Don’t you have capable team leaders?”

“I do. I don’t have anyone as powerful or intelligent as you are. I don’t have anyone more capable than you are.

But if you don't agree to be a leader, to think of the team and Irina first, I can't trust you with the job."

Rhiannon looked at Brenna, then at Irina. Turning to Collin, she said, "Damn you, Collin Doyle. Damn you and your concubine. The two of you are bound and determined to turn me into a responsible Clan member, aren't you?"

"If it's possible," Collin said.

She deflated. "I don't like being responsible for other people. But yes, I'll do it. As long as you tell your team leaders not to argue with me when the shit's hitting the fan. If I'm going to play general, I expect them to follow the script."

"Done."

Rhi,* Brenna sent directly to her alone, *remember plan T. If things get too hairy, I can pull you and Irina out. If you need me to be your nuke, I can do that, too.

Rhiannon met Brenna's eyes and gave her a tight smile. **Thanks.**

~~~

When the meeting ended, Rhiannon moved to leave with the rest. A sharp look from Seamus caused her to sink back into her chair. After the others filed out and Rebecca closed the door behind her, Seamus fixed Brenna with a baleful eye.

"What the hell happened? Why was Miss Kendrick even there? Corwin denied her for thirty-eight years. I find it hard to believe he had a sudden attack of conscience."

Brenna squirmed in her seat. "I didn't think that was right. She deserves her birthright. You knew Delilah. I figured that if he actually saw her, he couldn't doubt she was his granddaughter."

"And did he acknowledge her?" Seamus asked.

"Yes, he did," Rhiannon said. "Hugh lied to him all
~~~

these years. He told Corwin that my mother was a fortune hunter and that he wasn't my father. As we know, Hugh was one of the greatest liars in history."

"And how did you manage to get yourselves into the situation of sharing Corwin's death gift? Do you realize how dangerous that is?"

"Uh, no," Brenna said. "No one ever mentioned that it was even possible. No one warned me."

"That's because it rarely happens. For a reason. History doesn't document many survivors." He turned to Rhiannon, closely studying her face as he asked, "Are you all right?"

Nervously, she said, "Yeah, I think so. Why?"

"Because in most of the instances that I'm aware of, when two people share a death gift, one or both of them go mad. Some never reawaken."

Both women's eyes popped wide open, staring at him.

"You're not worried about me?" Brenna asked in a small voice.

"Of course I worry about you. All the damn time. But if you'd gone off the deep end, either Collin or Rebecca would have told me."

He sighed. "There are a number of complications to what you did. Corwin had the O'Neill Gift, which you also have. Miss Kendrick doesn't. I'm sure that having a seventeen-level mind emptied into hers made for a far more difficult integration than normal. And there are those who go mad from a death gift under the best of circumstances."

He rose, went to the sideboard, poured himself a fresh cup of coffee, and loaded a plate with fresh fruit. Returning to his seat, he said, "The larger risk is the process of integrating another living mind. When you receive a death gift, you get the person's memories. But you two shared each other's living souls. I'm surprised Corwin didn't take the both of you with him."

Rhiannon and Brenna shared a look.

"Have you had any issues?" he asked. "Any problems either with integrating his memories or with what you shared of each other?"

"No, I haven't," Brenna said. "It's weird having some of the memories, or meeting someone for the first time and knowing who they are. It's especially weird to meet an old woman and have a memory of making love to her as a man."

"Yeah," Rhiannon said. "That has to be the weirdest. That and the guy who had his head split by an axe."

Brenna nodded vigorously. "I have dreams sometimes, and that one comes around a lot more that I'd like."

Seamus shook his head. "Amazing. The only thing I can imagine is that you're far more alike than even your looks or your power. Your souls have to be compatible. You're very lucky."

"Do you know what a Pathfinder is?" Rhiannon asked.

Seamus froze, then turned to her in what seemed like slow motion. "Where did you hear about a Pathfinder? And what was the context?"

"After we woke, after Corwin died, the Goddess said that Rhiannon was the Pathfinder," Brenna said. "She said that the Pathfinder completed the triumvirate with me as the Power and Rebecca as the Shadow."

He closed his eyes and took a deep breath. "I'm glad I have a strong heart. Granddaughter, I never imagined I would be challenged the way I constantly feel since you walked into my study that night."

Opening his eyes, he looked at Brenna, then turned his eyes on Rhiannon. "Goddess touched? How in the hell do I manage to live a hundred and sixty years and never know anyone who was Goddess touched, and then meet three of you? Yes, I know what a Pathfinder is. She's the one who finalizes turning my hair snow white."

Brenna leaned forward. "Grandfather, please. Be serious."

"The Pathfinder completed the triumvirate," Seamus repeated. "Brenna, I don't know exactly what any of this means. You say the Goddess can't tell you what your future might bring. I guarantee I can't. I only know that my memories carry knowledge of two other triumvirates. In each case, they saved the Clans from extinction."

He looked at Brenna, and the expression on his face was one she'd never seen before. "You've been worrying about apocalyptic scenarios since we first met. You don't have to convince me anymore. I'm on board."

~~~

Chapter 12

I have learned over the years that when one's mind is made up, this diminishes fear; knowing what must be done does away with fear. - Rosa Parks

Eating dinner in a small Italian restaurant near the train station in St. Petersburg, Roman said to Irina, "I'm rather surprised at your Russian. For someone who is here for the first time, you have a rather strong Moscow accent."

"My mother lived most of her life in Moscow before I was born," Irina replied. "We spoke mainly Russian in my home until I started school. After that, my parents made a point of speaking all the languages they knew. One day would be Russian day, the next English, the next Arabic or German or Dutch. I was expected to keep up." She smiled. "A girl could get mighty hungry if she didn't remember the proper words on the proper day."

"Roman," Rhiannon said, "I've felt a lot of telepaths the past couple of days. Sometimes I feel a really strange,
~~~

hostile vibe, as though there's a silent war going on."

"Yes," he said, "in part that is a reflection of the conflicts within Russian society. But there are members of multiple Clans here, and none of them like each other. There are also factions within the Romanov Clan that controls St. Petersburg. The rumor is that Alexander, the Clan Chief, is dying. We just have to be careful."

Irina and Rhiannon had stepped off of the ferry from Helsinki and looked around at the grandeur of St. Petersburg. The spire of the Admiralty and the dome of St. Isaac's Cathedral rose above the city in one direction, and the steeple of Peter and Paul's Cathedral scraped the sky in the other direction. The rest of their view was a continuation of the many palaces they had seen on their slow crawl up the Neva River.

Carrying Russian passports identifying them as Larisa Mikhaylovna Orlova and Ekaterina Andreyevna Kuznetsova, they allowed the Protectors who accompanied them to direct them to a minibus that drove them to a flat in an old mansion on a canal near the center of the city. Their internal passports with their propiskas, or residency permits, listed their addresses as being in Moscow.

St. Petersburg was founded as an imperial capital, and palaces built during the Czarist period lined the streets. During the Bolshevik Revolution, most were turned into apartment buildings or offices, but the original facades were still impressive. Traveling through the streets, Irina bounced around and squealed like a kid with a new toy. She'd dreamed of seeing Russia all her life, and now she was there.

O'Donnell had purchased one of the old palaces and renovated it to provide apartments and offices for its Russian operations. Their stay in St. Petersburg was intended to be only a brief stop. The plan was to spend a week, acclimating Rhiannon and Irina and getting to know their team before proceeding to Moscow. The unspoken agenda was for their team to try to train them to work with the team, in the hopes of keeping both alive.

Their first day, Roman, head of O'Donnell's St. Petersburg operatives, toured them around the city and patiently accompanied them as they shopped. At Rhiannon's insistence, Irina had packed light. Rhiannon wanted to shop for clothes after they arrived in Russia, intending to ensure their wardrobes reflected current fashion and that the clothing would be of a quality and cut that wouldn't call undue attention.

The following two days were spent at the Hermitage, the great art museum, and Peterhof, the palace of Peter the Great outside of the city. Rhiannon and Roman agreed that keeping a low profile was critical, so they avoided the upper-scale restaurants and nightclubs. She expected some resistance to this from Irina, but was relieved to discover the young succubus agreed with them.

Roman paid the tab and they rose to leave the restaurant. Ivan, the other Protector eating with them, preceded Rhiannon out to the street. The rest of their team floated toward them from the stations they had taken outside the restaurant.

They had walked about half a block when Rhiannon heard the characteristic spit of a silenced pistol and Ivan crumpled. She turned and saw a man step from the shadow of a doorway toward Roman and Irina. He shoved his hand toward Roman, and Rhiannon heard three more spitting sounds in rapid succession. Roman clutched his side and went down. The man grabbed Irina as more men emerged from an alley and from around the corner.

Covering herself with an air shield, Rhiannon moved toward Irina, extending the shield to try to cover the younger woman also.

The man who had grabbed Irina jerked and stumbled

away as the succubus spun toward him. Two other men leaped toward her and she cut them down with Neural Disruption. Rhiannon saw a flicker of light from the syringe held by another man. He grabbed Irina's hair, plunging the syringe into her shoulder. Then he jerked and fell on top of Irina as she slumped to the ground. Springing to Irina's side, Rhiannon pulled the syringe out of her and saw that it was empty.

A curse in Russian and the sounds of blows from behind her caused Rhiannon to glance over her shoulder. A few feet away, one assailant was on top of a face-down O'Donnell Protector, beating him, while another was standing and kicking him.

Rhiannon couldn't use neural energy without also hitting the Protector. Dropping her air shield, she reached into her blouse and pulled her pistol. Taking a deep breath to steady herself, she shot one man and then the other. Beyond them, she saw that her team was badly outnumbered but were holding their own.

As suddenly as they had appeared, the attackers melted away. Spinning around, Rhiannon stared in horror at where Irina had lain. The little succubus was gone.

~~~

I lost her, Rhiannon reported to Brenna.

Lost her? Like you left her on a bus? She wandered off when you were shopping for souvenirs? What do you mean, you lost her? Brenna didn't have to ask who the 'her' was.

We were attacked. Badly outnumbered. They drugged her and we couldn't stop them.

How did Gorbachev even know she was in the country? What the hell is Derek thinking? There's a leak somewhere, and I want an accounting. Show me a landing spot. I'll ream his ass nine ways from Sunday. Derek was
~~~

Roman's real name.

Derek is dead. We lost three of his team and four more are wounded. If you feel the need to come here and do something, I'm sure Spencer could use your help. Spencer, aka Boris, was the team's Healer.

Through the link, Rhiannon felt Brenna hesitate, her anger diminishing and tinged with sorrow.

It wasn't Gorbachev, Rhiannon sent. **We captured one of them. He's from the Romanov Clan. Unfortunately, he's just muscle. He doesn't know a damned thing except they were told to snatch the blonde girl.**

Rhiannon let a bit of her weariness and frustration leak through the link. **Brenna, what's so damned special about Irina that every Russian Clan seems to want her?**

I don't know, Brenna answered. **We don't have a clue why they want her. You said she was drugged?**

Yeah. I can feel her when I try, but I can't make contact. She burned out four men, but I saw one of them inject her with something. She went down like Sleeping Beauty biting the apple. If she comes out of it, we'll find her, but after the performance she put on here and the one in London, I wouldn't count on her kidnappers giving her the chance to do anything.

I've been drugged before, Brenna said. **The stuff the slavers use is a complex cocktail that's meant to make it difficult to decipher. You can't detoxify it quickly enough to prevent it knocking you out. Damn! I can't believe you exposed her like that.**

Rhiannon caught herself before she reacted and took a deep breath. **Well, too late to worry about what we should or shouldn't have done,** Rhiannon sent. She had Brenna's memories from the kidnapping that had landed Brenna in the hands of a homicidal sadist. **Can you let Moscow know what's happened, and ask them for reinforcements? We* *have about forty-five operatives here in St. Pete. I could use a couple of hundred if we're going to find her and get her back.**

I'll see what I can do. Are you safe for right now?

I think so. I doubt anyone will bother us. We lost people, but their losses were greater. Even if they know where we are, I don't think Romanov would be very anxious to tangle with us again.

Okay. Hang tight and let me see what I can do about getting you some help.

~~~

O'Donnell Protectors flooded into St. Petersburg from Moscow and other Russian cities, along with a contingent of O'Neill Protectors from Helsinki.

"Andrei Galkin," the head of O'Donnell's operatives in Moscow introduced himself. **I'm Jerome Murphy, District Manager of O'Donnell Russian operations.**

"Ekaterina Kuznetsova," Rhiannon replied. **RB Kendrick. Brenna O'Donnell's representative on this mission.**

Murphy's hair was iron-gray but he carried himself with the grace of a trained fighter. RB conducted him to a small parlor. Over cups of strong Russian tea, she filled him in on the disaster the operation had become. After some discussion of the overall mission, and his status update on the situation in Moscow, the talk turned more personal.

"Collin said you'd been in Russia a long time," Rhiannon ventured.

"Almost sixty years. I came here with Seamus during the Silent War."

"Were you ..."

Andrei sighed. "Yes, I was at the Battle of Leningrad.
~~~

Everyone asks." He smiled. "A lot of the current situation has roots back to that battle. I assume you've either read the history or heard the stories. What is important for this situation is that the Russian Clans were decimated. Over ten thousand dead while our losses were a couple of hundred with a few hundred wounded. We decapitated their leadership structure. The top seven Romanovs were killed. The Clan Chief of Gorbachev, along with his two brothers and three oldest sons, were killed. Sergei was holding down the fort in the south and inherited by default."

"The numbers have always seemed staggering to me," Rhiannon said. "It's difficult to wrap my mind around a battle that lopsided."

"Picture the battle at Ayr on a grander scale," Andrei said, watching her carefully.

She jerked, spilling her tea. Setting the cup down, she reached for a napkin and mopped up the small mess. Not looking at him, she asked, "What have you heard about Ayr?"

"The official report, and a conversation with Collin before you came to Russia," he answered. "The battle here was kind of like that. It lasted three days, and we were outnumbered, but man for man, we had superior strength. We also had Seamus and Jack. The first night, Seamus found the enemy commanders, and in the early hours of the morning, he killed them all. And yes, the legends are true. Their camps were between one and three miles away."

He caught her eyes. "The difference in power from one telepath to another isn't just a minor difference. If Jack's O'Donnell Gift was a bazooka, Seamus's Gift was a howitzer. And my power is that of a musket. I have twelve Gifts, and there are few men I fear, but the kind of power you wielded at Ayr is truly unique."

Rhiannon picked up her teacup and took a sip to hide her embarrassment. "You were saying about how that battle influences our issues here?"

"Yes, well, you know that the distribution of Gifts isn't uniform. I've never heard of a Russian having one of the Rare Gifts, or a Russian succubus. Sergei used to have one, but she ran away."

"Irina's mother," Rhiannon said. "But she was born in Ireland."

Andrei nodded. "He's been buying them recently." It was Rhiannon's turn to nod. "Anyway," Andrei continued, "the Russian Clans rode out the Bolshevik Revolution and had an alliance with the German Clans until the Nazis invaded Russia. That fight was costly to both sides. And then the battle here crushed them. Alexander was a third son, and the weakest, but he was the only one left to inherit."

"Like Sergei," Rhiannon said.

"Exactly. They've built up their numbers since then, but the gene pool is thin. If I could pick our ground, I wouldn't be afraid of taking on either Romanov or Gorbachev at five to one odds."

He leaned forward, waiting until he was sure he had her full attention. "Rhiannon, what are we going to do if we do kill Sergei? He's never named an heir, and I don't blame him. There's no one to name. I could have taken him out several times over the years, but the thought of who might succeed him stopped me. It's a topic that's above my pay grade, but you should discuss it with Brenna and Seamus. And with Fergus, I suppose. There's going to be a civil war here at Romanov. Is that what we want at Gorbachev? It could have some nasty repercussions."

She thought about it. "I'll talk with Brenna. You never did tell me why you're still in Russia. No offense, but you're a little old to still be a Protector."

He chuckled. "My title is Director of Russian

Operations. You gave me an excuse to get back in the field for a while. But the answer to your question is that after the battle, I was part of the units that Seamus detailed to keep an eye on the retreating Russian forces. One night in Pskov, I took advantage of a pretty young Russian girl. A year later, I asked her to marry me. A couple of years after that, I began to question who took advantage of whom. That was fifty-five years ago. We have three grown children, and a new one in the oven. I've never regretted a minute of it."

~~~

Donald O'Conner, operational name Vladimir, was a few years older than Rhiannon. O'Neill's Chief of Operations in Finland, he and his team had taken the ferry in from Helsinki. Tall and powerfully built with dark blond hair and pale blue eyes, he stopped a few feet away from her and gave a slight bow.

"Lady Rhiannon, I'm Donald O'Conner. Lady O'Neill asked us to lend you any assistance you may require," he said. His body language struck her as almost too casual for his words. For some reason, he put her off stride, as though he was mocking her.

"Thank you for coming," she said, trying to regain her balance. "Andrei is out right now, but I can brief you and then we can discuss strategy when he gets back."

She led him into the office she'd appropriated. It had been Roman's. O'Conner's shields were very good, shutting off almost all emotional output, but she still sensed amusement from him, and that he was diligently studying her ass as he followed her. Sitting behind Roman's desk, she gestured to a chair and he took a seat.

Leaning forward, she began filling him in on the events leading up to Irina's disappearance. He didn't even glance at her breasts. Not once. Not even when she took an unusually deep breath. Not even when she arched her back and stretched and leaned back in her chair. His eyes never
~~~

left her face.

And why the hell does that matter? she asked herself. *Why is that suddenly so important?* It normally bothered her when men focused on her body, treating her like a sex object. Here she was practically begging this guy to do it, and it irritated her that he didn't.

As they talked, she found herself overly conscious of his broad chest and shoulders, the high cheekbones and straight, narrow nose. And his eyes. While his face showed complete seriousness, his eyes made her think he was secretly laughing at her. She tried to work up some indignation, some anger, but the effort was a complete failure.

"You know that Gorbachev has the Rivera Gift, don't you?" he asked.

"I'm aware of his Gifts," she said. "She's a succubus, and I'm here to make sure she succeeds."

"Yes, and she's only twenty-five years old, still a little girl. Do you have the O'Neill Gift?"

Rhiannon shook her head.

"Well, if you manage to find him, I don't even want to be in the neighborhood when they cut loose on each other."

"Andrei will provide the support we need," Rhiannon said, irritated at O'Conner's attitude. "We just need your manpower to help us find her, then you can go back to Helsinki and do whatever it is that you do there."

He stood up. "Miss Kendrick, Lady O'Neill said that you're in charge here. The only thing I have to say is that you'd better get your shit together. It appears this has been a pretty slipshod operation so far. I won't put my men in danger for you and some succubus with delusions of grandeur."

Rhiannon felt her emotions hit a slow boil as he turned and sauntered out the door. But she found herself distracted by his ass. *Shit, RB, he's right. Get your act together.*

A large conference room had maps of Russia and St. Petersburg on two of the walls. A third wall was covered with a white board. Rhiannon met with Vladimir, Andrei, Spencer and Mikhail, O'Donnell's Kiev team lead, to attempt to work out a strategy for finding Irina. Spencer provided a quick briefing on Romanov properties and interests, colored pins marking their locations.

Then Andrei provided a high-level overview of the relations between the Romanov and Gorbachev Clans, and shared the intelligence profiles O'Donnell had built on Alexander Romanov and his children.

Alexander Romanov was the Clan Chief. He had three sons and a daughter, who intelligence had identified as the strongest and smartest of the lot. His oldest son, Viktor, was the named heir, but he was generally considered the weakest of the candidates to succeed his father.

"The old man's dying," Andrei finished. "He hasn't been in good health for years, and the bickering between his kids has been building the whole time. As I was telling RB, there are very few truly strong telepaths in the Clan. The Silent War decimated their strength. Alexander has seven Gifts, and the strongest of his sons, Alexander, has seven. Viktor, the heir, only has five. And I would be ashamed if any of my kids were that stupid."

"What about the daughter?" RB asked.

"She's another story," Andrei said, running his hand through his hair. "Twelve Gifts, including the air, fire, water trine. No Rivera, no Krasevec, no Rare Gifts. She also got all the brains in the family, Goddess knows where. Her mother was a party-minded shopaholic. My wife speculated once that the mother was screwing around when Galina was conceived."

"Your wife is Romanov, isn't she?" Vladimir asked laconically.

"She was. She married into O'Donnell fifty-five years ago," Andrei said, a dangerous glint in his eye.

Vladimir smiled. "Not casting aspersions, old man, simply providing some context and credibility for those who don't know Yelena." He turned toward RB. "Yelena is Alexander's great-niece. As I'm sure you know, the women's gossip network often produces more credible intelligence than all the time and money us men spend attempting to justify our existence."

Andrei chuckled. "You have that right. Yelena's sister is married to a guy who is one of the Romanov insiders. An accountant. Under-appreciated and under-compensated." He shrugged. "You know how it is. In Russia, you marry a girl and you marry her family. I'd never hear the end of it if I didn't help the poor guy out occasionally. And his information is always rock solid. As to the gossip, I never discount anything my wife tells me. It wouldn't be healthy."

Looking at the map of St. Petersburg, Vladimir said, "So, we have the manpower to put all those locations under surveillance, but how are we going to know if this girl is inside one of them?"

"I spoke with Thomas earlier today, and he's sending a plane load of equipment that will arrive in the morning," RB said. "The latest laser and parabolic microphones, tiny wireless bugs that can be attached to clothing or under a table, equipment for cell phone monitoring, that sort of thing. He's also sending a dozen technicians to set it all up and train your people to use it. The techs don't speak Russian, so this is an in-and-out for them. And we can repurpose the equipment when we move from this operation on to Gorbachev."

Vladimir stared at her. "Thomas?"

"Yes, Thomas O'Neill."

"Hell. How did you do that? I've been trying to get

new equipment for the past two years," Vladimir said.

She smiled at him. "I just batted my eyelashes. Try it. Maybe you're his type."

"Bullshit."

Spencer turned to him, a puzzled look on his face, and said, "She's the heir."

"Huh?" Vladimir stared at him, then turned to RB. "The heir to what?"

"Are you sure you're in the right profession?" RB asked with a smirk. "Are you so far out in the hinterlands that you don't know what's going on at home?"

His eyes grew large. He opened his mouth and shut it. Then tried again. All of the others watched him in amusement. Finally, he said, "Lady O'Neill has named an heir?"

"Over my strident objections, I assure you," RB said dryly. He continued to stare at her, rapidly blinking his eyes. For some reason, she was finding immense pleasure in his reaction.

Finally, Andrei took pity on him. "Vladimir, she's Hugh's daughter. Corwin's granddaughter and Brenna's cousin. I thought you knew."

"Didn't you hear about the operation at Ayr?" Spencer asked. "Hell, I'm not even a member of O'Neill and I heard about it. The operation that broke Hugh's rebellion?"

"I heard something about a massacre," Vladimir said. "I didn't pay too much attention to the details. I just made a note to myself to stay the hell away from Ulster and not to do anything to get on Brenna O'Donnell's bad side."

RB felt her face heat. To hear someone actually come out and call what she had done at Ayr a massacre triggered even more guilt than she already felt. "Brenna wasn't there," she said. "She didn't order that. No one did. It just sort of happened."

Vladimir looked at her incredulously. “It just sort of happened? As to your question earlier, yes, I do pay attention to things outside of Finland and Russia. I was told that over three hundred rebels were slaughtered without mercy. They weren’t even given an opportunity to surrender. How does something like that just sort of happen?”

Biting her lip, she looked down at her lap. The room was dead silent. Out of the corner of her eye, she saw Andrei looking at her, waiting for her response. Taking a deep breath, she squared her shoulders and looked directly at Vladimir.

“I hated Hugh O’Neill. The bastard shamed me and treated me like crap. He refused to acknowledge me, and lied to Corwin that I wasn’t his daughter. He denied me my birthright. He treated my mother like a whore.”

She took another breath, looking around at the other men. “There were heavy machine guns and light artillery defending his position at Ayr. They were dug in, and it was pretty obvious that we were going to take casualties. As to an opportunity to surrender, that they were given. Their response was to commence firing. I broke down one of Hugh’s men and discovered Hugh wasn’t even there. He’d gone to Belfast to meet with Finnian to wreak more havoc on perfectly innocent people. And I lost my temper. I swore that no more loyal clansmen would die because of my fucked up father. So I ended the battle.”

“I don’t understand,” Vladimir said.

“I killed them all.”

“Three hundred men?” Vladimir’s face turned pale.

“From three hundred yards away,” Andrei said. “Collin told me the story when he briefed me for this mission.”

Vladimir turned to him, searching his face. Turning back to RB, he said, “You lost your temper?”

“Yeah. And when we find the cute little succubus we’re searching for, tread lightly. She’s got a hell of a lot worse temper than I do.”

~~~

After three days of discreet searching, they had turned up no sign of Irina. Rhiannon was increasingly frustrated and called a meeting with all the team leads.

“We’re not getting anywhere with our current approach,” she told them. “I think we need to ramp things up a bit.”

“What do you have in mind?” O’Conner asked.

“Start identifying mid-level leaders of Romanov teams and rousting them. Someone knows something.”

“Not a good idea to get Romanov stirred up,” he said. “They have at least three thousand bully boys in this city and we have three hundred. One-on-one we may be stronger, but you see how they fight. We’ll be going up against people who have no compunction in using submachine guns in public.” As the head of O’Neill’s security force in Finland, he had more than two decades of experience operating in Russia. Even O’Donnell’s Protectors tended to defer to him.

“Vladimir’s right,” Andrei said. Rhiannon knew Andrei had twelve Gifts, including Distance Communication. He very well might be the strongest telepath, other than her, in the city.

“What we have picked up,” he continued, “is that there are some deep divisions within Romanov at the moment. One of my men confirmed the rumor that Alexander Romanov is severely ill, possibly dying. If that’s true, then the jockeying for position among his sons may be the reason the city feels so unsettled.”

“If that’s the case, then we can probably narrow our efforts to the succession candidates. Let’s concentrate on
~~~

discovering which faction is most likely to have kidnapped her," Rhiannon said.

"Why would any of them kidnap her?" Andrei asked. "Even if they knew who she was, what would taking her have to do with the succession?"

"Perhaps they see her as a bargaining chip," Rhiannon answered. "They may not know why Gorbachev wants her or her relationship with him. They might offer to trade her to Gorbachev for help in backing their succession bid. Or possibly use her as a hostage to keep him out of the succession, to keep him from backing another candidate."

"That's pretty wild speculation," Andrei said.

Vladimir shook his head. "Actually, that makes a lot of sense." He cocked his head and looked at Rhiannon in a way that made her think he was really seeing her for the first time as more than a pretty girl. "That makes a hell of a lot of sense. It would be in Gorbachev's interest to see the weakest candidate take over. Viktor could have kidnapped her to ensure Gorbachev backs him or one of the others may be trying to use her to keep Sergei on the sidelines."

"That still doesn't explain how they knew who she was," Andrei said. "Hell, it could be that Gorbachev paid Romanov to snatch her. She might have already been moved to Moscow or even south."

Rhiannon looked around the room, her eyes settling on Spencer, the O'Donnell Healer who was the surviving senior Protector from the St. Petersburg team.

"There are only three possibilities," she said. "Either someone who recognized her from London tipped off Romanov, Sergei paid Romanov, or there's a mole inside O'Donnell's team. Anyone want to convince me the last option isn't true?" She looked at Spencer.

"I'll open my shields to a superior from O'Donnell," he said, "but not to you. No offense, ma'am, but you're not

Clan."

Rhiannon nodded and looked at Andrei.

"Spencer, gather your team in the dining room," Andrei said. Spencer stood and left the room. "Do you trust me?" Andrei stiffly asked Rhiannon.

"I'm not going to insult you," she answered. "I'm sorry about Ivan." The dead Protector had been Andrei's nephew. "I don't mean to insult any of the people on our team," she continued, "and I don't think anyone voluntarily betrayed us. I'm simply trying to eliminate any doubts in all of our minds. But I think you should include a construct artist in your interrogation."

Andrei's eyes widened. "I'll do that," he said. He motioned to the team lead from O'Donnell's Kiev operations and they left together.

Lady Brenna told me that I should trust your instincts, Vladimir sent on a spear thread. **I'm starting to see why.**

I'm only a pretty face with big tits, Rhiannon sent back, looking directly into his eyes. **Anyone who was at Ayr can tell you that.**

He checked his shields. They weren't leaking. She hadn't read his mind, but she had obviously picked up on what he was thinking, whether through Empathy, facial expressions or body language. Only a thin ring of green surrounded her pupils. He shuddered, realizing that Irina's kidnapping had Rhiannon close to the killing edge. This wasn't just a job for her, it was personal.

Roman's team checked out. There weren't any traitors in the group. When Andrei informed Rhiannon, she went to the dining room to talk to the people on that team.

"I apologize," she told the men and women gathered there. "I hope you understand we had to do this to eliminate any suspicion."

"It's okay," Spencer said. "Once I saw Mikhail, I understood what you were thinking." The Kiev team lead was a construct artist. "No hard feelings."

The others nodded. "Scary for us to think someone we trusted might have been compromised," a woman said. "Better we know."

"Thank you," Rhiannon said and turned to leave.

"Katya," Spencer said, using the familiar variation of her operational name. "I may be the senior person on this team now, but I don't have any experience leading a team. As a healer, I have to think differently if we get into a scrap. Collin said you're in charge. I know that you deferred to Roman's experience, but I'd feel a lot better if you really take charge of this team. We saw you in action when Irina was kidnapped. You know what you're doing."

She looked around and saw nods of agreement and heard some soft, "I agree" comments.

"Anyone disagree?" she asked. No one spoke up.

"Shit. I really hate responsibility," she said.

"Tough," one woman laughed. "You're stuck with it, and with us."

~~~

O'Donnell had a mole inside the Gorbachev Clan in Moscow. Checking with him revealed that, to his knowledge, no one had been contacted about Irina. He hadn't noticed any unusual activity and even Sergei's closest lieutenants didn't show any concern. But he also didn't know where Sergei was. Two of the Clan Chief's confidants were also missing. The mole assumed they were at the Black Sea estate.

It was decided that they would start with the weakest of the Romanov non-heirs. Leonid Romanov was the youngest of Alexander's children and the only child of his second wife. A playboy who didn't seem to harbor dynastic
~~~

aspirations, he was not only the least likely suspect, but also the one with the least political power, wealth and protection.

A scouting foray of his estate outside the city provided the intelligence that he was throwing a large party the next day. Tonight, there would be numerous deliveries of food and booze to his home, along with employees of the caterer coming in to prepare. His security force appeared to be about thirty men.

One hundred Protectors positioned themselves outside Leonid's perimeter. Andrei's team stopped a delivery truck with a load of vodka and champagne. They captured the driver and the other two men riding with him, blanked their memories, and put them to sleep. Unloading the booze, the team climbed into the back of the truck and Andrei drove on to the compound.

Once they were inside, another truck appeared at the gate. When the guard approached the truck, Rhiannon blasted through his shields and took control of his mind. He turned and waved to his fellow guard to let the truck through. Halfway through the gate, the truck stopped. Rhiannon took control of the second guard as Protectors swarmed out of the back of the truck and spread out around the compound.

The Protectors from the first truck were now in the house, capturing and neutralizing everyone they encountered. Rhiannon heard a few scattered gunshots from inside, then a submachine gun from the front of the house. She saw the flare of light that indicated a fireball, and the gun fell silent.

RB, we have them all, Andrei sent from the house.

Status? she sent to her team outside.

All good. No casualties on our side, Spencer sent.

She decided not to inquire about casualties on the

Romanov side. Slipping around to the front, she saw a charred spot on the side of the building with an equally charred body lying on the ground. Spencer waved her toward the front door.

"He was a bit uncooperative," he said, following her eyes toward the dead man.

He led her into the house and up a large staircase. Upstairs, she was ushered into a room where a visibly upset man in his forties, but looking about twenty-five, was pacing the floor, shouting about how his father was going to fry them all.

Leonid Romanov, I presume? she asked Andrei.

In the flesh. He hasn't offered any resistance.

Have you tried his shields?

No, we were waiting for you.

Rhiannon tested Leonid's shields and he resisted. Taking a deep breath, she assaulted his shields, breaking through to his ninth level and capturing his mind. Gazing on his soul, she found that although he had a few blemishes, it wasn't as bad as she expected. Several red spots that indicated rape or other types of coercion, a few light brown smudges that were the result of cruelties he'd inflicted, but no black that would be the result of murder.

Ransacking his mind, she found that he really was just a playboy. He had no expectation of becoming Clan Chief, and had done his best to remain neutral in his siblings' maneuverings. As to Irina, he had no idea she even existed.

"Nothing," she announced. "Andrei, Spencer, come on in and get whatever knowledge you feel is useful. His father is dying, and he has information on locations, codes, some bank accounts, things like that. But he has no power within the Clan, and he never heard of Irina."

It was almost morning when they returned to the safe house. Before going to bed, Rhiannon was relaxing in a warm bath when she felt a tickle in her mind. As it grew stronger, she realized that it was her link to Irina. The succubus, wherever she was, was regaining consciousness.

~~~

Chapter 13

Trust everybody, but cut the cards. - Finley Peter Dunne

The blackness gradually faded and Irina groggily fought to open her eyes. She felt terrible. Her eyes seemed crusted together, her mouth felt as though she'd swallowed a desert, and her stomach was churning. To top it all off, she couldn't move. Trying to lift her hand, she discovered it was tied to something. Her chin rested against her chest, and it took all her strength to lift her head.

Movement in front of her drew her attention, but she couldn't seem to bring whatever it was into focus. Her head felt as though it was filled with cotton.

"Irina Gorbacheva," a woman's voice said in Russian.

"Huh?" Irina's voice came out as a rough croak.

"Give her some water," the woman said.

Someone pulled her head up by grabbing her hair. The spout of a bottle was forced between her lips and water flooded her mouth. It tasted so good, but then she choked, coughing the liquid over the front of her dress.

"Idiot. Don't drown her. Just a little water. Let her swallow it. Fool," the woman said.

When Irina finished coughing, the bottle was pressed against her lips again, but only a trickle of water poured into her mouth. She greedily swallowed it.

"Irina Gorbacheva," the woman said again. "I need you to say hello to your grandfather."

Irina managed to bring the woman speaking into focus.
~~~

Very tall and thin, large breasted with auburn hair, she could have been someone they had passed on the street, but Irina didn't recognize her.

"My name is Larisa Orlova," Irina managed to whisper. "I don't know who this Irina person is."

The woman shot a glance at someone outside of Irina's line of sight. After a moment, she returned her attention to Irina.

"We know who you are. And if you are not Irina Gorbacheva, succubus and granddaughter of Sergei Gorbachev, then we have no reason to keep you alive. Do you understand?"

Irina attempted to touch the place in her mind where her Neural Disruption Gift was triggered. To her dismay, the drugs prevented her from touching any of her Gifts. Drawing a ragged breath, she tried to think, to concentrate on her situation. Her mind was so foggy. All she wanted to do was go back to sleep.

A small microphone was shoved in her face. Looking up, she saw a man aiming a camera at her.

"Say hello to your grandfather," the woman said.

"I'm going to kill you," Irina said.

"Is that really what you want to say to him?" the woman chuckled. "I think your threats are rather empty. We are in control here, not you."

"I'm going to kill you, too," Irina mumbled.

The expression on the woman's face changed from amusement to dismay. "Your message for your grandfather is that you're going to kill him?"

Irina shook her head. "Don't want to talk to him at all. Why would I warn him?"

Although Irina couldn't trigger her Gifts, Empathy didn't need a trigger. The emotional feel of the room changed. The woman's body language changed from arrogant to nervous and unsure. Irina tried to organize her thoughts, but she was so tired. She tried to start detoxifying the drugs in her system, but she couldn't concentrate.

The basic telepathic Gifts--Telepathy, Empathy and Charisma--don't have triggers. They are simply part of who the telepath is. But all telepathic efforts require energy, and that energy is drawn from the person's personal life energy.

Frustrated by her own lethargy, Irina began draining the life energy of the people in the room. As she strengthened, she began to feel people outside the room and pulled energy from them as well. As her focus sharpened, she began detoxifying the drugs. She was able to identify four drugs. Testing each of them, she found the one that was blocking her telepathic abilities and concentrated on it.

Next, she cleared the drugs that caused the lethargy and sleepiness. Soon, her mind began to work again and she was able to assess her situation. At the same time, three of the men in the room had moved to sit on tables or chairs. The woman facing her leaned against the wall, weariness showing in her face.

The first thing that surfaced in Irina's thoughts was the fact that her kidnappers had not broken down her shields and captured her mind. The only reason not to have done so was that they couldn't. None of her captors had a Dominance Gift, and even combining their strength, they weren't strong enough to breach her defenses. Her confidence soared.

And then, as her mind cleared, she felt Rhiannon.

Irina? Are you there?

Rhi! Goddess, am I glad to hear you!

Are you all right? Rhiannon asked Irina.

Yeah, I think so. I'm really hungry and I'm tied to a chair, but I've cleared most of the drugs out of my system.

Where are you?

In a room without windows, tied to a chair. I realize that's not terribly helpful.

What about the people holding you?

Everyone's asleep, Irina replied. *_They'll be out for a couple of days. But I don't know if anyone else will come here._*

Rhiannon got out of the bathtub and began drying off. She sent a spear thread to Andrei. *_I've contacted her. She's all right!_* Then what Irina had said hit her.

They're all _asleep? How many are there?_

Six in this room, another dozen in other rooms.

You shagged them all?

Irina sent the mental equivalent of a giggle. *_No, silly. I told you, I'm tied up. But I don't have to touch someone to drain them._

Rhiannon took a few moments to process everything Irina had told her.

If they're all asleep, can you read any of their minds to find out where you are? she finally asked.

No, they're all shielded, Irina answered.

Yes, I understand that. But can you break through their shields?

I don't know, Irina sent. She was silent for a few moments. *_I'm not sure how to do that. I've never done it._*

Biting back her initial response, Rhiannon knew that she'd let some of her frustration seep through the link when Irina sent, *_I never had to do it, and no one ever taught me. It's rude, you know._*

And you don't think someone kidnapping you is rude? Rhiannon chuckled. *_Can you let me into your mind? I can show you how to do it._*

Irina opened her mind and Rhiannon slipped in. She

directed Irina to test the shields of the sleeping people around her. The woman's mind was locked and solid. Rhiannon might have been able to break through if she'd been there in person, but at a distance she was limited to what Irina had the power to accomplish.

Irina tested the men, and as she brushed the mind of the third one, Rhiannon detected thoughts leaking through his shield. She pointed it out to Irina, then coached her to follow the faint random thoughts back to their source. Inside the man's mind, it didn't take long to identify Irina's location. Her kidnappers hadn't taken her far. She was a five-minute walk from where they had captured her.

Rhiannon sent the information to Andrei and Vladimir while she dressed, then turned her attention back to Irina and the man's mind. As they burrowed down through the layers of his mind, Rhiannon picked up additional information about the organization and motives of the kidnappers. By the time she and the Protectors reached the building, Irina had breached all of the man's shields and controlled his mind. Unfortunately, his energy levels were so low that she couldn't wake him to untie her or let her friends into the building.

Walking down the street with the Protectors, Rhiannon looked around at the people sharing the street with them. The buildings originally had been townhouses of minor nobility or rich merchants, but now they were apartment houses, most with businesses on the first floor. A cafe was on the first floor of the building on one side of their target address and a photo shop was on the other.

Irina, we're here,* she sent. *Are you sure everyone in the building is asleep?

Yes, I'm sure.

You're in an apartment house. What about the buildings on both sides?

There are people there, but they're all norms.

Rhiannon stopped, closing her eyes and getting her emotions under control. *Do you suppose any of them know where they are?*

I'm sure they do, Irina replied. *Why?*

Do you suppose you could have picked your address out of their minds?

Irina was silent, then sent, *I'm sorry. I didn't think of that.*

It wasn't Irina's fault. Rhiannon could feel that the succubus's mind was still foggy from the drugs. But Rhiannon blamed herself for not asking more questions earlier. Irina had drugs as an excuse for not thinking clearly. Rhiannon didn't have an excuse.

She keyed in the code for the security system and walked through the metal door. She found herself in a foyer with stairs in front of her, a door to her right, and a long hallway leading away to her left. Protectors flowed up the stairs and down the hallway. A projected air shield blew down the door to the right, revealing a room that obviously served as an armory.

Searching through the building, they found Irina on the fourth floor. They untied her and Rhiannon handed her half a roasted chicken, some potato salad and a bottle of wine. Irina's rescuers waited until she finished eating, and it didn't take long.

"Thank you," Irina said with a smile. "God, it feels as though I haven't eaten in a week."

"What do you remember eating last?" Andrei asked.

"Spaghetti, the night they snatched me."

"That was more than six days ago," Rhiannon told her.

Andrei pointed to the redheaded woman peacefully sleeping on the floor near the door. "That's Galina Romanova," he said.

"She's definitely the one in charge," Irina said. She pointed to the video camera on the table. "She wanted to send a greeting from me to my grandfather. That's why they woke me up. I think they wanted to prove I was alive. I got the feeling they thought he and I are on good terms."

"Bargaining chip," Rhiannon said. "We'll have to get into her mind to find out what her intentions are."

In addition to Rhiannon, Vladimir and Andrei also had the Dominance Gift. The three of them systematically broke through the shields of all the telepaths in the building, then turned them over to other Protectors to interrogate.

Galina was definitely the most difficult. The woman's shields were rock solid. When Rhiannon finally broke through, she understood why.

Donald, Jerome, would you please join me? she sent to Vladimir and Andrei. They joined with her mind and then entered Galina's.

Alexander Romanov's daughter had twelve Gifts, including Distance Communication, which strengthened her other Gifts. She didn't have any of the Rare Gifts, or the Irish Gifts of Dominance and Strong Shielding, and she wasn't a succubus or a carrier. But she was an exceptionally strong telepath, and she'd never met one stronger. She was in for a very rude awakening.

"Andrei, your information isn't entirely correct. She has the Krasevec Gift," Rhiannon said.

He was bending over one of the men, but he snapped upright at her pronouncement. "Are you sure?" he asked.

Rhiannon checked again in Galina's mind. The trigger for Distance Communication was there on her fifth level. "Yeah, I'm sure." Searching further in Romanova's mind, she said, "She hides it. Only a few close confidants know. On the other Gifts, your intel is correct. But if you're correct about Gifts in the Russian Clans, she's formidable."

"I know that guy," Irina said. Everyone's attention shifted to her, then followed her eyes to the man at Andrei's feet.

Rhiannon shifted her attention back to Irina. Sitting in a chair, the young succubus was hanging on to the table and weaving like a drunk. Obviously, she still hadn't shaken off the effects of the drugs.

"Where do you know him from?" Rhiannon asked.

Irina slowly looked up at her, and took a few moments to focus. "He was the guy I shagged in London last spring. Don't you remember? I took him upstairs in that hotel, and in the middle of things, his friends came out of the bathroom and tried to capture me."

Andrei? Rhiannon sent.

Andrei was quiet for a few moments, then he said, "This is the link. He's a member of Gorbachev, and he did try to kidnap her in London. He's also on Galina's payroll. He saw you outside the bookstore on Nevsky Prospekt and reported you to Galina."

"Does he know why Sergei wants her?" Rhiannon asked.

"No. He has several speculations."

"Spill."

"He has two main theories. One is that Sergei wants his granddaughter because he doesn't have an heir he believes in. He wonders if Sergei is hoping that Irina is strong enough to hold the Clan together after he's gone. The second, and the one he thinks is more plausible, is that he wants to breed his own succubi, because the price von Ebersberg's charging is too expensive. That theory is bolstered by Sergei's fetish for very young girls." Andrei shot a look at Irina, then sent a spear thought to Rhiannon. **He was around when Sergei had Irina's mother. Are you* *aware that he's not only her grandfather, but also her father?**

Yes, and she knows it, too. That's why she's so set on killing him.

Irina looked up at Andrei. "You don't have to talk around me. I know what kind of incestuous bastard I am."

His eyes jerked toward her, a guilty expression on his face.

"That's why I'm going to kill him," she said. "Wouldn't you, if you knew that's what he wanted to do with your daughter?"

He strode toward her and placed his hand on her shoulder. "My lady, I didn't understand before, but I do now. We'll get the son of a bitch. I promise. "

"Am I missing something?" Vladimir asked.

"Probably," Rhiannon said. "Use your charm and ask her for her life story."

Irina shifted her attention to Rhiannon. Her vision wavered, and it was obvious that she was still having problems bringing everything into focus.

"Do you want him out of commission for three days?" Irina glanced at Vladimir. "I won't cut him any slack. He's a dumbshit who doesn't respect women. You're welcome to him. As far as I'm concerned, he's just prey."

Rhiannon felt her face flame. Looking away from Irina, she turned and found herself face to face with Vladimir. His mouth hung open, staring at Irina.

"Shall we take care of business?" Rhiannon said, nodding toward Galina.

Rhiannon and Vladimir met in Galina's mind and began to set blocks on the triggers for her Gifts while Andrei went to organize the transport of their prisoners. The mental work with Galina presented a major effort because of the number of Gifts she had.

The intimacy of working with Vladimir in Galina's mind was both stimulating and uncomfortable. They sat several feet apart, but the feeling was that they were wrapped around each other. Every time her mind brushed against his, it sent a chill through her, and the looks he occasionally shot her told her that he wasn't immune to the contact.

After almost an hour of work, Rhiannon turned to Irina. The young woman was slumped over the table and appeared to be asleep. Rhiannon rose from her chair and shook Irina awake.

"We need your help. She has Gifts we don't have, and I need you to block them."

Blinking at the light, Irina said, "Okay. What Gifts?"

"She has Orgonekinesis, both projection and draining. From reading her thoughts, I can see that she has them, but since I don't, I can't see the triggers to block them."

Yawning widely, Irina said, "Okay. Uh, RB, I don't know how to do that."

"It's okay, honey. I left one of the Gifts that we all have. I can show you, and then you can block the others."

Rhiannon showed Irina how to block the Electrokinesis Gift, and then entered Irina's mind and watched as the young succubus placed the necessary blocks in Galina's mind. Then they set compulsions for obedience, and to keep Galina from attempting to use her Gifts that didn't have triggers. The obedience compulsion was set to Rhiannon, Vladimir, Andrei and Mikhail. The final compulsion was against her escaping. The last thing Rhiannon did was place a keyhole into Galina's shields. Even after the blocks and compulsions were removed, Rhiannon would have an entrance into Romanova's mind.

"There's something I don't understand," Vladimir said.

"If she has those Gifts, why didn't she realize you were draining all of them?"

"Because, sweetie," Irina said with a smile, "normal telepaths are amateurs at life energy manipulation. I play in the world championship league."

When they were finished, Rhiannon lifted Galina using Telekinesis and carried her down the stairs to a waiting van.

"You're pretty proficient at that kind of work," Vladimir said, his voice flat. Rhiannon picked up the accusation in his statement. Blocks and compulsions were considered severe ethical and moral breaches in telepathic society. Protectors were taught the skills, but were strongly cautioned against using them indiscriminately. A person caught manipulating other telepaths in such ways could expect sanctions, ranging up to exile and or mind wipe.

"My mum and grandmum are healers," she said. "I don't have the Gift, but they thought I should know how to deal with psychological trauma. Also how to calm someone who was wounded or injured until medical help could arrive."

As she spoke, her anger grew at his insinuation. She leaned into him, the space between their faces only inches. It had been a while since any of them had showered, and the smell of man, sweaty, testosterone-laden man, filled her nostrils. It triggered warmth between her legs, but also fueled her indignation.

"And for the past two years, I've been breaking up trafficking rings. I've recovered dozens of telepathic girls who have been sold into slavery. The slavers use drugs, compulsion and constructs to control their merchandise. I laid the compulsion that turned Siegfried von Ebersberg away from trafficking succubi—after I neutered the son of a bitch. So take your holier-than-thou shit and fuck yourself with it. If you don't want to be part of the O'Neill Clan, I'll release you from your obligation right now. Otherwise, I suggest that you fix your attitude. If you don't like taking orders from women, then you don't want to meet Brenna. She'll take you apart and make you wish you'd never grown a pair of balls."

She was trembling with anger. It was amazing how strongly he affected her.

Irina stepped between them. "Vladimir, unless you're tired of living, I suggest you walk away," she said.

He tore his eyes away from Rhiannon's, which were completely black without any green at all. Looking down at Irina, he saw that the fuzzy, stumbling, drugged demeanor she had displayed earlier was gone. The depth of what he saw in her eyes, the intelligence and awareness, and the lethal threat, staggered him.

She's either going to shag you or kill you in the next sixty seconds, Irina sent him. **I'm giving even odds on both options. Are you a betting man?**

He took a staggering step backward, then another. Irina stood in front of Rhiannon, the top of her head barely reaching the taller woman's shoulder. *She came here to kill a Clan Chief, and she has no doubts that she can do it,* he realized.

He shifted his gaze upward, toward the most magnificent woman he'd ever met. He'd pushed her to the killing edge, and that was the last thing he wanted to do. He bowed deeply.

"My apologies, my lady. You're right. I'm out of line. It won't happen again."

Irina bowed her head toward him in acknowledgement. **I'm glad you're not as stupid as you've been acting,** she sent. She turned toward Rhiannon, who was starting to shake as the adrenaline in her system found no outlet. An expanding green ring began to form around her shrinking pupils.

"Come on, Rhi," Irina said. "I'm tired. Let's go home."

~~~

Chapter 14

Luck is a very thin wire between survival and disaster, and not many people can keep their balance on it. - Hunter S. Thompson

After eating again, Irina went to bed and slept through the rest of the day, the night, and the next morning. She appeared in the dining room around noon.

"Oh, good! I was afraid I'd missed breakfast," she said, bouncing into the room and sitting down at the table.

"You did," Rhiannon laughed, placing a bowl of soup in front of her. "This is lunch."

In between spoonfuls, Irina said, "What's the plan? Fill me in on what I've missed. And where did all these good-looking men come from? Can I have a couple?"

The group related the events of the past few days, and then Vladimir said, "I have the same question she does. What's the plan?"

Rhiannon looked to Andrei. "Any ideas?"

"I like Galina's plan," Irina said. In the silence that followed, she filled her bowl with more soup. "I think that taking a video of me, captured, and sending it to Sergei might draw him out."

"Do you enjoy being bait?" Rhiannon asked.

"Not particularly. It's kind of scary, but I'm really good at it," Irina replied. "I have another question. What are we going to do with Galina and her men?"

"That's a very good question. Andrei, Vladimir, what do you think about the Romanov succession?" Rhiannon asked. "Should we just cut them loose and let the
~~~

succession bloodbath run its course? It would mean a weakened enemy Clan. Or should we think about alternatives?"

Vladimir looked up at the ceiling. "I think that's a little above my pay grade." Andrei nodded.

"Well, it's not above mine, damn it," Rhiannon said. "That's why I would appreciate ideas, suggestions, maybe a few informed opinions, before I speak with Brenna and Lords O'Byrne and O'Donnell."

"We haven't talked about what we're going to do with Gorbachev, either," Irina said. Andrei froze and then slowly turned to look at her.

"After I kill my grandfather," she said, "or maybe before, we're probably going to have to take out the Clan leadership, including his sons. He doesn't have an heir. Are we going to just waltz out of there and leave what's left of them to figure it all out? Or should we decide for them?"

"Do you want to be Clan Chief?" Rhiannon asked with a smile.

"Maybe," Irina said. Rhiannon's smile died.

Irina continued, "If we help Galina take over here, and we install a new Clan Chief in Moscow so that we control Gorbachev, we'd have two eastern allies and cut off a huge amount of the slave trade. Plus we'd have the German Clans in a pincer."

"We?" Andrei asked.

"O'Donnell. And the other Irish Clans. Someday, Brenna will hold all three seats. Anyway," she turned to Rhiannon and shrugged, "you asked for suggestions, those are mine."

"The drugs still haven't worn off, have they?" Rhiannon said.

Irina giggled.

They spent the rest of the afternoon discussing various plans and alternatives, then hashed out several contingency plans. Late in the evening, Rhiannon contacted Brenna.

Can you set up a conference call with Lord O'Donnell and Lord O'Byrne?

Sure. What's up?

We have an idea about controlling the Romanov succession. We have Galina Romanova under our control and she's planning on killing her brothers and taking the seat. I figured I should check with the Clan Chiefs before I try to play queen maker.

It took a few minutes, but Brenna called back with Seamus and Fergus channeled through her mind. Rhiannon had prepared a thought package consolidating the afternoon's discussions. She pushed it into their minds, then sat back and waited while they processed it.

Seamus was the first to respond. **Pretty damned ambitious. I knew no good would come of you sharing Brenna's mind.**

Didn't you read the dossier I sent you? Brenna asked. **She displayed this attitude of oblivious invincibility before she met me.**

Rhiannon, Lord O'Byrne sent, **would you need more manpower to pull off either of these schemes?**

I'm not sure, she answered. **We would need to be very judicious in deploying Irish troops. We need this all to appear to be driven by those inside the Russian Clans. You know how the Russians are. At the first suspicion that outsiders are manipulating them, or driving what's going on, that would be the end of it.**

Telepathic communications are far faster than if they were conducted verbally. Within twenty minutes, the various plans had been discussed, decisions made, and Rhiannon had her orders. The only thing that caught her by surprise was that one more person from O'Donnell would be joining her team.

~~~

When Galina returned to consciousness, she found herself in a windowless locked room with a bed and a bathroom. No chairs or tables, not even a mirror, the room was as bare as a cell. The only clothing she could find was the simple cotton petticoat she was wearing. She tried to send her mind out to assess her environment, and found that she couldn't. Panic set in.

A few minutes later, she heard the door being unlocked. A man and a woman walked in, and she became very aware of the skimpy covering she wore.

"Galina Alexandrovna," Rhiannon said, "I'm Ekaterina Andreyevna Kuznetsova, your hostess. I trust you slept well."

"How did I get here?" Galina asked. The last memory she had was questioning Irina in the safe house near the train station.

"You made a very grave mistake," Rhiannon said. "You kidnapped our friend and killed several of our employees. You were set up by Vasily Lapin on orders of Sergei Gorbachev, and you fell for it. And now we need to determine what to do with you." Of course, Lapin wasn't working on Sergei's orders, but Galina didn't need to know that.

"What have you done to me?" Galina's panic at not being able to access her Gifts was growing. She didn't know what it felt like to have her Gifts burned out, and physically she didn't feel any different than before, but she couldn't figure out another explanation.

"You're a prisoner. We've taken away your weapons, your defenses and your ability to call for help. Isn't that what you did to our friend? Filled her full of dangerous
~~~

drugs so she couldn't use her Gifts? But Galina, we aren't fools. As you've proven, drugs aren't foolproof."

"I don't understand," Galina said.

"It doesn't matter. Why don't you tell us of your plans to kill your brothers? I think that's a far more interesting subject."

Rhiannon already knew Galina's plans in great detail. But their plan hinged on Galina willingly switching sides and making an alliance with the Irish Clans. The first step was convincing her that she had no choice, then to make her understand that actually it was in her best interest to do so. Rhiannon and Andrei were in the woman's mind through the keyhole Rhiannon had created in her shields. They could hear all her thoughts, and could push all the right buttons to keep her anxiety at a fever pitch.

"One of the men who were killed on your orders was my nephew," Andrei spoke for the first time. "I haven't told my sister yet. What do you think I should tell her about you? What should I say to her when she discovers I've captured her son's murderer?"

"I didn't tell those fools to kill anyone. I only ordered them to capture the girl."

"You didn't tell them *not* to kill anyone," Andrei said.

"We need to decide what to do with you," Rhiannon said. "Execute you? Wipe your mind? Turn you over to Sergei Gorbachev? Or turn you over to your brother Viktor? There are so many tantalizing possibilities." She turned to Andrei. "It's too bad that she doesn't have anything to offer us. I think it would be fascinating to hear her try to bargain for her life."

Andrei moved to answer a knock on the door. Vladimir walked in with a small platter of sandwiches and finger foods. He looked Galina up and down with an undisguised leer on his face.

"She's not bad looking. It would be too bad to waste her. I still say we should mind wipe her and implant a construct. We should be able to get pretty good money for her." Vladimir put the tray on the bed.

Rhiannon felt the terror in Galina's mind spike. None of the other options for punishment had inspired that much fear. Even the suggestions of a mind wipe hadn't affected her as much. She had seen the disgust in Galina's mind for the sex trade her Clan engaged in. But she hadn't previously detected that the woman's fear of such a fate was so strong. Her memories and insecurities burst to the surface.

From the time Galina was six until she reached puberty and came into her power, her brothers had systematically abused her, both sexually and physically, and used their mental powers to prevent her from telling anyone. As a forty-five year old adult, she had never had a sexual relationship. Indeed, she could barely stand to have a man touch her.

Rhiannon shrugged. "Vladimir will stay with you while you eat." Turning to him, she added, "I don't care what you do, but be careful not to damage the merchandise. Our superiors still haven't decided what to do with her." She motioned to Andrei and they left the room. Galina's panic escalated.

In the hall, RB slumped against the wall.

"Are you all right?" Andrei asked.

"I feel dirty. Goddess, I hope my mother never finds out what we did in there."

With a grim face, Andrei said, "My mother wouldn't be proud of me either, nor would my wife. Torture is a nasty business."

RB shuddered.

Vladimir, who had been with them mentally the whole

time, sent, **She's almost catatonic. She just stares at me and shakes. We can't push her any farther. I don't think she's going to be able to eat with me in the room. RB, if you need a volunteer to kill her brothers, I'll do it.**

I don't think she can do any damage with that metal tray, Rhiannon sent. **Take the plates but leave the food.**

Vladimir emerged from the room a couple of minutes later carrying the dishes. "Holy Mother," he breathed, "that was ugly."

"I think I need to contact Lady O'Byrne," Rhiannon said. "If we need that woman to be a useful ally, I think a Clan psychologist is more in order than the interrogation techniques we're used to using."

"Yeah," Vladimir said. "We extracted her deepest, darkest secrets, but that isn't going to make her cooperative. I think that you did some real damage. Up until you told me to do what I wanted with her, she was hopeful that a woman would protect her."

"Water under the bridge. I wasn't too worried about her psyche because I figured she was responsible for killing Ivan and Roman."

"Yeah," Andrei said. "I'm not sure that supposition was correct. She's intelligent and in some ways tough as nails, but rather naïve. I don't think she really understands the real culture Romanov has cultivated the last few decades."

During the interrogation, Galina's memory of ordering Irina's kidnapping surfaced. She had given explicit orders that no one was to be harmed. "We don't need Gorbachev coming after us looking for blood. I want this clean and smooth. No violence. We can afford to take some time." But her men had disregarded her orders.

A spear thread from Brenna drew Rhiannon's attention away from their conversation. **Are you in a place where* *you can visualize a landing spot?**

Yes. Why are you coming here?

I'm not.

Confused, Rhiannon sent the image of the empty hallway in front of her. Almost immediately, a woman appeared with a large roller suitcase. Andrei and Vladimir whirled around, staring at her.

"Hello, Jerome," she said with a smile. "And you must be Rhiannon. I'm Jill."

Jill McConaghy was Seamus's youngest child. Slender and pretty with shining brown hair and sparkling blue eyes, she served as O'Donnell Group's regional manager in Hong Kong, overseeing all of their Asian interests. In addition to Japanese, Mandarin and Cantonese, she was also fluent in Russian.

They took her downstairs, and after calling the other team leaders and Irina, briefed her on the situation. Jill listened, asking few questions. When they got to the point of explaining the interrogation of Galina, Jill pursed her mouth and said, "I agree about bringing in a psychologist. Just a moment."

Closing her eyes, she sat for several minutes in silence. Then she stood and walked to an empty space of floor in the corner of the room. "I'll be right back. Please keep this area clear." Then she disappeared.

"Holy Goddess," Vladimir said. "So that's what one of Seamus O'Donnell's kids is like."

"Jill's the soft, cuddly one in the family," Irina said. "She doesn't have any weapons among her Gifts."

Rhiannon had pulled up Brenna's memories of her aunt. "Yeah, soft and cuddly. Also frighteningly intelligent and competent. She runs a seven billion dollar a year division in a hostile part of the world. When I presented our plans to the Clan Chiefs, they said if we're going to launch a major world-changing initiative, we need a strategic thinker on board. I knew she was coming. I just didn't expect her so soon."

"What Gifts does she have?" Vladimir asked. "Teleportation and Distance Communication, obviously ..."

"Telekinesis, Aerokinesis, Kilpatrick and O'Byrne, and the base Gifts. Ten in all," Rhiannon said.

"I've known Jill for over twenty years," Andrei said. "She spent four years studying at the Moscow State University. My wife absolutely loves her. Hell, everyone does."

"Except the Chinese," Irina said. "She controls Hong Kong and Canton, most of Southeast Asia, and has pulled the Japanese Clan in as an ally. She's almost like a Clan Chief in that part of the world."

"She's how old?" Vladimir asked.

"Forty-five," Rhiannon answered. "About your age. Makes you feel kind of like you've been wasting your life when you really could have been accomplishing something, doesn't it?"

Jill reappeared holding the arm of another woman carrying a suitcase. "Sorry it took so long. I had to give her a chance to pack. When something is this important, you don't half-ass things. You bring in the best. This is Dr. Moira O'Reilly."

Irina leaped up from the table and embraced Moira. She then poured her a cup of tea as Jill and Moira seated themselves at the table.

Rhiannon had met Dr. O'Reilly a couple of times, usually at the O'Byrne estate, and once in London. Those meetings had involved Rhiannon's recovery of trafficked girls from prostitution rings she'd broken up. She was struck with how much the psychologist resembled Galina. A couple of inches shorter, her auburn hair was shoulder length, whereas Galina's was waist length, and Moira was probably ten or fifteen pounds heavier with smaller breasts. But at a distance, it would be difficult to tell one from the other.

"I've given Moira the gist of what's going on," Jill said. "For some added background, I know Galina. We went to university together in Moscow, and we still keep in touch. I think for the time being, we'll keep all men away from her. Moira, me, Irina and RB will be her only contacts."

"I'm not sure she's going to be comfortable with me," Rhiannon said.

"We'll repair that," Moira said, taking a sip of her tea. "Once she knows your feelings toward sexual abuse and the role you've played in recovering girls from the sex trade, she'll understand that you would have never carried through on your threats."

"Hell, none of the men here would do anything like that," Vladimir said. "And if there are men like that working with us, they wouldn't survive very long."

Moira smiled. "I understand that. But you have to realize that in her experience, men like you don't exist. Romanov is a major conduit for sending Russian women to the west. They make more than a billion dollars a year from the slave trade."

She shifted in her seat, leaning forward and scanning the faces of those at the table. "You need to understand the ramifications of what you're proposing to do. According to the intelligence that O'Donnell and RB have gathered, almost a third of Romanov's total yearly revenue comes from trafficking women. Another third comes from other illegal businesses."

"This isn't just a matter of installing a new Clan Chief who will be sympathetic to us," Jill said. "You're talking about a complete culture shift. Thousands of Clan members will be out of a job. And given the chauvinistic nature of Russian society, and of the Clans, many of them won't be happy or willing to make a change. This isn't a quick operation. If we do this, we're making a very long term commitment to supporting Galina."

"We face the same challenges with Gorbachev," Irina said. "Only there, we're also looking at changing the direction of an entire nation. That's why I asked Brenna to send Jill here. This thing has grown far beyond a simple assassination."

Jill and Rhiannon both looked startled. "You're the one who suggested Jill be assigned to this mission?" Rhiannon asked.

"Yes. Not just to this mission. If we're successful, I want her to stay in Russia." Irina looked at Jill. "If you're willing, of course."

~~~

Chapter 15

Our greatest glory is not in never falling, but in rising every time we fall. – Confucius

Galina sat on the bed with a half-eaten sandwich lying on the tray beside her. Rhiannon could read the fear in her eyes. The four women filed into the room, and a look of amazement spread across Galina's face. "Zhillian!"

"Hello, Galina," Jill said, motioning toward the psychologist. "Moira doesn't speak Russian. Do you mind if we switch to English?"

"No, that is fine." Galina's English was heavily accented. "I wasn't aware that I was being held by O'Donnell."

"O'Donnell and O'Neill," Jill said. "Let me introduce you. This is Rhiannon Kendrick, heir to O'Neill, Moira
~~~

O'Reilly of O'Donnell, and I believe you've met Irina Moore, who is also a member of O'Donnell. I'm sorry I didn't come sooner, but I only recently learned that we were holding you."

Jill sat down on the bed and hugged Galina to her. Galina immediately started sobbing. In Russian, she said, "They wiped my mind. They took my Gifts. Oh, Goddess, Zhillian, they crippled me."

Rhiannon felt as though she'd been slapped. It had never occurred to her to explain to Galina that they had merely blocked her Gifts. No wonder the woman was terrified. She thought they had permanently maimed her.

Although she didn't speak Russian, Moira had access to Galina's mind through the Rhiannon's keyhole in her shields. She immediately began searching through Galina's mind, finding the trauma from her childhood, beginning to blur the memories and laying a Comfort on her.

"No, they didn't," Jill said in English. "They only placed blocks on your Gifts and a compulsion on using your telepathy. Nothing they've done is permanent. They only wanted to make sure you didn't escape, or contact anyone."

"Or kill us all," Rhiannon said softly. "Galina, I apologize for what we said earlier. I would never allow anyone to abuse a woman that way. None of our men would do that. We were trying to scare you, but we went too far. I'm sorry."

The sobbing slowed and Galina studied her face, then turned to Jill. "The heir? I thought your niece was the heir at O'Neill."

"Corwin is dead," Jill said. "Brenna is now the Clan Chief. Rhiannon is Corwin's granddaughter."

"A woman Clan Chief. And a woman heir. I never thought I would see such a thing."

"That surprises me," Rhiannon said. "Isn't that your ambition?"

"I never thought I would succeed," Galina said. "My father is dying. And no matter Viktor or Alexander takes over, one of first things they do is kill me. So I don't have anything to lose."

Her backup plan, in case everything else failed, was to go to Hong Kong and hope Jill would take her in, Moira sent to the group.

Jill's eyes filled with tears. **We were friends, but I didn't consider us that close. Does she really feel that alone in the world?**

Completely alone. You're the only person she's ever known that showed her kindness. The emotional scars are impossible to erase without changing who she is. But I think we can give her a life going forward, Moira sent.

"Galina," Rhiannon said. "Do you want to be Clan Chief, or do you want asylum? If you want out of Russia, we can take you to the British Isles or America, or even to Hong Kong."

"You make it sound as if I have two options. Why would O'Neill and O'Donnell care who sits in the Romanov seat?"

"Because I plan to kill Sergei Gorbachev," Irina said. "If we had an ally in Romanov, then we might also consider taking control of the Gorbachev Clan. But we can't do that with Romanov as an enemy."

"And because we're trying to end the slave trade," Rhiannon said. "We don't want telepathic women trafficked anymore."

"I don't know if I could do that," Galina said. "The business is so profitable."

"Von Ebersberg got out of the business," Rhiannon said. "At least the trafficking of telepaths. I wish I could have ended all of his trafficking, but that probably would have gotten Siegfried deposed by his sons."

Galina's eyes widened. "You! You're the woman von Ebersberg's sons were looking for. Rimma Gorbacheva!"

Rhiannon smiled. "I might have used that name once or twice."

~~~

Over the following days, Moira and Jill worked with Galina. Sometimes Irina joined in. Using the intelligence they gleaned from her, much of it with her active cooperation, the Protectors began laying plans to assault Viktor and the younger Alexander on news of their father's death.

Galina's captured men were carefully vetted for loyalty to her and several manipulations to their motivations were implanted. Then they were used to gain access to her country estate and various business interests. Rhiannon led those efforts, ruthlessly searching for spies from the other Romanov factions or from Gorbachev.

Anyone who was found to be less than loyal disappeared. Vladimir's team took them to the train station, put them to sleep, and put them on a train to Minsk, in Belarus, without their papers.

The joke was that Belarus was still a Soviet state at the time, and without a passport or visas, they were detained by the Belarussian KGB. At that point, they would be considered spies by the Kovalchuk Clan who controlled the KGB.

When Moira announced that it was safe to take the blocks off Galina's Gifts, Rhiannon contacted the Irish Clan Chiefs. That evening, Galina was invited to the dining room. In addition to the four women she'd had the most contact with, Vladimir, Andrei and Mikhail also were there.

"Galina," Rhiannon said, "our information is that your
~~~

father has at most days to live. Do you want to visit him?"

Galina shook her head. "It's too dangerous. Besides, he wouldn't know me. He's been almost comatose since his last stroke. But thank you for asking."

"What do you want to do?" Jill asked. "We can get you out of the country."

"You've spoken of backing me as Clan Chief. Was that just talk, or are you willing to take the chance I can do it?"

"It depends on what you plan to do if you take the seat," Rhiannon said. "In exchange for our help, we want a number of assurances."

"I understand that. If you want me to end the slave trade, I'll need support for an extended length of time. And the war that will result won't be quick or easy."

"Yes, we know that. We would want the slave trade ended, yes. In return, we would offer trade and business opportunities to help fill the gap in your revenues. We would also want an alliance, an agreement of mutual assistance. The Irish Clans would support you against any aggression, but we would expect you to support us, also."

"Yes. I've had a chance to think about this. I would agree to that."

Rhiannon looked at Jill, who nodded. Almost immediately, Seamus, Fergus and Brenna appeared in the room.

"I'm not the one to work out an agreement with," Rhiannon said. "That's something Clan Chiefs do. But if you're on our side, I'll make sure you win that seat."

~~~

The older Alexander was at the Romanov estate near Strelna, southwest of St. Petersburg. Viktor's estate was nearby. The younger Alexander had an estate on the Neva River, southeast of the city. Both of the brothers' estates
~~~

were fortified and guarded in anticipation of a conflict. In contrast, Galina's forces abandoned both her country dacha and her house in the city. As far as her brothers might know, she and her followers had disappeared.

In Russia, a *dacha* usually refers to a summer house outside the city. Usage of the term has changed somewhat over time, and currently it might be used for anything from a small shack to a huge mansion. The Romanovs' dachas were definitely not shacks.

Jill had teleported to Ireland and brought Collin and Rebecca back to help with planning the operation. Andrei was the most experienced commander of the group in Russia, but none of them had ever been involved with a battle plan of the magnitude they were considering.

"I was talking with Antonia Federicci," Rebecca said the morning after she arrived. "She was telling me that a true Storm Queen was able to do more than manipulate lightning. Everyone focuses on the ability to channel lightning because it's flashy." She paused, a crooked grin on her face, waiting for the pun to sink in. Amid the groans and a few chuckles, Collin threw a pencil at her, which she caught.

"What's involved in a storm?" she continued. "Wind and rain or snow, sometimes lightning, right? Now, what is the basic threshold of talent to join the Protectors? Aerokinesis, so they can form an air shield. But the Gift can be used for a lot of other things."

A breeze stirred in the still room, becoming stronger until papers began to flutter and the women's hair fluttered. Then it died.

"If you have a hundred people with Aerokinesis, they should be able to link and create a hell of a lot of wind."

"Goddess," Rhiannon said, as memories of ancient battles surfaced in her mind. "Clan armies used to do that. Not only can you create incredible winds, you can move storms to deluge your enemies. But for an assault on a fixed structure, such as a castle, you can use the Corliolis effect to create a tornado."

Collin looked thoughtful. "Do your memories include actually being involved in creating something like that?"

"Yes, and I have the Gifts to do it. In order to do it safely, you need someone as a focal point. Someone strong enough to dissipate it after it's done its damage." She was quiet for a while, searching her memories. "Rebecca, according to what you said, and what I can find in my memories, Antonia doesn't have the Gifts to be a true storm queen, and neither do I. But we have someone sitting here who does."

She turned to Galina. "Aerokinesis, Cryokinesis, Electrokinesis, and Magnetokinesis, with the Krasevec Gift. The perfect combination to create a storm." She looked around the table. "I have what I'd need to create and control a tornado, so I can be the focus at one location. Galina can be the focus at the other."

Galina didn't look too sure. "I've never done anything like that. I wouldn't even know how."

"No problem. I have the knowledge in my memories, and I can transfer the knowledge to you."

Collin spoke up, "Forgive my skepticism, but something that you've never tried isn't something I'd want to hang the success of a battle plan on. I can envision all sorts of things going wrong."

"Such as the tornado taking out all the friendly forces and leaving the enemy to die of laughter?" Andrei asked.

Rhiannon glanced at Jill. "We could go someplace to practice. How many people can you transport at once?"

"About a dozen," Jill replied. "My range is unlimited, but I'd need a landing place. And we need someplace that's completely uninhabited to practice."

"I know the perfect place," Rebecca said. "Last summer, Carlos and I went hiking in the Blue Stack Mountains in Donegal. We came across a dolmen that, to my knowledge, no one had ever reported. I called Brenna on my sat phone, and she and Collin teleported in. I can give you the image I sent Brenna."

She projected the image to Jill, who said, "Yes, I can use that. You're sure we won't land on top of any hikers?"

Collin nodded. "It's completely uninhabited and no one ever goes there, as evidenced by the fact the dolmen was completely unknown. There are some deer and other small wildlife, but I don't think that will be a problem. If you can bring us in ten feet from the ground, I can use Telekinesis to lower us safely. It would work."

He turned to Rhiannon. "Would a dozen people provide enough power?"

"I could create the tornado on my own. But we need to test if a linked circle can supply the power to make it larger and more powerful. A dozen people could do that. I mean, we don't want to destroy the whole countryside."

"When should we try it?" Andrei asked.

"Right now," Collin said. "We need to know if it would work before we plan any further."

Jill looked around the room, counting the people involved in the planning session. "Are all twelve of us aerokinetics?" Everyone nodded. She motioned to a clear space of floor, rose and walked to it. "Lock the door. We don't need anyone coming in here and interfering with our return. Who besides Collin is a telekinetic?"

"I am," Rhiannon said.

"And so am I," Jill said.

They all gathered around her and held hands. The world turned black and they were in a place without light, sound, gravity, or any other earthly force. The sensation lasted less than a second, and then light returned. Hanging in the air, the group looked over a meadow high in the mountains. Rugged, rocky peaks ringed them. A golden eagle soared overhead and a small herd of red deer grazed several hundred yards away.

"Where's the dolmen?" Jill asked as they floated to the ground.

Rebecca pointed up a hill. "It's behind that copse of trees. It's not very large, only about five feet tall. What's unusual about it is the size of the rocks. Brenna speculated that it was built by children, just coming into their power. They used over thirty rocks, all between two hundred and three hundred pounds." Modern scholars believe dolmen are Neolithic tombs, built with rough stones that usually weigh tons. The most well-known site of such building is Stonehenge.

"That would make sense," Rhiannon said. "I used to build things like that when I was a teenager."

Jill nodded. "So did I. What's the largest stone you ever lifted?"

Rhiannon blushed. "Well, if you promise you won't tell the English authorities, I got curious about the stones at Stonehenge when I visited."

Jill laughed. "So did I. I lifted a couple of the bluestones. I think they're around four tons."

"I lifted one of the sarsen stones completely out of the ground," Rhiannon said. "Then I got worried about whether it would stand when I put it back. Luckily it did."

Jill's laughter died. "The sarsen stones weight forty or fifty tons."

"I didn't try with the largest ones," Rhiannon said.

"You scare the hell out of me," Collin said. "Don't tell Brenna you did that. She'll probably want to rebuild the damn thing."

"Perhaps we should play with the wind," Rebecca suggested. "We don't have a lot of time to spend here, and we didn't bring lunch so we can't have a picnic."

Under Rhiannon's direction, the group linked minds and then triggered their Aerokinesis Gifts.

"Okay, now don't release the power, just channel it to me," Rhiannon said. She felt the power flow into her, then projected it about two hundred yards in front of her, directing the air flows as her ancient ancestor had done.

The wind whipped up around them, growing stronger. The women's hair flew about, and everyone braced themselves. The young eagle overhead gave an alarmed cry and dove to the shelter of the trees behind them.

A funnel of air gradually grew in the sky, pulling earth and debris into it. Soon, a hundred-foot dust devil whirled in front of them.

Can you move it? Collin sent.

Rhiannon pushed and the whirlwind moved away from her. A different push caused it to move to their right.

Is that as big as it's going to get? Jill asked. **Is that all of our power?**

Rhiannon poured more power into it, and the whirlwind grew, growing taller and wider. **I could probably make it a lot larger,** she sent. **Do we want to do that?**

I don't think so, Collin answered. **Do you still feel in control?**

The control really isn't a problem. What I'm worried about is having enough power to wind it down. I don't think it will just stop if I withdraw my control.

Enough, then, he sent. **Show us how to wind it down.**

She pulled power out of her creation, surprised to

discover the whirling winds contained more energy than she had put into them. The winds rippled the grass and bushes as it dissipated in an expanding circle away from where the whirlwind had been.

"Do you understand what I did?" Rhiannon asked Galina once the meadow returned to its natural morning stillness.

"Yes, I can do it," Galina said. The group once again gathered their power and fed it into Galina. The whirlwind she built was larger than Rhiannon's, and she moved it around the landscape for about five minutes before she disbursed its power.

"My turn," Jill said eagerly. "I want to try."

Once again, they built a whirlwind and Jill proved to be as adept as the other two women at controlling her creation.

Back in St. Petersburg, Rhiannon had food brought to their war room. The amount of energy they had expended left everyone ravenous.

"And that's a problem," Rebecca said. "It would be nice to have an external energy source to feed the people in the circle."

"What do you propose?" Collin asked. "A couple of hundred succubi? If we had two hundred Irinas, we wouldn't need the tornado. We could just drain all the defenders and walk in without doing any damage."

"I don't think the energy drain will be that bad," Rhiannon said. "If I had a hundred Protectors feeding me power, the drain on each person would be minimal. I think I could probably build a real tornado with the help of just one or two hundred people."

Jill and Galina agreed. "It really does start to feed on itself past a certain point," Jill said. "You don't need to keep feeding it. As RB said, the issue is controlling it and winding it down."

~~~

Chapter 16

Never think that war, no matter how necessary, nor how justified, is not a crime. - Ernest Hemingway

Rhiannon deployed her forces for simultaneous attacks on the two brothers. In addition to two hundred Russian-speaking Irish Protectors, she had another thousand O'Donnell Protectors who had flown in from England over the three days since Galina signed the alliance. Galina had five hundred soldiers who had been checked and their loyalty assured.

"I can't believe the force you're able to commit to something like this," Galina said. "Romanov only has a trained force of three thousand men."

"The combined size of the Irish Clans is much larger than yours," Rhiannon said. "O'Donnell alone has more members than all the Russian Clans combined. But you'll also notice that a third of our forces are women. You make a mistake limiting your training to men."

"Perhaps you can help me overcome that," Galina said. "Russian women were soldiers in the Great Patriotic War. I think many women would welcome such training. And I'll need the soldiers after so many of the men are purged."

That gave Rhiannon an opening to discuss something that had been worrying her. "What do you plan to do with your brothers? Assuming they're captured, that is."

"Kill them," Galina answered without hesitation.

"You could just burn out their Gifts and exile them," Rhiannon suggested. "Neither I nor my Protectors will execute anyone."

"That's good. I'd rather kill them myself. But your
~~~

idea would work for the others, my brothers' loyalists. Also for those involved in the slave trade who won't change." Her eyes were hard as she looked at Rhiannon. "It's personal."

The logistics of moving that many people unnoticed were daunting. Galina solved the problem by renting the entire fleet of buses from two tourist companies. It only took twenty of the enclosed double-decker buses to transport the entire force and their equipment to their staging areas.

Rhiannon commanded the force that would assault Viktor's compound, while Andrei took command of the troops sent to the younger Alexander's estate. Galina was assigned to Andrei's force. Jill stayed at the safe house in the city with Collin, Rebecca and Irina to provide communications between the groups.

Viktor's dacha overlooked the Gulf of Finland, just as Peter the Great's palace at Peterhof just up the coast did. From what Galina told them, Viktor's estate was much grander than their father's. Viktor had been considered the heir since his father became Clan Chief shortly after World War II. He had spent much of that time partying. Galina said he kept a stable of girls, but recently he had sold most of them to western slavers. He needed to raise money and his advisors were building up their treasure chest for the expected conflict with his brother.

As darkness fell, Rhiannon's troops moved into position. Their listening devices confirmed that Viktor was at home, along with a five hundred-man security team and his closest advisors. The house nestled next to the Gulf behind a thirty-foot seawall, with terraces that extended to the water. That proximity gave her an idea, and she contacted her commanders to explain the deviation from the plan.

She moved from her post, and with a team of thirty

circled to the left, skirting the compound. It took her half an hour to reach a vantage point overlooking the water. As the moon started to rise, she gave the signal, and a hundred O'Donnell Protectors triggered their Aerokinesis and fed her their power.

A light breeze blew in off the Gulf. Focusing the energy from her assistants, Rhiannon began weaving the complex air currents necessary to create a vortex. Soon, the winds began to swirl over the water, and as they gathered force, the whirlwind began pulling water from the sea.

She poured energy into her creation, and a gigantic waterspout formed only yards from Viktor's home. Rhiannon had never seen a tornado, except those they had created for practice in Donegal. She definitely had never seen a waterspout. The roar of the swirling winds surprised her. She realized that they didn't need so many telepaths feeding her energy.

Showtime, boys and girls, she sent, and directed the waterspout toward the house. It hit the seawall and danced over it, across the terrace, and blew into the house. Rhiannon began drawing energy out of the storm and it faltered. Thousands of gallons of water fell as if in slow motion. The roof collapsed, as if someone had stepped on a dollhouse. The entire compound flooded, washing debris, furniture and people over the seawall as the water returned to its origin.

Rhiannon stared, appalled at the massive devastation she had caused. She'd thought that simply flooding the place would be less destructive than a tornado hitting the compound. Too late, she realized how much the weight of the water would increase the force of the storm.

That was rather spectacular, Vladimir sent. **I think I'll wait a while before I send anyone in to mop up. If there are any survivors, I don't think they'll be in much of a mood to fight.**

~~~

Sixty kilometers away, Andrei's force closed in on the younger Alexander's estate. He had built his mansion on an artificial hill overlooking the Neva River east of the city. This wasn't just an affectation as the Neva delta had been swampland when Peter the Great conceived building a city there to give Russia a seaport. The river still rose significantly in the spring.

Galina was nervous, fidgeting and pacing, occasionally peering through a pair of night binoculars toward her brother's compound. It was raining lightly, but she didn't seem to notice.

Andrei was nervous, too, but he suspected for different reasons. Although he had watched her and the other two women create and control the vortex storms, he didn't trust her to perform according to script when the action started.

Lights from the village across the river were a constant reminder of how close they were to inhabited areas. Small towns dotted the banks of the Neva, along with dachas and small farms. If Galina didn't control the storm, or if she got carried away, the destruction could spread far beyond her dispute with Alexander.

He had expressed his concerns to Rhiannon, who didn't brush him off. "I didn't remove the keyhole in her shields," she reminded him. "If you feel the need to take control, you'll be able to do it." It was some comfort, but not enough.

When they received Rhiannon's message that the assault on Viktor had started, Galina turned to him. He nodded and said, "Be careful. You need to maintain control."

She sent the order to the Protectors, **It's time.**

Licking her lips as the Protectors' power flooded into her, she triggered her own Gift, directing the air flows in
~~~

the sky, twisting them into new patterns. As the vortex began to form, halfway between her and the wall of the compound, she became afraid that the wind alone wouldn't be strong enough to breach the wall. Remembering what Rebecca had said about storm queens combining Gifts, she triggered her Cryokinetic Gift. The rain caught up in the vortex froze, turning the whirlwind white. She gave it a push with her mind, and it began drifting toward Alexander's compound.

"What did you do?" Andrei shouted.

She didn't answer him, concentrating on guiding the ice tornado. It grew as it picked up speed and slammed into and through the brick walls surrounding the compound as though they were made of paper.

"Shut it down!" Andrei yelled. Then he switched tactics, **Galina, pull it back! Pull the energy out of it!**

She stood frozen, eyes wide, seemingly unable to respond.

CEASE FIRE! Andrei sent to all of his troops. **Stop broadcasting!**

The vortex ripped through the main house and tore a hole through the riverside wall of the compound, dropping down the hill and into the river. Sucking up the water, it grew, towering a hundred yards into the air.

Andrei slipped through the keyhole into Galina's mind. **Galina, you have to pull the energy back. There are innocents. You have to stop. Now!"*

She seemed to become aware of him for the first time. Turning slowly toward him, her eyes still wide, she suddenly jerked her eyes back to the ice storm.

"Goddess," she breathed. "Ohhhh, no."

He felt her frantically begin pulling energy out of the storm. But instead of dissipating the energy as she had done in Donegal, she poured it into freezing the waterspout. As the winds slowed, more of the water froze, until the column began to tilt. Ice fell away from it, and then the whole thing slowly toppled into the river.

Water splashed almost as high as the column of ice had stood. Andrei saw a huge wave spreading toward both shores. Boats washed up on the shore, a dock on the other side splintered, and water rushed into the village's streets. Eventually, the water retreated to the river. Ice flows rode away down river, a scene from early spring. Alexander's compound looked as though it had been hit by a bomb.

~~~

Andrei rode with a silent Galina to meet Rhiannon in Strelna. Vladimir had called on his mobile and told him what had happened at Viktor's. From a tactical standpoint, the evening's operations had been a resounding success. All of the enemy were vanquished and the allied forces hadn't suffered a single casualty. But from any other point of view, the results were as horrifying as the Battle of Leningrad sixty years before. It had been a massacre. He thought about what Rhiannon had done at Ayr.

He decided he should talk to Collin. It was time to retire and find another career. Before some woman killed him.

As the bus slowed and pulled into Viktor's estate, Galina turned to him. "I'm sorry. It got away from me. I really didn't mean to kill all those people."

She looked miserable, as though she was ready to burst into tears. Andrei had a daughter her age, and his heart melted. Without thinking, he spread his arms. To his shock, she stepped into him, her arms around his back, and laid her head on his shoulder. She was as tall as he was. He held her for a minute or so before she pulled away. Her eyes were dry, and her face was more relaxed.

"Thank you," she said. "Your children are lucky to have you." Then she turned and walked away.
~~~

“Status?” Andrei asked Rhiannon and Vladimir as he stepped off the bus.

“No idea of total enemy casualties,” Vladimir reported. “We found about ninety bodies, including those we retrieved from the Gulf. There are over a hundred prisoners, and our healers have their hands full with them. Some of the buildings are still intact, but the main house is a total loss.”

“Total loss,” Andrei repeated, looking around at the wreckage. “You haven’t seen a total loss. Alexander’s compound is nonexistent. I’m not even worried about containment. I brought all of our force with me. I’ll let the authorities try to figure out what happened there, and good luck to them.”

“Now you know why they name hurricanes after women,” Collin said as he stepped from the darkness with Jill and Rebecca. Rebecca punched him in the arm.

He held out a mobile phone. “Galina, your stepmother has been trying to call you.”

They all knew that Maria, her stepmother and Leonid’s mother, was her only ally in her family. Maria knew that Alexander’s older sons would either kill Leonid or at best exile him. She had pledged her support to Galina in exchange for a pledge of her son’s safety.

Galina snatched the phone from him and punched buttons. She walked away from them, holding the phone to her ear.

When she came back, she said, “Maria says my father died a couple of hours ago. Dmitri, my father’s head of security, is holding her prisoner. He’s trying to contact Viktor, but hasn’t been able to reach him.”

“Viktor’s mobile probably doesn’t work underwater,” Vladimir said, waving toward the wreckage of the house. “We did find his body, though. He wasn’t one of the ones who washed away."

Rhiannon looked at Andrei. **Did you find Alexander's?**

We didn't even look. There were some body parts mixed in with the match sticks that were left of the house. The only way he would have survived is if he wasn't home.

"She also said that she received a call from Leonid's house," Galina continued. "Alexander's men were there looking for him. But there was another raid a couple of weeks ago, and Leonid decided it would be safer in Paris until things were settled here."

Rhiannon exchanged looks with Vladimir and Andrei.

"What is the situation at your father's place?" Collin asked.

"Dmitri holds the estate. He has about a thousand men."

"Do you think he'll see reason, or will we have to assault the place?"

"I don't know," Galina said. "If we tell him that Viktor is dead, he may decide to accept my authority. Or he may hold out hoping to get a better deal from Alexander."

"Well, let's you and me go talk to him," Rhiannon said. She looked at Jill. "Can I talk you into coming?"

"Wait a second," Vladimir said. "You're not going alone. You may be the strongest set of telepaths here, but you need someone to watch your back."

Rhiannon started to object, but Jill placed a hand on her arm and gave a small shake of her head. **We don't have time to argue.**

"Pick two men and let's go," Jill said to Vladimir.

To her surprise, Collin stepped forward, holding Rebecca's arm. "If you get killed, Seamus will use my hide for a sofa cover. I might as well make sure I go down before you do. Getting shot will probably be less painful."

Galina contacted her stepmother telepathically, and then gave Jill the image for a landing spot. The party linked hands and Jill teleported with them into Maria's bedroom, every nerve on edge and ready to jump them out again. Through her link to Andrei, she heard him move their troops into position around the estate.

Maria Romanova wasn't much older than her stepdaughter. Tall and blonde, she spoke Russian with a Czech accent. Obviously distraught, she sent a beseeching look toward Galina. It wasn't just Leonid's survival that worried her, Rhiannon realized, but also her own.

"This is very risky," Maria said. "I'm sure Viktor and Alexander are looking for you, too. And Dmitri might try to use you to bargain himself a deal."

"Your husband's sons are dead," Rhiannon told her in Czech. "We're here to ensure Galina becomes Clan Chief, and we have over a thousand men waiting to assault the estate. The only bargaining Dmitri will do is with us."

The blood drained from Maria's face and she staggered to a chair.

"Who are you?" she asked.

"I'm the heir to the Irish O'Neill Clan. The other women are Seamus O'Donnell's daughter and granddaughter. Are you going to help us?"

Maria looked to Galina. "Will you protect us? You promised."

"Jill, why don't you take her to Andrei and then come back?" Rhiannon said. "If things get sticky here, she could get hurt."

"That's a good idea," Galina said. Jill strode over to Maria, grasped her elbow, and disappeared. She returned to her original landing spot less than a minute later.

"Okay," Jill said. "What do we do next? I assume you

had some sort of plan prior to dropping into the lion's den."

"If I had a plan, I wouldn't need you," Rhiannon said with a grin. "What is it that Brenna calls it, Plan T? If everything goes to hell, teleport out."

"If that's the case, you'd better stay close to me. I'm not Brenna, and I can only take you with me if we're in physical contact."

Wrapping themselves in air shields, Rhiannon picked the lock to the door and stepped out into the hall. The guards stationed there startled and reached for her. She downed them both with light shocks of Neural Disruption, not enough to do lasting damage. Turning to the other women, she motioned them to follow her and strode off down the hall, looking for Dmitri.

As she walked, Rhiannon drew her pistol and held it against her leg. Looking over her shoulder, she saw that the rest, including Galina, were also armed. Vladimir carried an assault rifle. Drawing on the household electricity, she filled her reserves and kept the link to the lines in the walls.

Rhiannon and Galina walked in front with Rebecca and Jill behind them. Collin and Vladimir formed their rear guard. Taking a turn into another hallway, they met two women.

"Hello, Olga," Galina said. The other woman responded, but since Galina kept going, the women didn't look back.

They came to an open, circular room filled with plush furniture and potted plants. Two men were sitting there talking, but they stopped abruptly and sprang to their feet.

"Where is Dimitri?" Galina demanded. "I need to talk to him."

"Who is that?" one of the men said, motioning to Rhiannon and the others.

"My friend Ekaterina," Galina replied. "Where's

Dmitri?"

"Who are these people?" the man demanded again.

"Really?" Galina said, putting her hand on her hip and trying to stare him down. "It's her boyfriend, my cousin and her husband, and her sister. Look, I don't have time for this. I need to talk to Dmitri. Something's happening at Viktor's."

"We've been trying to reach Viktor for the past three hours. His communications are down. We've sent men over there, but no one has returned."

We've captured all the men who came out of here, Rhiannon sent.

"I guess my communications are better than yours," Galina said. "There's been an attack at Viktor's. Probably that bastard Alexander. Now, where is Dmitri?"

"He's in his office," the other man replied.

"Thank you," Galina said, spinning on her heel and heading for another hallway. Rhiannon went with her. Behind them, there was a dual thump, and when they turned back, they saw the two men sprawl on the floor. Collin and Vladimir hurriedly dragged them to two of the couches and dumped them. They looked like they were sleeping.

Collin slammed them into the ceiling telekinetically, Rebecca sent.

Rhiannon looked up. The ceiling was made of birch planks held up with heavy beams.

They crossed into another wing of the house, and here there were more people, mostly armed men. The men eyed Galina's party, but no one tried to stop them. Eventually, they came to a large office with an open door. The six of them walked in, and Vladimir closed the door. Sitting behind a desk and surrounded with computer monitors sat a thin man with gray hair.

"I heard a rumor that my father has died," Galina said. "I also heard that you are looking for me. Well, here I am. Let's talk."

Dmitri Sholokhov regarded her, his eyes shifting to her entourage and back. "Yes, Alexander is dead. I've been trying to contact all of his children. We need to ensure that the succession is smooth. The other Clans are probably waiting to pounce. All of these ridiculous rumors about a succession squabble must be put to rest."

"Oh, is that all?" Galina said, flopping into a chair. "Well, that's all taken care of. Viktor and Alexander are dead, and Leonid is out of the country. The other Clans, at least those that know, are backing my claim. So everything is taken care of. You can tell your security personnel to stand down. I'll begin going through the rosters and deciding who I'll keep in the morning. For now, my guard will take over here."

Rhiannon slipped through the keyhole into Galina's mind. The woman was as nervous as a cat trapped in a dog kennel, but outwardly, one would never know it.

"How do I know Viktor is dead?" Sholokhov asked, his hand slowly slipping into a drawer out of Galina's sight. Rhiannon slammed the drawer shut using Telekinesis.

"Ahhhh!" Sholokhov shrieked, jumping backward.

"That would be a very silly thing to do," Rhiannon said, raising her pistol from her side and showing it to him. "As to Viktor, his dacha was hit by ... a tidal wave earlier this evening." She turned to Vladimir. "Did he drown?"

"Crushed. He was in an upstairs bedroom with a young woman when the roof collapsed. The healers think she'll live, but she'll probably never walk again," Vladimir said.

"And Alexander's dacha was hit by a tornado earlier this evening," Galina said.

"A tornado or an ice storm?" Jill asked.

"Well, a frozen tornado. It doesn't really matter. We haven't recovered his body, but there were eight hundred and thirty-two people in the compound. As far as we know, there were no survivors," Galina said. "So even if he wasn't there, he doesn't have much to back him up."

She stood. "Dmitri, please cooperate. Call your men and tell them to stand down. If they don't, we'll open the gates," she nodded toward the control panel for the security systems next to him, "and signal our forces to take the compound. I'd really prefer to keep the house from damage."

"You said other Clans were backing you. Which ones?" Sholokhov said with a sneer.

"Donald and I are from O'Neill," Rhiannon said. Pointing to Jill, she said, "She's representing O'Donnell." She looked at Rebecca. "Who's representing O'Byrne?"

**I guess you are. Lady O'Byrne is your aunt*,* Rebecca sent.

"Oh. And I'm also representing O'Byrne."

"You sold us out to the Irish?" Sholokhov snarled.

"We also have a representative from Gorbachev," Rhiannon said. "But she needed to get a manicure, so she isn't with us tonight."

"Who do you think will protect you when your friends go home?" Sholokhov asked.

"The loyal members of the Romanov Clan," Galina answered. "But you and your thugs won't be around to challenge them. I'll give you one more chance. You can walk out of here with your mind intact, out of deference to the service you gave my father, or I'll burn out your Gifts before I exile you. You have five seconds to order your men to stand down."

Rhiannon had been working on the man's shields since she walked in the room. She was almost in when Rebecca said, "Screw this." The English words were jarring.

Dimitri's eyes flew wide and he stiffened. A panicked look crossed his face, then he slumped. Turning toward his console, he flipped a switch and began speaking. At the same time, he sent out a mental broadcast.

Both messages told everyone that the elder Alexander was dead, and that attacks by the Gorbachev Clan had killed Viktor and the younger Alexander. Luckily, said Dmitri, Galina had rallied the Romanov forces and dealt with the intruders. Galina now was assuming the leadership of the Clan and her orders were to be followed without question. In the light of the treachery by Gorbachev, her security forces would be assuming control of the compound until everyone could be checked for loyalty. Then he turned off all the security systems and opened all the gates to the compound.

"Do you mind explaining that?" Collin asked.

"Take a look in his mind," Rebecca answered. "The son of a bitch has been planning this for years. He wasn't looking for Viktor to secure the seat. Dmitri planned to kill him. Then he'd tell Alexander that Galina did it, and tell Galina that Alexander did it. Play them off against each other and kill them both. Then this would become the Sholokhov Clan."

Looking in Dmitri's mind, Rhiannon confirmed what Rebecca told them. Sholokhov had been an independent Clan that was absorbed after it was almost destroyed during the Battle of Leningrad.

"Okay," Jill said after reading Sholokhov's mind, "but why did you implicate Gorbachev?"

"Galina needs an external enemy to rally her people. She can't just say that she killed all the opposition and have people trust her. But if they were killed by outsiders, and she prevented the Clan being conquered by the nasty Gorbachevs, she's a hero."

Galina looked startled, and then smiled. "Are you sure you're not Russian? That is a masterful piece of Soviet-era propaganda you're spinning."

"Thank you," Rebecca said, returning the smile. "The other thing is that after the losses tonight, and the purge that's coming, Romanov will be severely weakened. The Gorbachev threat provides cover for the alliance with the Irish Clans. And the whole story justifies us moving against Gorbachev to protect an ally."

"Tell me you had this all planned out," Rhiannon said. "If you tell me you came up with this spiel in the last few minutes, I'm going to be terrified." She paused. "Actually, the fact that you thought it up at all terrifies me. Have you been studying Machiavelli?"

"Every night before I go to bed."

"Give me a break," Collin said. "She plans better than you or Brenna do, and I'm willing to concede that she probably had bits and pieces of this swirling around in her head, trying to figure out how it all fit, but it came together after we reached this office."

"Shhh," Rebecca said, putting a finger to her lips. "You're blowing my cover as a master strategist."

"Any problem with any of this?" Jill asked Galina. Receiving an enthusiastic shake of the head as an answer, she said, "Tell your people to come in and take charge. We'll keep our people out unless you need us."

Jill stayed with Andrei and a contingent of O'Donnell Protectors. The rest of their force withdrew to Viktor's estate for the night. Rhiannon and Vladimir accompanied Rebecca and Collin back to the city.

"You really figured all of that out in a few minutes?" Rhiannon asked as they shared a bottle of vodka on the bus.

"There were a lot of possible outcomes to this thing," Rebecca said. "You have to see the endgame to figure out what the final spin is going to be. With you and Galina going off script, we need to go for the big lie. You're a telekinetic. Don't you know how much water weighs? And Galina had to do you one better and freeze the damn water. I envisioned a hammer to lessen casualties. You two used a fucking howitzer to drive a nail."

~~~

Chapter 17

A woman is like a tea bag - you can't tell how strong she is until you put her in hot water. - Eleanor Roosevelt

"What do you plan to do with the Gorbachev turncoat that led Galina to Irina?" Andrei asked one evening over dinner.

"Turn him into a sock puppet," Rhiannon said. Vladimir choked on his drink, and Irina broke into giggles.

"And?" Andrei pursued the subject.

"Let him go back to Moscow with his new girlfriend."

All eyes at the table turned to her.

"You want someone inside, right? Well, does anyone have a better idea?"

A few days later, Irina sat tied to a chair, several shots of vodka in her to make her appear drugged while Galina made a video. She told Sergei that she was Clan Chief now and she needed Gorbachev to stay out of Romanov business. The camera cut to Irina, who tried to mumble something, and then a voice over by Galina saying that Romanov had Sergei's granddaughter. If he didn't play ball, Galina would give her to the sharks.

The original purpose of the video wasn't a concern anymore, but Irina hoped it would draw Sergei out of hiding. Rhiannon's new 'boyfriend', Vasily Lapin, would deliver the disk.
~~~

To reinforce the boyfriend perception, after Rebecca implanted a construct and a new set of memories in his mind, Rhiannon had taken Vasily to the bank and emptied his account. Then he'd taken her shopping, where she bought presents, mostly amber jewelry, for Brenna, Morrighan, Rebecca and Lady O'Byrne. She also bought some jewelry and clothes for herself, including a sable coat. She sent the gifts with Rebecca and Collin when they flew back to Ireland with the majority of the Protectors.

"We're in St. Petersburg," Rhiannon explained. "I won't get the same kind of deal on amber in Moscow. Besides, Vasily can afford it, and winter's coming, so I need a warm coat."

Vladimir objected to Rhiannon going into Gorbachev with the turncoat.

"What if they figure out that he was on Galina's payroll? They may take the disk and shoot him in the head," Vladimir said, continuing the litany of reasons he'd offered for changing the plan.

"So they shoot him," Rhiannon said. "They aren't going to shoot me." She batted her eyes. "I'm just an innocent bimbo he picked up. I have no idea what he's doing, or who he's doing it for. I just want to party and he showed me a good time. I'm flexible. If he dies, I'll let someone else show me a good time."

"And what if that someone wants you to really show him a good time?" Vladimir asked.

"Why, Donald, are you concerned about my virtue? That's sweet."

Watching the exchange, Irina giggled. "It really is sweet. Donald, are you concerned about my virtue, too?"

He cast a disgusted look at her. "I'm not worried about your virtue, something I suspect fled long ago. I'm worried about your safety."

"Did he just insult me?" Rhiannon asked. "I think he called me a slut."

Vladimir's face turned bright red. "I didn't mean that at all. Dammit, you know that isn't what I meant."

They laughed him out of the room. But in the end, he went along with her to Moscow. He won by calling Brenna, who overrode Rhiannon and ordered security on her heir. The rest of the O'Neill Protectors would provide out-of-sight security. Half of Andrei's Protectors returned to Moscow the day before Rhiannon and Vasily did and restored O'Donnell's presence in the capitol.

~~~

They booked private compartments on the overnight train from St. Petersburg to Moscow. As soon as they boarded, Rhiannon put Vasily to sleep on one of the bunks. She tried to sleep herself, but was too keyed up. Sending out a tentative mental probe, she found that Vlad/Donald was still awake next door.

She knocked and he slid back the door, dressed only in boxer shorts and holding a pistol.

"I can't sleep," she said.

He stepped back and with a wave of his arm invited her in. He had made up one of the two bunks. A paperback book, a classic American science-fiction book translated to Russian, lay open there. She sat on the other bunk.

"And what can I do for you, my lady?" he said, reaching for a bottle of juice and pouring some in a teacup. She nodded at his raised eyebrow, and he filled the other teacup on the small table.

"I just figured that if we were both awake, perhaps we could keep each other company," she said. "We've never really gotten to know each other." She hoped he didn't take that the wrong way. His body was even better without clothes, but as tasty as he looked, she wasn't trying to
~~~

seduce him.

Flashing her a lop-sided grin, just short of a leer, he plopped down on his bed. "You're looking for small talk?"

"Yeah, I guess so. I've read that in English," she said, pointing to the book.

"So have I. I was curious to see how well they translated it."

They talked for almost two hours, telling each other about their lives, their personal histories. She grew up in a small telepathic town in Wales, while he grew up in Belfast during the Troubles. She went to Oxford and he went to the University of Edinburgh. He had been engaged once, but his fiancée had been killed in an automobile accident. She, a bit uncomfortably, admitted that she'd never had a relationship that lasted more than three months. Even then, she hadn't been very serious about it.

At times, when the conversation flagged, the atmosphere became a bit uncomfortable. He was almost nude, and she wore only an old t-shirt and jogging shorts. It was slightly embarrassing that her nipples had tightened when he first answered the door, and she couldn't seem to get them to settle down. Her face warmed a bit every time he glanced at them.

"Well, I guess I should try to get some sleep," she said, standing to go. "Who knows what the hell our day is going to be like."

"You'd rather sleep with Vasily than stay here?" he teased.

"I think I'm probably safer with Vasily. Good night, Donald."

As she locked the door to her compartment, she reflected that it wasn't Donald she was worried about. She didn't trust herself if she stayed with him. He did things to her that made her feel nervous and tingly and warm in uncomfortable ways. And there was an undeniable charge any time they happened to touch each other, however inadvertently. But it had been a long time since she was comfortable with quick, easy sex.

Undressing, she turned out the light and crawled between the sheets. It seemed only an instant before she heard a soft knock on the door. Donald's voice softly called, "It's time to get up. We're on the outskirts of Moscow." Glancing at the window, she saw it was morning.

Telekinetically unlocking the door, she slid it open a few inches. Donald stuck his head in. She was sitting up, covered only by the thin sheet, and she saw his eyes light up.

"That telekinetic stuff is neat," he said. "I could think of a use for it right now, if I had it."

Her face grew warm and her nipples betrayed her, presenting sudden peaks in the sheet.

"Get out of here and let me get dressed," she said.

Donald looked at Vasily, still asleep in his clothes on the other bunk. "Why is he privileged to attend the show and I'm not?"

"Do you really want to know? I'm actually going to wake him up and let him watch me. I want good, fresh, real memories in his mind. Hopefully, if anyone reads him to find out information about me, the images will distract them from probing deeper."

"You don't trust the construct Rebecca planted?" he asked, his forehead furrowing with sudden worry.

"Yes, but reinforcing the artificial memories we planted won't hurt anything."

Donald withdrew and Rhiannon threw back the sheet. Waking her companion, she rose and began choosing her clothes for the day. In the process, she showed Vasily views of her anatomy that only her lovers had ever seen. A lump grew in his trousers, but she ignored it. He was completely under her control and his physiological reaction confirmed that he would react naturally in spite of the construct and the compulsions Rebecca had set in his mind.

After a few minutes, she leaned over him, her breasts bobbing in front of his face. "Why don't you go to the washroom, use the toilet, and brush your teeth? Straighten yourself up so we can leave the train."

Obediently, he left the compartment. Following him with her mind, she confirmed that he did exactly as she had ordered. By the time he returned, she was dressed and ready to go. They disembarked with their luggage and walked through the station. Vasily called for a limousine and gave the driver his address.

Vasily owned a flat in one of the Seven Sisters. The baroque-gothic Stalin-era skyscraper was one of the most prestigious addresses in the city, overlooking the Moskva River and the Kremlin. The flat was spacious by Russian standards and furnished with heavy, nineteenth century elegance. Rhiannon took possession of the master bedroom, clearing closet space by taking all of Vasily's clothes that she didn't like and throwing them in the rubbish bin downstairs. Donald was relegated to the guest bedroom.

"You're going to continue sleeping with him?" Donald asked with a mournful, hurt expression.

"I'm not sleeping with anyone," she answered. "He'll sleep on the floor, across the doorway to ensure my safety from sleepwalking marauders. A girl has to protect the tattered remains of her virtue, you know." She smiled, trying to project a bright, flirty, sickly-sweet countenance.

"I've never sleepwalked in my life. Anytime I maraud, it's entirely intentional," he said, drawing a laugh from her.

They sent Vasily and the video disk off to talk to his boss. Vasily was a tall, well-built man, handsome in a brutish sort of way. A dapper dresser, he was a mid-level thug in the Gorbachev Clan hierarchy. A member of the KGB when the Soviet Union fell apart, he had been assigned to work for a normal human in St. Petersburg. That official was now President of Russia and Vasily had transitioned into a job for the FSB, the Federal Security Service. His rank was Deputy Section Chief, and he oversaw the President's security detail. Yuri Gorbachev, his boss, was one of the highest-ranking telepaths in the FSB.

Vasily was fairly intelligent and highly ambitious. However, his two failed attempts at kidnapping Irina in London had not been well received by his superiors. That, combined with the fact he had been missing without contact for a month, worried Rhiannon, and worried Donald even more. It was a major hole in their plan.

Rhiannon rode in Vasily's mind as he entered the Lubyanka, the infamous headquarters of the Soviet KGB. Seemingly unconcerned, he sought out his boss.

"My, what a pleasant surprise," Yuri Gorbachev, Sergei's nephew, said. "I thought you'd defected, or maybe run off with a rich heiress."

"My apologies," Vasily said. "I ran into some difficulties in St. Petersburg and was detained."

"Where the hell have you been?" Yuri thundered.

"I told you, in St. Petersburg. Alexander Romanov has died. The succession battle was very nasty, and every telepath in the city, at least those with any brains, kept their heads down."

"You've been gone for weeks. Don't tell me that all of the phones in St. Petersburg were blocked."

At that moment, three men walked into Yuri's office, men that Vasily recognized, and Rhiannon felt his fear explode in the portions of his mind behind the construct.

One of them battered down his shields and took control of his mind. Of course, he only saw the construct. At least for a while, Rebecca's carefully detailed creation held. It all depended if his interrogators believed what they read there. It became obvious very quickly that they didn't.

"I think he's wearing a construct," one man finally said.

"Get Gennady," Yuri replied. "We need to get to the bottom of this."

While they waited for Gennady, Yuri took the video disk and slipped it into a secure reader. When he finished viewing it, he said, "When Gennady gets here, take Vasily to the house in Odintsovo. I'll be there." Then he took the disk, put on his jacket, and left.

"Shit!" Rhiannon said. She had been broadcasting what she saw and heard from Vasily, and Vladimir raised an eyebrow.

"I think things are going quite well, don't you? They read the disk, and Sergei's Moscow residence is in Odintsovo."

"Things aren't going as direly as you predicted," Rhiannon said. "They haven't shot him."

"Yet. Don't you think we should get out of here?"

"No, they're preoccupied. They may think about us later, but so far, no one has said anything about checking his flat. Besides, I'm not worried about dodging anyone they might send here."

"Oh? Can you fly?"

She gave him a tight smile. "Damn near. But if we have to jump out the window, behave yourself. I've been known to drop things when I get distracted."

She thought through the possible scenarios, then went to the wine cabinet, opened a bottle, and poured two glasses.

"Why don't you call O'Donnell's office and ask them to send a couple of people around to collect our luggage. I'd hate to lose that coat if we have to leave here in a hurry."

He smiled. "You forget. We have fifty Protectors surrounding this building."

A few minutes later, he went to the door and opened it. People Rhiannon recognized came in and collected their bags and Rhiannon's coat.

After they left, she said, "Donald, if we do get in a scrap, stay out of my line of fire. And tell your people, also."

She saw his jaw tighten as he nodded. He was probably remembering the night at Viktor's, or maybe the tales of Ayr.

"So, what are they doing?" he asked.

"Still waiting for Gennady. They're sifting through his mind, or rather the construct. It appears they're spending most of their time looking at the fake memories we planted of him having sex with me. Sort of watching a psychic porn show."

"Any chance of sending that to me?"

She scowled at him.

"I didn't think so. Let me know if anything interesting happens."

Gennady took over an hour to get to the Lubyanka. Almost immediately, he pronounced that Vasily did have a construct implanted. There was some discussion about collapsing the construct, and Rhiannon held her breath. But whoever had the most authority decided they weren't authorized to do that. Yuri had said for them all, including Gennady, to go to Odintsovo, so they should wait.

They loaded Vasily into a car and the group took off for the country.

“And what do we do now?” Vladimir asked.

“Sit tight. I can read him as well from here as I could if I was sitting next to him. More comfortable and safer here.” She took a sip of her wine.

They waited. Vladimir had one of his men bring them some food, and he and Rhiannon finished the bottle of wine.

When the FSB men finally dragged Vasily into the Gorbachev compound, Rhiannon started paying attention again. They took him to a room in the basement and waited. After some time, Yuri came in with two other men. Vasily recognized them as Boris Gorbachev, one of Sergei’s sons, and Georgy Kalugin, the Clan’s head of security.

“That was an interesting disk,” Yuri said. “So, Alexander’s dead. And who is the new Clan Chief?”

“Galina,” Vasily said. “Both Viktor and the younger Alexander are dead.”

“And how did you come to be in possession of the disk? How did you get so friendly with Galina Romanova? And why in hell should we believe anything you say?” Yuri said. “Remove the construct. Let’s see if we have a traitor or a fool.”

Rhiannon withdrew from Vasily’s mind.

“What’s going on?” Vladimir asked.

“They’re going to collapse the construct,” Rhiannon said. “Rebecca booby trapped it, and she said it was completely undetectable. When the construct is collapsed, it will trigger a command to wipe Vasily’s mind. She says it will also wipe the minds of anyone who is in his mind at the time. That will get the construct artist for sure, and the psychic backlash might damage anyone else who’s close.”

She took a deep breath and stared into her glass. Abruptly, she downed the wine and rose, striding to the wine cabinet and pulling out another bottle.

"At least a couple of them were in his mind when I pulled out. Goddess, Vladimir, he was terrified. He knew he was going to die. It was so hard to watch."

She uncorked the bottle and poured her glass full with a shaking hand. Then her head snapped up and she froze. Putting her hand out to the counter in front of her, she braced herself and then slumped.

"He's gone. I could still feel him up until a few seconds ago, but he's either dead or mind wiped." She took a deep drink of her wine. "Well, what do you think we should do now?"

~~~

Rhiannon contacted Andrei in St. Petersburg. **Do you have a mole or two in the Lubyanka?**

One or two. Why?

I'm curious as to whether Yuri Gorbachev shows up for work tomorrow. He had a construct artist collapse Vasily's construct and I wonder how well Rebecca's booby trap worked.

She told him what had happened since they arrived in Moscow.

I think we should move Irina to Moscow, Rhiannon sent. **I don't know if Sergei is here, but that video certainly got their attention.**

Galina will loan us a plane, Andrei sent. **We can land at Domodedovo and take her to a dacha we own near there.** Domodedovo is one of two international Moscow airports and lies south of the city. **I think it's safer than having her in the city itself.**

Andrei, do you have someone who can change a property registration? Vasily doesn't need this flat anymore, and it's a prime location. Are my papers legitimate? My passport and propiska?
~~~

Yes, you're a legal Russian citizen. Should I put it in your name and have your propiska transferred? How much should we use as a purchase price?

Register it in my Ekaterina Kuznetsova name. Record the purchase price as thirty million rubles. That's way under value, but enough to make the sale look realistic.

"Vladimir, I've been thinking," Rhiannon said. "You may be right. Perhaps we should relocate."

"The O'Donnell safe house?"

"I was thinking more of that fancy new hotel next to Red Square."

"Your expense account is better than mine."

Rhiannon laughed. "No expense account. I took thirty million rubles out of Vasily's account in St. Petersburg. He doesn't need it anymore."

Vladimir whistled. "Goddess, that's almost seven hundred thousand euros."

"A drop in the bucket. His Swiss and Cayman Islands accounts held about forty million euros."

"Held? Past tense?"

She smiled. "Like I said, he doesn't need it anymore."

Laughing, he said, "You're a goddamned thief!"

"No, I'm not, and I'm deeply offended at your implication. I'm an international financier," Rhiannon said with a flip of her hair. "I'm simply continuing in one of the family businesses. I deposited it in my grandfather's bank in Switzerland. Now, do you want to quibble, or do you want to check into a fancy hotel and go have a steak dinner on Novy Arbat?"

Sipping cocktails after they ordered dinner, Vladimir said, "What are the other family businesses?"

Rhiannon felt her face grow warm, and then became angry with herself. She wasn't ashamed of how her family earned their money, at least she never had been. Thinking about her reaction, she realized it wasn't shame but shyness. Vlad/Donald confused her. He irritated her and attracted her, and she wasn't sure how to deal with him.

"Most of the women in my family are courtesans. Some of them are also Healers, but I don't have that Gift. And the men, well, the Kendricks aren't much for marrying. Men are transient."

His eyes narrowed and he shook his head. "And what made you decide to become a private investigator instead of becoming a courtesan? Isn't that what most Druids do?"

It took a minute for his statement to make sense, then a sudden awareness blossomed. A slow smile spread across her face.

"I'm afraid you're operating under a mistaken impression, sir. I'm not a Druid."

"But ... I thought ...," he stammered. "Oh, come on. Normal women don't look like you do. You can't bullshit me. You're the most beautiful woman I've ever met."

"Thank you. I think." She shrugged. "You're not the only one who's made that mistake."

He studied her, and then his face grew red. "Oh, shit. I apologize. I'm sorry I've been such an ass."

Surprised, Rhiannon's head jerked up and she studied him. "You thought I was playing games with you? Teasing you? No, not teasing, you thought I was taunting you. Trying to put you in your place." She cranked up her empathic awareness.

His face flamed. She looked around quickly, wondering if he glowed enough that other people would notice.

"What do you have against Druids?"

She didn't think he was going to answer her, but finally he said, "I had a girlfriend when I was younger. I didn't handle it very well."

"I'd say you're still not handling it. Is that why you're in Finland rather than Ireland?"

"I don't need any psychoanalysis."

"No, I don't guess you do. Don't worry. I'm not looking for a boyfriend, and I'm not into casual sex. Especially not with a man who doesn't like women. I hope you don't have a problem working with a woman. But if you do, you don't have to stay close to me. I told you that I don't need security."

The shock in his eyes slowly faded to hurt. Rhiannon didn't care. Men always felt women should be careful of their feelings, but seemed to think women's feelings didn't matter. Screw the son of a bitch.

~~~

Chapter 18

Scientists now believe that the primary biological function of breasts is to make males stupid. - Dave Barry

Rhiannon and Vladimir met with Irina and the O'Donnell Protectors at their dacha the next day. The O'Donnell Clan had bought several farms and a large forest tract, then built a compound that resembled a small village. It didn't look like much, but after entering a small house, Rhiannon discovered that the majority of the facility was below ground.

"Cute little basement you have here," she told Andrei, looking around at what looked like a large log hunting lodge with no windows. "Does this extend very far?"

"It's fairly large," he answered. "We have garages, storage areas, and an armory. Seamus began building the complex in the early sixties, when the Soviets still banned private ownership of property. We needed a secure base to
~~~

monitor the Russian Clans, and at that time, we weren't sure if the U.S. and the Soviet Union might start throwing nukes around. We expanded things quite a bit after the Soviet Union broke apart."

Andrei's wife Yelena greeted them and escorted them to a large dining room. Irina and a couple of dozen Protectors sat around a table laden with food.

"My sources inside the FSB tell me that there was a bit of a stir inside the FSB this morning," Andrei told Rhiannon after Yelena placed a loaded plate in front of her. "Neither Yuri nor Vasily showed up for work, and no one can contact them. No one seems to know who is in charge of the President's security detail."

Rhiannon nodded. "I thought that Jill would be coming with you."

"She's going to stay in St. Petersburg until the situation stabilizes a bit. There was an assassination attempt on Galina the night before last."

"What happened?"

"Some of Sholokhov's men managed to sneak through all of our security measures," Irina said, taking a sip of her wine. "Jill, Galina and I were having dinner when they came crashing in and started shooting up the place. It was very rude. We had to have our dessert out on the terrace because the parlor was such a mess."

The prim expression on Irina's face caused the group to laugh, and Rhiannon asked, "Did any of them survive?"

"Yeah, we captured one of them. Jill did."

"Out of how many?" Vladimir asked.

"Their force was about a hundred men," Andrei said. "Twenty of them got through to Galina. We probably should have let them all through and taken fewer casualties." He shook his head. "A bunch of thugs against three of the most powerful telepaths in the country. Assault rifles against air shields and Neural Disruption made for a short fight."

"It seems there are a lot of pitched battles here. Is that normal in Russia?" Rhiannon asked.

Yelena laughed, "Only when the Irish come to town."

~~~

The next day, Jill contacted Rhiannon. **Sergei sent an emissary, asking about Irina. He flew in last night and flew out after talking with Galina.**

Oh? What did he have to say?

Give Irina to him or Sergei would consider her kidnapping a declaration of war. Gorbachev knows that Romanov is weakened, and Galina was told that if she wanted to keep her seat, let alone her head, not to fuck with them. The guy wasn't very diplomatic.

And you said?

Galina told them that she wanted reassurances. If Sergei doesn't sign at least a neutrality pact and stay out of Romanov business, then he'll never see Irina. His man said that wasn't going to make Sergei very happy and she said she didn't care. Those were her terms. She also told him that Irina wasn't being held in St. Petersburg and that attacking Romanov wouldn't get him anything. So the ball is back in his court.

Rhiannon reported this to the group at the dacha.

"There was a lot of activity at the Gorbachev compound early this morning," Andrei said. "Of course, it could have been a party for all we know. We don't have anyone inside."

"So, we still don't know where my grandfather is," Irina said softly, not really asking a question. She seemed to gaze off into space, obviously lost in thought.

"Okay," she finally said. "I think we need to find out if
~~~

he's there, somewhere in Moscow, or in the south. Any ideas about getting inside without a full-scale assault?"

The group brainstormed ideas for about half an hour without any brilliant plans emerging. Finally, Irina said, "This isn't getting us any closer than all the other discussions we've had."

Shifting in her seat, she leaned her elbows on the table and said, "While I was in St. Petersburg, Seamus held a conference call with me, Brenna, Rebecca, Jill, Morrighan, a Druid historian from O'Neill and Fergus O'Byrne. It seems Seamus has been giving this problem of how to get to my grandfather a lot of thought. He delved into his memories, and came up with something from our fight against the Romans."

She turned to Rhiannon. "Brenna said you should pull up the memories of Maeb O'Conner, around 1600 AD, for something similar."

Rhiannon sorted through the memories she'd received from Corwin and found Maeb. "Blackwater," she announced. "The Battle of the Yellow Ford, August 14, 1598. O'Neill and O'Donnell forces destroyed an English army."

Irina nodded. "It seems Seamus has memories of one of Boudica's daughters who escaped to Ireland after the Roman's crushed her rebellion. Boudica was a Druid, as were her daughters, and the British Clans wreaked havoc on the Romans until they were defeated. And for those who don't know, Morrighan has the memories of the Irish High Priestesses going back to the Cataclysm. Every Druid High Priestess for the past twenty-six centuries."

"Yes, so she told me," Rhiannon said. The others at the table looked duly impressed.

"This is a rough outline of what we discussed," Irina said, and proceeded to explain how Druids had participated in ancient battles.

~~~

Dressed in a skin-tight black leather catsuit and knee-high boots, her hair loose and flowing over her shoulders, Rhiannon stepped out of the O'Donnell limousine carrying a pistol with a silencer in one hand. Irina followed, wearing a loose summer dress and sandals.

Irina chuckled. "I guess we have the answer to one question. If Gorbachev's men are as distracted by what you're wearing as ours are, then that suit was a good idea."

Those with the Kilpatrick Gift of Power Shielding are able to extend their strong mental shields to someone they are touching. Rhiannon took Irina's arm and covered the succubus with her mental shield, then created a dome of hardened air with Aerokinesis. The two women walked down the road away from the limousine and the Protectors following it.

When they came within sight of the Gorbachev compound, they stopped, and Rhiannon scanned the compound with her mind.

There's a guardhouse outside the gate, Rhiannon sent, **with two guards inside. A door with an electronic keypad goes through the wall from the back of the guardhouse. Six more guards are patrolling the front of the compound inside the wall. Another two are in the foyer of the main house, and there's about forty men and twenty women inside. Another two hundred men are patrolling other parts of the compound or in two barracks behind the house.**

Irina nodded, then proceeded to pull her dress over her head and drop it on the ground. Other than her sandals, she was completely nude. Taking Rhiannon's arm, they continued walking toward the compound.

As they neared the guardhouse, Irina turned on her Glamor, the specialized manifestation of Charisma that is part of the Succubus Gift, and gave it full power. She shone
~~~

like a goddess, spectacularly beautiful. At the same time, Rhiannon boosted her own Charisma to its highest level and lifted Irina off the ground using Telekinesis, then resumed walking toward the compound.

Projecting Influence, another manifestation of the Succubus Gift, Irina drew the men inside the guardhouse out. They walked toward her transfixed, their faces blank with wonder. Rhiannon dropped the air shield and Irina sent a massive blast of pheromones toward the men.

Floating to the first man, Irina put her arms around his neck and kissed him. To Rhiannon, the kiss seemed to last forever, but checking her watch showed it was only a minute until he slumped to the ground. Irina floated to the second man and kissed him until he passed out. Rhiannon set her back on the ground and they entered the guardhouse.

As they did, she felt Irina push life energy into her, replenishing what she had used and filling her reserves. One of Rhiannon's reservations about the plan was the amount of energy she would be expected to use.

Irina had laughed, telling her in the limo, "Don't worry about it. I took five lads, all volunteers, this afternoon." Indeed, the blond succubus Glowed with life energy. "I'll feed you with everything you can hold, and then replenish you as we go with what I drain from the men we disable. You're the girl who's protecting my sweet ass, so you can bet I'll make sure you're in fighting shape."

Rhiannon read the keypad sequence from the mind of one of the guards and unlocked the door. While she was doing so, Irina was busy draining the guards on the other side of the wall.

How fast can you drain someone? Rhiannon asked.

Enough to disable them? About a minute without touching them. But it doesn't matter whether it's one or a dozen. I don't have to do them one at a time.

You took a minute to drain each of those outside guards, and you were touching them.

They aren't merely disabled, Irina sent. **They're close to death. It will take them days to recover. They'll be able to sit up and eat the day after tomorrow, but they won't be doing any talking or shooting tonight.**

Pushing the door open, Rhiannon peeked around the compound. Two men were sprawled on the pavement. Another sat slumped next to the door, and fifty feet away two more lay on the dacha's front porch.

There are a couple more you can't see, Irina sent. **Don't worry, all the men near us are out of commission. The ones we need to worry about are those monitoring the security systems. Let's hope they aren't paying too much attention to their cameras.**

Irina paused at the front door, and Rhiannon felt the minds of the guards in the foyer beyond gradually dim and then slip into unconsciousness. Irina nodded, and opened the door.

Showtime again, Irina sent, once again beginning to Glow. Rhiannon lifted her up, holding her hand, and floated her through the doorway.

Rhiannon blasted through the shields of one of the men lying there. **Irina, Sergei is in the house.** Rhiannon sent her a floor plan and pointed to the area Sergei would be.

They cautiously crept through the house, Irina blasting pheromones and broadcasting aversion using Influence. At the same time, she was draining everyone she came into mental contact with and feeding Rhiannon with as much energy as she could hold. The lights dimmed ahead of them as both women drained the house's electrical circuits.

A klaxon sounded in the compound outside.

Shit! Irina sent. **Someone set off the alarms. Rhi, I can't drain that many people. We need to get this done* *now!**

Rhiannon opened a new channel in her mind. **Brenna! I need you now!** She sent an image of the room they were standing in. Brenna appeared in front of them, wearing a loose, soft cotton shift.

I like the outfit, Brenna sent to Irina as she pulled the shift over her head and began to Glow, quickly matching Irina.

We need your O'Neill Gift, Rhiannon sent. Pulling a second pistol from the holster at her waist, she offered it to Brenna. To her surprise, Brenna reacted by taking a step back.

God, don't give her a gun! Irina sent. **She's more likely to blow her foot off than hit anything she aims at.**

Brenna nodded. **I have all the weapons I need. What's going on?**

Both women sent her images of the situation.

Rhi, manage the air shield for you and Irina. I'll take care of our mental shields, so don't worry about the Rivera Gift. Tell your Protectors to stay back and send me a landing spot outside the compound. Now, where are we going?

Brenna floated off the floor, and she and Irina preceded Rhiannon down a hallway. The klaxon outside continued to blare its message of alarm. Then the lights dimmed even more and the klaxon stopped.

Thank God, Rhiannon sent. **That thing was driving me crazy.**

I wonder why they turned it off, Irina sent.

They didn't, Brenna replied. **I did. I drained its power source.**

Brenna knew of their plan, and was prepared in case her friends needed her. The ability to teleport them out was their main contingency plan, but Rhiannon had earlier revealed that Sergei's Rivera Gift was her major concern. While Rhiannon's Kilpatrick Gift might deflect or reduce Neural Disruption energy, it wouldn't block it the way Brenna's O'Neill Gift would. The other advantage was that Brenna didn't need to be in contact with either of them to give them that protection.

They approached a pair of French doors at the end of a hallway on the second floor.

Rhi, don't cover her with your air shield, just hold it in front of her, Brenna sent. Glancing toward Irina, she sent, **Ready?**

Irina nodded. Brenna sent a projectile of hardened air at the doors and they blew open, banging against the walls inside. The succubi drifted into the room, blasting pheromones in such quantities that Rhiannon wondered why she couldn't see a cloud forming.

Four men stood facing them. They all recognized Sergei Gorbachev from their briefings, but he looked older than the pictures they had. Gray haired, thin and shorter than average height, Brenna could see elements of Irina's features in his face. Two men stood to his right and one to his left. Something about the man standing directly to his right gave Brenna the shivers.

Brenna, capture the man to Sergei's right, Irina sent. **Rhi, take out the guy on our left.**

"Hello, Grandfather," Irina said.

"Irina," Sergei said, a leering smile spreading across his face. "How good to meet you at last." He looked her up and down and licked his lips.

The creepy man next to him screamed as Brenna breached his shields with her O'Donnell gift. Without any warning, Irina lashed out with Neural Disruption, pouring power into Sergei and the man on his left. They jerked, dancing an epileptic jig, and fell to the floor.

The other man raised his pistol and Rhiannon released a bolt of electrical energy at him. He flew backward, slamming against the wall ten feet behind him, then slid to the floor and lay still.

"God, Irina," Brenna said. "You killed him."

"That's what I came here to do," Irina said, her face a stoic mask. "I don't have any interest in anything he might say."

"So who is that?" Rhiannon asked, gesturing to the man standing alone with blank eyes.

"Holy shit!" Brenna exclaimed. "He's Lavrentiy Beria!" The man she had captured was the notorious head of Stalin's NKVD, the secret police force that was later renamed to KGB.

"I thought he was dead."

"People think Seamus died seventy-five years ago," Brenna replied. She searched through the man's memories. "The communists thought he was dead. But he's a telepath. Instead of being executed, he escaped. Sergei's father gave him asylum in exchange for his knowledge of the NKVD's internal workings."

"And all the dirt he held on the Communist Party's ruling elite," Irina said.

"How did you know who he was?" Brenna asked.

"He was one of my mother's rapists," Irina said. "I saw him in her mind, and then I saw a picture of him in a history book. As to why I want him alive? Because I'll bet you he knows all the internal workings of Clan Gorbachev. Every bank account, every closet containing a skeleton, every secret. Am I right?"

Brenna was silent for a couple of minutes. "Maybe not everything, but everything that matters. If all you do is loot his bank accounts, you'll be a billionaire."

"That's all fine," Rhiannon said, "but what do we do now? We're in a compound, surrounded by hundreds of hostiles. Do we teleport out?"

Brenna turned to Irina with a questioning look on her face.

Taking a deep breath, Irina said, "Let's see if we can find some clothes. I don't want to make my first speech to my new Clan naked."

"We have clothes for Irina back at our car," Rhiannon said, "but I doubt we have anything that will fit you."

"I'll be right back," Brenna said and disappeared. Less than five minutes later, she reappeared wearing a blue cocktail dress, and holding Rebecca by her hand.

"She caught me dressing and insisted on coming. Don't ya just hate tagalong older sisters? I keep telling her she needs to develop her own social interests."

Then Brenna teleported to the limo waiting outside the compound and brought back a dozen Protectors and Irina's clothes. The young succubus discarded several articles of clothing and quickly dressed in a red evening gown with matching four-inch heels.

"What the hell is going on here?" Rebecca asked. She walked over and looked at Sergei's body. "Oh. I guess that answers my question. I take it we're in Russia. Who's the guy who looks like Lavrentiy Beria?"

~~~

Chapter 19

Think like a queen. A queen is not afraid to fail. Failure is another steppingstone to greatness. - Oprah Winfrey

After climbing to the third floor, Irina opened French doors to a balcony overlooking a lake and the back of the compound. "Can you drop the air shield for a moment
~~~

while I get their attention?" she asked.

Rhiannon dropped the shield and Irina loosed all the electric energy she'd been holding. A small bolt of lightning shot from her outstretched hand to the ground, lighting the compound with a loud, sizzling crack. Immediately, fifteen air shields enveloped the balcony.

How many layers of air shield does it take to protect from a nuke? Rebecca sent to Rhiannon.

About as many as it takes to protect one short, blonde succubus, Rhiannon answered with a smile.

The bolt of electricity had its intended affect. Everyone in the compound looked up and then spotted Irina standing on the balcony. Even in the dark, she was hard to miss, the blonde in the red dress with electricity dancing on her hands. To help light the scene, Rebecca and Rhiannon stood at the edges of the balcony with fireballs on their palms.

"My name is Irina Gorbacheva," Irina shouted, also broadcasting her words telepathically. "My grandfather, Sergei Gorbachev, is dead. I claim the seat of Clan Chief of Clan Gorbachev. Is there anyone who wishes to contest my claim?"

A spray of automatic weapons fire bounced off the air shield. Irina pointed at the two men who had fired and cut them down with Neural Disruption.

"Thank you. Is there anyone else? Come on, don't be bashful. Let's get this over with."

No one in the compound moved.

"Lay down your weapons," Irina shouted. "All of your weapons, boot knives, ankle guns, everything." She raised her voice as loud as she could. "*I will kill* anyone stupid enough to disobey my order. I've had a hell of an evening and I'm not in the mood to argue with anyone."

Most of the men began laying down their arms, but

some were being very slow about it.

Don't hit anyone, but drop those fireballs to get their attention, Irina sent to Rebecca and Rhiannon.

Two fireballs arced through the air, one hitting the driveway and setting the asphalt on fire, the other landing in a fountain with spectacular results. Both women immediately created another fireball and stood holding them. The laggards got the message and soon everyone below stood with their hands above their heads.

Brenna had hung back, and noise from the hallway beyond the room they were in attracted her attention. She slapped an air shield over the room's doorway, then strolled over to look through it. A dozen men stood in the hall, some taking shelter in doorways as she approached.

"You have fifteen seconds to lay down your arms," she said. "After that, I start killing people."

She stood looking at her watch. After fifteen seconds, she looked up. Using a tight stream of Neural Disruption, she cut down the man closest to her, aiming at his knees. She shot the next stream at the arm of a man holding a pistol. The hallway erupted with gunfire, bullets bouncing off the air shield. Without flinching, she downed the next man standing with a weapon, then the next. The gunfire ceased and weapons clattered to the floor.

She began draining energy from the men in the hallway until all of them were asleep on the floor, then turned and walked across the room to the balcony. "You're lucky I'm not Irina," she muttered to herself. "She probably would have killed you."

As she passed the Protectors who had followed her, she said, "Keep an air shield around this room. It was rather careless not to cover our backs, don't you think?"

The man closest to her turned red. "Yes, my lady."

When she got back to the balcony, some of the men in

the compound were opening the gates. O'Donnell and O'Neill Protectors flooded in, rounding up the Gorbachev men.

The confusion finally got sorted out, and things calmed down. The Irish Protectors controlled the compound. Andrei notified Collin that the operation had succeeded, and asked for a thousand Protectors to help with the next phase. With fifteen thousand members, Irina's control of the Gorbachev Clan was far from complete.

"Jerome," Brenna said to Andrei as she prepared to leave, "if Seamus or Callie or Collin ever asks, I wasn't here. Understand?"

"I understand perfectly, my lady," he answered with a smile. "And thank you for the help you didn't provide."

She turned to find Rebecca, and heard Jerome say, "By the way, Brenna, have you had a chance to look at that increase in my budget allocation I requested?"

Slowly, she turned back. His face was a study in innocent expectation. She pursed her lips and studied him. "I think with the changed circumstances in Russia, that request was a bit premature. Rework it for the current reality and get it to me by the end of next week."

"Thank you, my lady," he said and bowed.

"My lady, my foot. You old pirate."

He beamed at her.

She spotted Rebecca talking to Rhiannon and Irina, and walked over. But before she reached them, she saw someone else she decided she should talk to.

Approaching Donald O'Conner, she said, "Mr. O'Conner. I don't think I've had the pleasure."

"Lady O'Neill," O'Conner said, bowing deeply.

"Do you think that you should keep your headquarters in Helsinki, or should we move you to St. Petersburg?"

“Considering the new alliance with Romanov, it probably would make more sense to be in St. Petersburg and make the Helsinki office a satellite,” he said.

“Get me a list of what you need, equipment, facilities, personnel. I’ll probably have Rhiannon supervise O’Neill operations here in Russia, so copy her on everything.”

His eyes bugged out and his mouth hung open. Brenna wasn’t sure why he reacted that way, and looked over his shoulder at Rhiannon, who had heard the exchange.

“Of course, Mr. O’Conner will be ecstatic to report to Ms. Kendrick,” Rhiannon said. “I’m sure it fulfills one of his deepest secret fantasies.”

He whipped around, face red, and stared at her. She smiled at him. “We do work well together, don’t we, Donald?”

“I think there’s something I’m not getting with those two,” Brenna muttered to Rebecca as they prepared to teleport out.

“Irina’s setting up a lottery,” Rebecca said. “She says it’s even money which happens first, either they shag each other or Rhiannon kills him. I put a hundred euros on them shagging.”

“I’ll put a hundred on her killing him,” Brenna said. “Make sure we get a competent second in command for him.”

“Now I’m missing something,” Rebecca said.

“Yes, you are,” Brenna said, thinking of the memories from Rhiannon’s mind concerning Brian O’Byrne.

~~~

Chapter 20

Time is a dressmaker specializing in alterations.
- Faith Baldwin
~~~

Brenna was in her office in Tyrone when her grandfather, Fergus O'Byrne, contacted her.

Brenna?

Grandfather! How are you?

I'm fine, but I have some unhappy news, Fergus sent. *Your grandmother has had a heart attack.*

Oh, no! Is she going to be all right?

Yes, the doctors say it was mild.

Do you want me to come and see her?

Yes, but wait a day or two until the doctors say she's strong enough for company.

There was a pause.

Brenna, she needs a softer climate and less stress. Some years ago, I purchased a home in the south of France. As soon as she's well enough to travel, I'm moving her there.

In other words, as soon as she was well enough to be teleported. Brenna didn't think Fergus would subject Caylin to a plane ride.

I had hoped to put this off a little longer, Brenna, and I'm sorry. I'm going to retire. I haven't told anyone as yet, but I think I need to announce it soon.

I understand, Grandfather.

Brenna understood, but she wasn't happy about it, and cursed her fate after her grandfather broke the connection. She contacted her other grandfather.

Seamus? Caylin had a heart attack. She went on to give her grandfather all the news. Afterward, she contacted her cousin Jared, who had been living at the O'Byrne estate in Ireland the past three years as her representative and transition coordinator.

While she was communicating with Jared, Rebecca walked into her office. Seeing Brenna staring off into space, Rebecca went to the refrigerator and pulled out a beer, holding it up to catch her sister's attention. Brenna nodded and Rebecca pulled out a second one.

When Brenna's focus returned to the room and she took a pull on her beer, Rebecca asked, "What's up?"

"Caylin's had a heart attack and Fergus is retiring," Brenna said. "We'll be going down there in a day or two. Send your team there to coordinate with Jared."

Rebecca's response was a stream of profanity.

"Rebecca, don't tell anyone. Tell your team that Jared will brief them when they get to Wicklow."

"Okay. Got it. So, are we moving to Ireland permanently?" Rebecca and her husband Carlos both traveled frequently, but had established a home in Washington. It would be a wrenching disruption if Rebecca moved. Since Brenna was a teleport, she could visit Collin any time she wanted.

"It kind of looks that way. I wish I could stay in Washington, but the next time we go home, we should probably pack for a long stay."

"Can I tell Carlos?" Rebecca asked.

Brenna nodded. "Of course, but tell him it isn't official yet, and he can't tell his family."

"Thanks. Maybe he can get a transfer to Dublin."

"Ecuador doesn't have an embassy in Ireland, only a consulate. The closest embassy is in London," Brenna said, feeling depressed. She'd checked long before. Carlos was a general in the Ecuadorian army and the Military Attaché at their embassy in Washington. "Maybe de Vargas can set up a trade mission in Dublin. We can trade Ecuadorian wool for Irish wool."

Rebecca snorted a laugh, then walked over to where Brenna sat behind her desk. Taking her sister in her arms, she gave Brenna a tight hug. "The good thing is that Caylin is going to be okay. We'll deal with the rest of it."

~~~

Fergus O'Byrne was a tall, slender man with white hair. He had been Clan Chief since the late 1800s and guided his people through Irish independence, two world wars, and the Silent War between telepaths in the late 1940s and 1950s. The O'Byrne Clan was prosperous and counted over twenty thousand members, controlling most of the Irish Republic, Wales, and had a small contingent of members living in Iceland.

Irish clan structure traced back to antiquity, and with their long lives, telepaths were much closer to their ancient roots than normal humans. Fergus's grandfather had fought the English conquest as an ally of O'Donnell and O'Neill. The rules of succession followed ancient feudal practices, and Brenna would be only the fourth Clan Chief since 1600.

Lord and Lady O'Byrne had produced three children, including Brenna's mother, Maureen. All three had died young. Lord O'Byrne had fathered four children with other women, Andrew, Michael, Brian and Morrighan. By tradition, the bastards were unable to inherit unless no one in the direct line was capable. Michael had been the designated heir between the death of Maureen and Brenna's discovery fifteen years later.

Brenna, Rebecca and Rhiannon teleported into O'Byrne, materializing in the middle of a large throw rug. Looking around, they saw Morrighan standing near the door.

"Welcome to Wicklow," Brenna's aunt said. "I wish it were a happier occasion, but it's still good to see you." She hugged each of the women. "Lady O'Byrne is expecting you."

Morrighan led them to Lady O'Byrne's bedroom. Caylin sat in bed sipping tea, propped up by several
~~~

pillows. She was pale and looked tired, but she smiled when her granddaughter walked into the room.

Their visit was short, and after being ushered out by Caylin's nurse, they trooped down to Fergus's study.

Jared was present, along with Fergus's sons Michael and Brian, Morrighan, and O'Byrne's head of security, Devlin O'Conner. Michael was president of O'Byrne Industries, while Brian lived in Paris and worked as head of the O'Byrne trade mission there. Morrighan served as head of O'Byrne's lobbying unit, keeping an eye on the Irish Parliament.

When Rhiannon walked in and saw Brian, she halted. Frozen, she stood and stared at him.

"Hello, Rhiannon," Brian said. "It's good to see you again. You're looking good."

"Hello, Brian. I didn't know you were here."

Brenna watched the two of them, wondering if she was the only one in the room with operating Empathy. Everyone else seemed to ignore the pain and longing both were sending out in waves.

Fergus called the meeting to order, and for security purposes, the conversation was conducted telepathically.

You all know why we're here, Fergus began. **The healers say that Caylin can travel next week, and I've already sent staff to prepare the house in Grimaud. I plan to move her there as soon as possible.**

When do you plan to announce your plans? Michael asked.

Tonight.

Brenna rocked back in her chair. She turned her head to look at Rebecca, and wondered if her own face was as wide-eyed and pale as her sister's.

Taking a deep breath, Brenna sent,**I've been expecting*

_this for two years, but I can't say that I'm ready for it._*

Do we have any idea where Andrew is? Rebecca asked. Fergus's oldest son was the major source of everyone's concern. Andrew was arrogant and abrasive with a bullying sadistic streak. Considered the black sheep of the family, he was hated by his half-brothers and half-sisters. He had clashed with Brenna on her visits to the estate.

We had word he was in Dublin, Devlin sent, *_but we were unable to locate him. He moves around quite a bit. He's been in Wales and Scotland. Obviously, he hasn't been keeping in touch since the bombing. We have an O'Donnell operative planted in his inner circle. Unfortunately, he hasn't been able to contact us much. Andrew's been gathering malcontents to him and recruiting non-Clan telepaths. He's amassed quite an arsenal over the years, and I don't think he plans on using it to go duck hunting._*

Where does he get his money? Brenna asked.

Lord O'Byrne met her eyes. *_He has always received a living stipend from me, but that's not enough to fund his activities. His mother had money and when she died three years ago, he inherited it. It would be enough for his lifetime if he invested it and lived sensibly, but he's chosen to go a different way._*

Brenna looked to Jared. *_That stipend ends as soon as I take over._*

Jared nodded.

That won't be necessary, Fergus said.*_I cut him off the instant he took credit for the bombing. We also froze his accounts in our banks. I know he has money elsewhere, but we can't control that._*

How many men can he field? Rebecca asked.

He has about a thousand adherents, Devlin

answered.

We figure that your support among Clan members is about fifty percent, Jared sent. *_Andrew's support is about ten percent, mostly from those who think they'll benefit directly if he takes the seat. About twenty-five percent view you unfavorably. About ninety percent view Andrew unfavorably._*

Sounds like an election opinion poll, Rebecca chuckled.

That's exactly what it is, Jared sent. *_Along with intelligence assessments gathered by my team and Devlin's. We each run our own intel, then share the results._*

Andrew lost favor with that bombing, Devlin sent. *_On the other hand, the war in Scotland and the scale of the casualties there have made some people view you with trepidation._*

So what can we expect from him? Brenna asked.

Andrew was fascinated with the IRA, Michael sent. *_The mayhem, the terror, it appealed to him. I think we're in for some unpleasantness._*

On a spear thread to her sister, Brenna said, *_Can we take him out?_*

If that's what you want to do, we can try. But we need to find him first. Jared can probably hook you up with our operative, but it will probably be his death warrant as well. Is that what you want to do?

Assassination. Such an ugly word. Brenna wasn't sure she could give the order, though she knew it was probably the best course of action.

~~~

Lord O'Byrne called all the people living on the estate and in the surrounding villages to a meeting after dinner. The gathering was far too large for the ballroom in the manor house, so they used the large lawn between the
~~~

house and the barns, where the Beltane and Samhain celebrations were held.

Climbing the steps of a large fountain so that he could be seen by the crowd, Fergus used both his voice and telepathic communication to address the crowd.

"The Goddess gives us our Gifts, and blesses us with a wonderful world to live in," he began. "The seasons bring us new life in the spring, and harvests in autumn. Just as the world has its cycles, so do our lives."

A murmur began. The members of the Clan had been waiting for this moment since Brenna was named heir.

"I have lived a full and happy life," Fergus continued. "I have had the great privilege of being addressed as your Lord, and the joy of seeing O'Byrne grow and prosper for almost a century and a half. And now I am entering a new cycle in my life. I am looking forward to simply being Fergus, and no longer Lord O'Byrne."

He paused, waiting for the crowd to quiet.

"I have had the honor and privilege of leading this Clan since 1875. I am tired. As you all know, my wife is in poor health. It is time for us to step aside and let those who are younger and have more energy do the work."

He motioned for Brenna to join him atop the wall surrounding the fountain.

"My granddaughter, Brenna Aoife O'Donnell, shall be taking my place as Clan Chief. I ask you all to show her the loyalty, love and patience you have shown me. She is young, and she will need your help as she grows into the role, but there is no one more qualified. This I believe with every fiber of my being. She is smart, she is strong, she is humble, and she is compassionate. As her other grandfather once told me, anyone who wants to be a Clan Chief is obviously too stupid to understand what the job entails. She has done everything in her power to try to talk me out of this, which tells me she is the proper person for the job."

Scattered laughter from the crowd.

Fergus stepped down, leaving Brenna standing alone facing her new Clan. She took a deep breath.

"Thank you for welcoming me," she began. "I don't remember the first time I lived here in Wicklow. You'll have to forgive me, but although I was born here, I was only eight months old when I left. I do remember coming back, but then my parents died when I was eight, and it was many years before I came here again. My mother loved it here, and I'm sure my parents planned to raise me partially here and partially in the United States."

She stopped, her composure slipping. The crowd was silent, and waited for her to continue.

"As I'm sure you know, in a perfect world my mother, Maureen O'Byrne, would be standing here. She was supposed to be the heir, just as my father was supposed to be the heir of O'Donnell. And in that perfect world, I would have another hundred years before I had to grow up."

She squared her shoulders, her chin jutted out defiantly. "But we don't live in a perfect world. We have enemies. The Clans have been fighting for survival for thousands of years, and there are dangers all around us. We are a vulnerable minority in a world with billions of norms. We have other Clans who would take our lands and force us to live as their servants. Many of you here remember living under the English yoke. Our enemies have burned us at the stake, slaughtered us in battle, starved us in our homes."

Looking around, she saw many, especially the older people, nodding.

"Some might think that being Clan Chief means living in a fine manor house and telling people what to do. Having servants and fancy clothes. Anyone who thinks that has never watched or understood Fergus O'Byrne. They have definitely failed to understand Caylin O'Byrne. I know that my place in this Clan is dependent on how well I serve you, protect you, and help you to prosper. The Irish do not suffer tyrants well."

She turned and held out her hand to Fergus, who took it in his. "My grandfather spent one hundred and forty years doing this job. I'm sure I won't do it very well at first, definitely not with the grace and understanding that he has. But I promise to do my best to fulfill my duties. I ask you to help me to fulfill them. I ask for your patience, your support, and your counsel. I don't know all of you. I plan to. Please feel welcome to stop by and have tea. I know that my grandfather never turned any of you away, and I don't plan to change that. Thank you for welcoming me to Wicklow."

Brenna took a deep breath, uncertain of how to address the next part. She looked around, seeing people patiently waiting.

"As you know, I recently inherited the O'Neill Clan. There were those who opposed me, opposed Corwin naming me his heir. During the rebellion that followed, we discovered that Hugh O'Neill, Corwin's son, was the man who killed my grandmother, my father, and my mother. In his efforts to eliminate all opposition, he attempted to kill me, and he did kill his own son, Finnian."

Looking around, she raised her voice. "War is a terrible thing. It tears families apart. It kills and cripples young people. But we, of all people, should know that there are things worse than war. We fought the Romans. We fought the English. We fought the fascists. I know that some blame me for the war in Northern Ireland and Scotland. I did not start that war. Instead of challenging me in the Clan Council, Hugh tried to assassinate me. He did assassinate three members of the Council. He and his partisans killed thirty-four children, one hundred and twelve non-combatant women, and the brothers, sisters, husbands, wives, fathers and mothers of thousands of loyal Clan members."

Her voice fell, but her telepathic voice remained strong. "I have ordered the exile of over a thousand people who fought for Hugh O'Neill. I have ordered the mind wipe of four hundred more. But Hugh killed almost a thousand people. It is my job to protect you. I could not allow those responsible for murder to walk away. Fergus and Corwin and Seamus told me this job would be hard. It is harder than I imagined."

She looked into the eyes of those in the front row, and tried to speak directly to them, and through them to the others farther away. "Andrew O'Byrne has now rebelled. He claims to have bombed one of our factories in Wales. He promises more death. I cannot look away from that. I will protect you. I will bring Andrew to justice. I will protect Clan O'Byrne, but I won't promise it will be easy. I ask for your help, your loyalty, and your good will. In exchange, I promise you shall have mine."

She stepped down from the fountain. Rebecca stepped toward her, gave her a small smile and nodded. And then some people started clapping, then more of them, and some started cheering. The crowd closed around her, people called out welcomes and shouted encouragement. She stood in the midst of her people, shaking their hands, hugging them, a smile on her face and tears streaming down her cheeks.

Back in the room Brenna and Rebecca shared, Rebecca asked, "What about Andrew?"

"If you can find him, take him out. But Rebecca, it has to be totally clean. No collateral damage. That's not the message I want to send to the Clan. Not a one of them is worth sacrificing to kill Andrew."

"I hope he doesn't kill you," Rebecca said.

Brenna chuckled. "That's why I have a bad-ass Protector sleeping in my room."

"Oh, please," Rebecca said, rolling her eyes and going off to the bathroom to brush her teeth and get ready for bed.

A knock on the door had Brenna casting her mind out to see who it was. She admitted Morrighan, who drew her into a hug.

"How are you doing, Lady O'Byrne?" Morrighan said.

"That shit has to stop," Brenna said, drawing away from her aunt. "I'm not Lady O'Byrne. At the most, I'm Lady Brenna, but not to you. This thing is already too complicated. I'll go nuts trying to figure out whether I'm Lady O'Byrne, Lady O'Donnell or Lady O'Neill, depending on which day it is and where I am."

Morrighan laughed. "It's going to take some time for the Irish Clans to break down centuries of formality. And some people may resent it."

"I really don't think so. The older people will remember Caylin, and appreciate me not trying to take on her mantle. And as young as I am, they won't have a problem calling me Lady Brenna. The younger people will be easier."

Nodding, Morrighan said, "You may be right."

She crossed to the sideboard and poured herself a snifter of brandy. "What are you going to do about Andrew?"

"Try to find him, limit the damage," Brenna replied. "If we're careful, hopefully we can avoid another war. I'm hoping we can draw him in and trap him. Give him enough rope to hang himself."

Morrighan shrugged. "If you need someone to tie the

noose, let me know."

"Do you and your brothers hate him that much?"

"You have no idea. He's tried to kill every one of us. When Michael was three and Andrew was twelve, Andrew tried to drown him. He pushed me off a horse and tried to trample me when I was eight. But he really screwed up with Brian. Brian is the strongest of all of us. He damn near crippled Andrew when Andrew tried to bully him. If it wasn't for Father, Brian would have killed him decades ago."

"That bad, huh?"

"Worse. He's a bloody sociopath. Murderous, sadistic, and narcissistic."

"C'mon, Morrighan, don't hold back. Tell us what you really think," Brenna said with a laugh.

"What do you expect him to do?" Rebecca asked, coming back into the room.

"Andrew grew up during the Irish fight for independence," Morrighan said. "During the Troubles in the north, he joined the IRA. Father wasn't happy. I don't think Andrew did it out of a sense of patriotism. I think he just liked blowing things up, killing and maiming people."

"Wonderful," was all that Rebecca said, shooting a look at Brenna.

"You know he had people in the crowd tonight," Morrighan said.

"Devlin has doubled security at all their facilities, cancelled leaves, and put everyone on red alert," Rebecca told them.

"You mean *our* facilities, right?" Brenna said.

"Yeah, our facilities. Damn." Rebecca looked from Brenna to Morrighan and back again. "This is for keeps, huh?"

She sat down in a chair and stared off into space for a few minutes.

"Where do I fit into all this? Formally, I mean," Rebecca finally asked.

Brenna looked at Morrighan.

"Security coordinator," Morrighan promptly said. "You're dealing with security apparatus in three separate Clans, and three separate security chiefs. They'd better all be on the same page."

Brenna nodded. "Do I have to give her a raise? Or can I continue to pay her with empty promises and good will?"

Rebecca barked a laugh and Morrighan chuckled.

"How about my own private plane so I can visit my husband occasionally?" Rebecca suggested.

"Want to go see him tonight?" Brenna asked.

"Yes."

"I'll be right back," Brenna told Morrighan. "Don't stand on that rug over there by the bed."

She took her sister's arm and sent a spear thought to Carlos in Washington. Then the two women disappeared. Five minutes later, Brenna reappeared on the rug by the bed.

"It must be nice to be able to just go anywhere you want, anytime you want," Morrighan said.

Brenna pursed her mouth and said, "I used to think it would be nice to have enough money to do anything I wanted. I've discovered that when you have that much money, you can't do everything you want. Hell, sometimes I can't do anything that I want to do. It seems like everyone wants a piece of me all the time. If I could teleport around the world on my own, like a jetsetter, then I'd get excited about it. But I can't. All the security and my responsibilities get in the way. The logistics prevent it."

Morrighan nodded. “So, what now?”

“I guess I need to get into the finances and business of O’Byrne so I understand what’s going on. I’ve tried to keep up with it the past two years, but I don’t have as good an understanding of this Clan as I do of O’Donnell. Then I need to figure out how to integrate the two Irish Clans with O’Donnell. I need to put Collin and Devlin together to get the security stuff straight. And I need to figure out what to do with Andrew and Rebecca.”

~~~

The next day, she teleported to Dublin to speak with Michael O’Byrne, then to Washington and had a second breakfast with Rebecca and Carlos.

“Have you two figured out what you’re going to do?” Brenna asked them.

“I’ve been toying with the idea of shooting you,” Rebecca said, raking her hand through her hair. “But Carlos thinks there are less drastic solutions to our problem.”

Brenna and Carlos both laughed.

Rebecca’s husband, tall, broad-shouldered, dark-haired and movie-star-Latin handsome, said, “I’m resigning my position in the military. I knew this would come, and I’ve stayed on in this job because it gave me an excuse to be here in Washington.” Carlos was a general in the Ecuadorian army and his country’s military attaché at their embassy in the United States. He was also heir to the Vargas Clan in Ecuador.

“My father plans to continue as Clan Chief for another forty years. We have talked about what would happen when you and Rebecca moved to Ireland. He says it’s time I became more business oriented, so I’ll be taking over our trade office in Paris. It’s not the ideal living situation, but we’re going to get a place in London so we can meet in the middle.”
~~~

"It's less than a two hour flight from Dublin to Paris," Rebecca said. "An hour from Dublin to London and an hour from Paris to London. We'll manage."

"Rebecca, what do you want to do?" Brenna said, leaning forward and looking directly into her sister's eyes. "I know that Morrighan's idea makes some sense, but I can find someone else to coordinate security. What do you want to do?"

Rebecca leaned back in her chair, sipping her coffee and staring off into space. Silence extended for several minutes, with Brenna and Carlos also preoccupied with their own thoughts.

"You know," Rebecca said at last, "I didn't object to that because it makes sense. Not just sense in a strategic way, but in a personal way. I enjoy being a Protector. Goddess help me, but the rush, the excitement of being in Scotland, of the work I did in Russia, was something I liked."

She took Carlos's hand. "As much as I love you, I don't want to sit around knitting sweaters and keeping house. Maybe someday, but I'm young and I need to be active. I enjoy all the travel, seeing new places. I feel as though I learn something new every day."

Turning to Brenna, she said, "That sounds good. Let's go with security coordinator for now, and see what it morphs into. I'm sure that we'll figure it out over time."

"Okay," Brenna said. "I have a present for you. I know it's not enough to make up for what the two of you are doing for me, but maybe it will help."

She held out a piece of paper to Rebecca.

Rebecca's eyes about popped out of her head. "Brenna, I wasn't serious!"

"What?" Carlos asked.

"She bought us an airplane! Jesus, Brenna. You can't

do that!"

"I already did. If you're going to be coordinating security for three Clans, you're going to need to be mobile. This plane will fit the runways at all three Clans and its range will take you from Paris to West Virginia. We'll write it off as a corporate expense to O'Byrne."

They stared at her with their mouths open.

"Now, señor de Vargas, what kind of business ventures do you plan to explore in Europe? Should I have Brian O'Byrne contact you to develop an integrated strategy for taking the Continent by storm? Should I put you in contact with the Clan Chiefs in Russia? I'm sure they have a need for warm sweaters, even if your wife refuses to knit them."

~~~

Leaving Carlos in Washington, Brenna and Rebecca teleported to West Virginia, where they spent the rest of the morning closeted with Seamus and Callie. Brenna had an intimate lunch with Collin, then she and Rebecca teleported back to Ireland in time for dinner, each carrying two large suitcases full of clothes.

Seated at the head of the table, with her grandparents to her right and Rebecca and their cousin Jared to her left, Brenna felt very uncomfortable. Only family attended, but there were sixty people at the table. She had gotten to know most of them over the previous two years, but her place in the Clan had undergone a major change in the past day.

Dinner conversation was subdued, with everyone focused on their new Clan Chief. Brenna assured them that she planned no major changes in the Clan or its business operations. She also told them that she was open to recommendations or suggestions, and encouraged them to meet with her to discuss anything they might want her to hear.

The following day, she traveled to Dublin for a
~~~

business meeting with her uncles Michael and Brian and her Aunt Morrighan. They rode in two limousines, sandwiched by two vans full of Protectors in front and two behind. Brenna was amused by Rhiannon and Brian trying to avoid sitting next to each other. Being the Clan Chief had its perks, such as micromanaging minor things when the whim took her.

Brenna directed Rebecca to join Morrighan in the lead limo with Michael. Brushing past Rhiannon, actually being a bit rude, she took the seat Rhiannon had targeted and set her briefcase next to her. The only empty seat left was the one next to Brian.

The sexual tension in the back of the limo was sky high. Brenna was sure the two people sitting across from her thought they were masking their feelings, but it's almost impossible to hide attraction from a succubus. She knew from Rhiannon's memories that her cousin was madly in love with Brian, indeed had been since she was a teenager. But Brian had brushed her off once, and Rhiannon had never gotten over the humiliation. It sat like an aching tooth in the back of her mind, and seeing Brian brought out the pain.

What Brenna couldn't figure out was why, since Brian was obviously smitten with her, he'd never tried to rekindle a relationship.

As they slowed to enter a roundabout before the M11 highway near the town of Rathnew, a streak of light from the trees on their left hit the lead van and it exploded. Immediately, air shields went up around the limos and the other vans. The second lead van skidded and barely missed hitting the flaming wreckage in the road.

A fireball hit the shield around Brenna's limo, and then an explosion rocked the vehicle. The driver pulled as far to the right as he could and stopped. The two trailing vans pulled up to their left, shielding them from the attackers in the trees.

Brenna scanned the area, finding a confusion of minds and telepathic communications. She tried to filter out what she could, concentrating on the trees to their left.

Dismayed at what she found, she told Rebecca, **There are over fifty of them.**

Brenna shifted her attention to the right, where there were no trees, only grass and low bushes inside the roundabout. She sensed two minds there and, using her O'Donnell Gift, shattered their shields and captured their minds.

Rebecca, I have the only two men on the right. They're armed with automatic rifles and a bazooka.

Just hold them, Rebecca responded. **Contact Jared and tell him we've been attacked.**

Fireballs flew from the trees and the chatter of automatic rifle fire filled the air.

Brenna sent a spear thread to Jared back at the estate. He told her that help from there was at least twenty minutes away.

The limo's driver began to inch forward, then gunned the engine and shot forward, driving on the shoulder of the road. They passed the burning van and took the on ramp to the highway. Looking back, Brenna saw the other limo following them and the battle continuing behind them. The surviving lead van followed the two limos. They hit the highway, and the driver pushed the limo up to over one hundred miles an hour.

Shortly thereafter, she felt her grip on the minds of the two men she held begin to fade. With a sick feeling, she stopped their hearts and slumped back into her seat.

"Did you lose them?" Rhiannon asked.

"Yeah, but I learned what they knew," Brenna answered. She telepathically sent the information she'd gathered to Rhiannon and her sister. It included where the men thought Andrew was hiding in Dublin, and then she transmitted it all to Jared.

When they arrived at the O'Byrne headquarters in Dublin, the building and the blocks surrounding it were swarming with Protectors. Brenna and her family were hustled from an underground garage to Michael's office suite on the sixth floor. The first thing Brenna noticed was that metal shutters covered all the windows. The Protectors were taking no chances.

A man in Protector-black gave them a quick report. "We hit both places where we expected Andrew might be. Both were abandoned. We found no weapons, money or computers, but they left some of their communications equipment behind. They left food and personal effects, including clothing, so obviously they bailed out in a hurry. The warehouse where Jared told us to look had beds for about a hundred men. After we've finished sweeping it, we'll use it as a barracks for the O'Donnell personnel when they come in."

"O'Donnell personnel?" Brenna asked.

"Yes, Jared said there are several hundred O'Donnell Protectors coming in. We expect two hundred from England tonight."

"I think your grandfather is concerned about your safety," Michael said, referring to Seamus.

As the largest Clan in the western hemisphere, O'Donnell had a security force almost as large as the entire O'Byrne Clan.

"What about our operations outside Ireland?" Brenna asked. People exchanged glances, but no one answered her.

Finally, Brian said, "I have one hundred Protectors in Paris. I think there are about the same in Cardiff."

Brenna turned to Rebecca. "Double Paris, triple

Cardiff."

Rebecca nodded and pulled out her phone.

"Please alert O'Neill," Brenna said to the Protector who had briefed them. "We had intelligence that Andrew and Finnian O'Neill were in contact with each other. With Finnian dead, some of his men might be looking for someone to take them in, and they might contact Andrew. If you can coordinate with O'Neill, maybe we can avoid something falling through the cracks. I'd prefer to avoid any nasty surprises."

The man nodded and left them.

"Well, if I can get a shot of whiskey to calm my nerves, shall we get back to the reason we came here?" Brenna asked, giving Michael a shaky smile.

The group was ushered to a conference room where a bottle of Irish whiskey sat with coffee and tea on a sideboard along with finger foods. Several aides showed everyone to their seats, handed them the business documents prepared for them and served drinks and small plates of food.

~~~

Chapter 21

The only way to make sense out of change is to plunge into it, move with it, and join the dance. - Alan Watts

The next two weeks passed like a whirlwind. Along with two hundred Protectors, Fergus and Caylin moved to Grimaud, France. Before she left, Caylin informed Brenna that she was to move into the Lord's rooms, and brooked no discussion on the matter. Andrew's room and the room next to it were converted to quarters for Brenna's grandparents when they visited.

One small group of Andrew's men had been
~~~

discovered and most were either killed or captured, but otherwise things were quiet. The attack on Brenna had shocked everyone, and the outpouring of support and sympathy from those at the estate was almost overwhelming. Jared and Devlin reported that Andrew's support had dwindled, while Brenna's had increased.

Collin flew in from the States and five hundred Protectors flew in from England and Scotland. He spent a week meeting with Jared, Devlin, Rebecca, and Thomas O'Neill. Although the circumstances weren't the best, Brenna enjoyed having Collin in her bed every night.

The third night he was there, Brenna reminded him of his promise to move to Ireland with her.

"We'll have to upgrade the communications and computing infrastructure here before I can do that," he said. "It will be expensive. I'll be able to spend considerable time here, but I'll also need to be in the States a lot until all the construction and cabling are complete and the new computers are installed."

He kissed her. "It may take three years before I can be here full time. Is that okay?"

She pulled him down on top of her. "Remind me of why I want you in my bed," she said with a smile.

Brenna called Michael the following morning. "I need sixty million dollars. I don't know how much that is in euros."

"More airplanes?" Michael's voice was flat.

"Communications and computing hardware and software to upgrade O'Byrne's capabilities and integrate us with O'Donnell and O'Neill," Brenna replied. "O'Donnell will take care of their end. I need to build a world-class computing and telecommunications infrastructure. It's not just for Clan business, but for our moneymaking business interests as well. Ireland is already a software development hot spot. Collin can leverage that and turn us into a major player in the industry. It will be a three-way partnership between O'Byrne, O'Neill and O'Donnell."

"What about O'Neill?" Michael asked. "How much are they contributing?"

"Another sixty million. O'Donnell will put in four hundred million, including our own transatlantic cable."

"Goddess, Brenna. How are you going to talk Seamus and Callie into that?"

"I don't have to. We had already allocated three hundred million to put in the cable. The ROI numbers look even better with O'Neill and O'Byrne thrown into the mix."

"Where are you going to put all this new infrastructure?"

"At Wicklow. We'll upgrade Dublin, of course, but I want the main computer centers in places that are defensible. It will mean new high-paying jobs in Wicklow, as well as in Dublin. We'll have to put in facilities at Dunany also, but I'll take care of that out of my own pocket." Dunany was the estate and horse stables Brenna had inherited from her mother.

"Michael, I'd also like to find some time for you to meet with a man named Jack Calhoun. He's the president of my development and construction company in the States. I'd like to explore opportunities for expanding in Ireland. He's already doing some work for me in Dunany, and I'd like to find some property in Dublin and maybe Cork to develop."

"For a pretty little girl in fancy dresses, you certainly think like a capitalist shark," Michael said.

She sputtered into the phone, completely at a loss for something to say.

Michael laughed. "You're as fun to tease as

Morrighan," he said. "I miss the naive little sister she used to be, but I think you'll do nicely until you catch on to me."

~~~

Brenna's base of support at O'Byrne was much stronger than at O'Neill. Rhiannon was popular there, and having her as heir reassured those who didn't know Brenna. Jared Wilkins, her cousin, steward, and Callie's son, had been working at O'Byrne as her transition manager for three years. Fergus had turned over day-to-day responsibility for running the estate to him long ago. It also helped that Jared, a lawyer by training, and Michael had long known each other and were good friends. Jared was easygoing and friendly, and people liked him. Young women especially liked him.

With Jared, Rebecca and Rhiannon at O'Byrne, Brenna felt secure in turning all of her attention to the situation at O'Neill. Recovering from Hugh's rebellion was going to be a long and expensive task. They had lost enough orders for new ships that the Glasgow shipyard would run at a loss for the next few years.

Andrew's support had melted away after the bombing in Wales and the attack on Brenna's motorcade, but his adherents had made occasional raids on O'Byrne facilities and transport. With Brenna's ascension, those were stepped up. Devlin speculated that many of these raids were aimed at acquiring supplies or goods that could be sold. Andrew's personal wealth was almost nonexistent, and without a means of support, he needed some way of feeding his troops.

Rhiannon and Rebecca took a day to drive up to Dublin and visit Morrighan. She had invited them to lunch and a day of sightseeing. Even such everyday activities were overshadowed by security needs. They traveled in a convoy of heavily armed Protectors, all the vehicles surrounded by air shields. When they reached Morrighan's
~~~

apartment in an O'Byrne-owned building, the security reminded Rebecca of a foreign embassy in Washington. A hundred Protectors accompanied them to lunch, with thirty in close support.

Sitting at a table in an outside courtyard of an upscale bistro, Rhiannon said, "Is this much security really necessary? I understand that Andrew's a threat, but this is overkill."

Rebecca and Morrighan exchanged glances and shifted uneasily in their seats. Rhiannon froze, studying them through narrowed eyes.

"What am I missing?" she asked. "What's going on that you're afraid to talk about?"

"I'm not sure what you mean," Morrighan started, then stopped as she saw the hard set of Rhiannon's jaw.

Rebecca cleared her throat. "Let me try to explain," she pleaded. "There are actually three security teams here. Morrighan's, mine, and yours. So it looks a lot worse than it actually is. It won't always be this way. Once things settle down, and Andrew is taken care of, you probably won't have more than fifteen or twenty men assigned to you. Maybe thirty."

"And why would I have anyone assigned to me?" Rhiannon said.

Rebecca squared her shoulders and looked Rhiannon straight in the eye. "Because you're the heir. Because you're Corwin's granddaughter. No matter what your last name is, you're an O'Neill of O'Neill. I get a team because Seamus insists that his blood kin get protection. The same thing with Morrighan being Fergus's daughter. You may pretend that you can take care of yourself, but the potential for blackmail if someone captures you is too high."

"I knew it was a mistake getting involved with the Clans," Rhiannon said, shaking her head and reaching for her beer. "Wait! I didn't get involved with you. Brenna kidnapped me! That bitch. I'm making a list. She's going to owe me into the next life."

Rebecca chuckled. "That's the proper spirit. You know she feels guilty about it, don't you? But that won't stop her from using you the next time she needs you to do something."

The three women clicked their glasses in a silent toast.

After lunch, Morrighan said, "I need to pick up a friend at the airport. You don't mind, do you?"

They drove out to Dublin airport and parked the limo. Two Protectors disappeared into the terminal, emerging a few minutes later with a tall, dark-haired man.

"Carlos!" Rebecca screamed, scrambling out of the car and running toward him. He scooped her up in his arms and spun her around like a little girl. Setting her back on her feet, he kissed her so hard and deep and long that every woman in sight stopped and stared in envy.

They walked back to the limo, arms around each other's waists, and Rebecca introduced her husband to Rhiannon.

"Morrighan told me you were easy on the eyes," Rhiannon said. "Do you have a brother?"

"I have several brothers, señorita," he replied with a smile. "Perhaps Rebecca will bring you to meet them the next time she visits Quito." He leaned down and kissed his wife, then looked around. "This is summer? It's quite pleasant."

"Sure is. It hasn't rained all day, and since we're in the midst of a heat wave, you're in for a treat. Most of the girls at Wicklow are probably out sun bathing," Rebecca told him. Turning to her friends, she said, "Quito is on the equator, but it's so high that it rarely hits 70 degrees, and during the wet season, it rains as much as it does here."

Don't tell him about Irish winters, Rebecca sent to her friends on a spear thread. *I don't want to scare him off.*

On the way to Wicklow, Carlos asked, "Do you have time to help me find a place to live in Paris?"

"Oh, I'd love to," Rebecca said. "I'll have to check and see if Brenna needs me for anything."

"My mother lives in Paris," Rhiannon said. "If you like, I can ask her to help you."

"That would be wonderful," Carlos said.

When they reached the O'Byrne estate, Rebecca led Carlos to her room.

"Nice room," Carlos said. "A bit smaller than the one at O'Donnell."

"It was Maureen's. Shut up and kiss me."

Taking her in his arms, he kissed her long and deep. His hand tangled in her hair, pulling her head back as he kissed her throat, her ears, her eyelids. She fumbled with his belt, but stopped when he covered her mouth again, draining her thoughts away as she lost herself in the softness of his lips, the heat of his tongue fencing with hers.

He was far more adept at belts than she was. Her pants skimmed down to her ankles before she knew they were unfastened. Picking her up, he carried her to the bed and laid her down, spreading her legs. She watched him undress, then he lay between her knees and kissed her while unbuttoning her shirt.

His tongue found her breast and toyed with her nipple before sucking it into his mouth. Arching into him, she gasped as his hand slid between her legs. Urgently, she pushed against him, circling her hips as a ravening hunger rose inside her. Writhing beneath him, she grabbed his hair and pulled his mouth back to hers.

"I want you. Now!"

Chuckling, he slipped away from her. She grasped at him, but he was too quick, and as his face disappeared between her legs and his mouth settled on her, she moaned, falling back on the bed. With tongue and clever fingers, he took her to the edge of madness and then sent her over. The orgasm started between her legs and exploded in her brain, her hips bucking so hard she knocked him off the bed.

Panting for air, her body jerking from the bolts of pleasure running through it, she felt him bump against her entrance. With a single thrust he was inside her, filling her as no one ever had. His mind merged with hers, and then their souls merged. Another orgasm shot through her, and into him. They cried out together as he shared her pleasure, continuing to thrust inside her. Wrapping her legs around him, she matched his rhythm and their intertwined souls soared.

~~~

Rebecca spent a week showing Carlos around Wicklow and Dublin, then they took her new jet and flew to Paris. Rhiannon continued to pour through the library at O'Byrne seeking information on the Power-Shadow-Pathfinder trine. Frustrated because she couldn't find a book that was referenced in the card catalogue, she contacted Lord O'Byrne.

My Lord?

Yes, Rhiannon. How can I help you? he responded immediately.

I'm trying to find a book in your library, but I've looked everywhere and I swear it's not here. Where else can I look?

When she told him the names of the books she was seeking, he sent, *That's my fault. I took some of the books with me. I have it here in France.*

*Is there any chance I can talk you into sending it to
~~~

*me?**

Send me an image for a landing spot.

A few minutes later, Fergus O'Byrne appeared in the middle of the library holding several books.

"Here's the book you were looking for and a couple of others that might interest you," he said. "Suppose you tell me what you're looking for."

Rhiannon called for tea and began explaining the research she and Rebecca were conducting. He asked her some questions, and that led to her telling him about the visitations of the Goddess and what She had told Brenna, Rebecca and Rhiannon at various times.

"You girls are over thinking this," he said when she finished. "The Pathfinder is really just what it says. The one who finds the way."

"But the way to what?" Rhiannon asked.

"You said that the Goddess told Brenna and Rebecca that She doesn't know where their path will lead. If She doesn't, then why are you spending time looking through old books? Evidently, you will discover that path."

"But where do I look?"

He laughed. "I would suggest that you just lead your life, and someday you'll stumble over it."

"That doesn't sound like much of a plan."

"Do you have a better one? If you don't know where you're going, what your fates will be, then how do you find the path? Rhiannon, it's very difficult to plan for the unknown. What I do believe is that you'll recognize it when you find it."

"Whatever *it* is," Rhiannon said.

"Yes," he chuckled. "Think about it. Last year, did you even imagine the path you're currently on? The world has a way of intruding on our fantasies about how it should work.

You're the oldest. Brenna and Rebecca haven't even reached thirty yet. And you want to know where you'll be a hundred years from now?"

He placed his hand on hers. "Rhiannon, think about what you did in Russia. A year ago, if you'd asked me or Seamus, the idea that we would have two Russian Clans as our allies would have been laughable. You led an expedition into an exceptionally hostile territory and won a victory that changes the entire landscape. No one could have predicted that path."

"But I wasn't a pathfinder. I was follower. Irina found that path."

"Did she? I was told that you volunteered to go with her. Everyone was surprised at that. What was your interest? You barely knew the girl. And then she was captured. Who drove the effort that rescued her and not only overthrew the Gorbachev Clan, but also captured the Romanov Clan as an ally?"

He took her face between his hands, capturing her eyes with his. "Rhiannon, the Pathfinder doesn't have to be a visionary, that's Brenna's role. The future is nebulous. There are multiple paths to take. Your role is to choose between paths. Whether it is the best path, or the easiest path, doesn't matter. At each decision point, someone must choose a path. Once done, it's up to Brenna to choose whether to go there. If she says no, then you'll look for another until she decides to follow one. At that point, you'll be presented with new possibilities, because every path has branches. Do you understand? The Pathfinder identifies possibilities. You'll give Brenna your best advice as to those that look most promising, and those that look most dangerous."

Standing abruptly, he paced across the room. "Rhiannon, I wish I could tell you something to comfort you. The Pathfinder is always looking, never finding, because time never ends. But that doesn't mean you won't find happiness, or contentment." He whirled, fixing her with a piercing look that made her understand how he had successfully led a Clan for over a century. "Not all of those who change history understand their role. And the points where history is changed are often not seen or understood at the time. The important thing is that you do what you think is right, and leave it to Brenna to make the final choices."

"Do you think she'll always choose the right path? Where does Rebecca fit into all this?"

"It doesn't matter whether she chooses the 'right' path," he said, making air quotes with his fingers around the word 'right'. Between you and Rebecca, she won't take a 'wrong' path." Again, the air quotes. "As for Rebecca, she is there to watch Brenna's back. In her spare time, she'll watch yours. And since both you and Brenna have some deficiencies in the arena of common sense, and Rebecca has an overabundance of that commodity, I assume she'll be your anchor to reality. Probably a very outspoken and profane anchor."

~~~

Chapter 22

He who is unable to live in society, or who has no need because he is sufficient for himself, must be either a beast or a god. – Aristotle

Brenna, Collin sent, *the O'Byrne offices in Paris are under attack.*

Paris? Are you in the command center? Brenna asked.

Yes.

I'm on my way.

Thomas O'Neill met her as she entered the security
~~~

command center in the basement of the sprawling manor house. The room was half the size of a high school gymnasium, packed with computers, television monitors, screens with flashing lights and graphs, and almost fifty people monitoring it all.

"O'Byrne received a message from Paris about ten minutes ago," he said. "They contacted us and tied us into their communications."

"What do we know about it?" she asked.

"Not much," Collin said, looking up from the computer screen he was watching. "We haven't had time to start integrating the communications systems, so we're on a relay. Someone in Paris sends a message to Dublin, then it's relayed to Wicklow, and only after that do we get it."

"What about our other offices in Paris?" Brenna asked. "Has O'Neill or O'Donnell been attacked?"

"No," Collin answered. "We're in contact with both of them, and things are quiet there."

"Andrew," Brenna said. "Son of a bitch!"

Then a thought occurred to her.

"Collin, Rebecca's in Paris with Carlos."

"Haven't heard from her. Hang on. There's another transmission coming in."

He adjusted the headphones he wore and listened for a moment, then reached over and flipped a switch on the control board in front of him.

Brenna recognized Jared's voice.

"...went off in the lobby and killed several people. When the Protectors swarmed the area, another bomb went off outside. That was followed by black-clad commando types with automatic weapons and grenades. We don't know the size of the attacking force or who they are, but the attack is very open and attracting attention. French police are responding."

"IRA tactics," Brenna said. "The first bomb attracts police and medical personnel, and the second bomb delivers the major damage." Collin and Thomas nodded. "I ordered the security force there doubled to two hundred," Brenna continued.

"There are two hundred Protectors assigned there," Thomas said. "Devlin, Collin and I hold a brief conference call every morning and exchange our duty rosters and let each other know the status of any operations we're running."

"They were hit just after the evening shift change," Collin said. "There would have been about seventy Protectors on duty. The O'Donnell forces that augmented O'Byrne aren't housed there, and neither are the O'Byrne Protectors. They just don't have the facilities for that. It's a business office. We'll have almost three hundred people there within half an hour, but that doesn't help us now."

Brenna nodded and wandered away. **Rebecca, where are you?**

In Paris. I'm with Carlos. We're looking at a building he's considering buying.

The O'Byrne offices have been attacked. Go somewhere you can see a TV. I want to know what's being broadcast. O'Byrne and O'Donnell Protectors are heading to the scene, but so are the French authorities.

A "will do" somehow came through the stream of profanity that ran through Rebecca's mind.

Whatever you do, Brenna sent, **I don't want you anywhere near there. Understand me? There have been two bombings already, and we can't discount the possibility of more. Rebecca, they're using IRA tactics.**

Okay. Damn. The hotel we're staying at is only a couple of blocks from here. I'll call your cell when we get* *there. Rebecca broke the connection.

Ten minutes later, Brenna's cell rang.

"Brenna," Rebecca gasped, "the gendarmes and TV crews showed up and two more bombs went off."

"Inside or outside?" Brenna asked.

"Outside. Lots of casualties, total chaos. There was also automatic weapons fire from the building into the street. They're shooting innocent civilians. The authorities are evacuating buildings for a three hundred meter radius. Gotta go. Need to contact O'Donnell HQ here."

The phone went dead.

"What?" Collin said.

Brenna updated him and Thomas. Their profanity at the news rivaled Rebecca's earlier. Brenna's phone rang again.

"Yeah?" she answered it without looking to see who the caller was.

"Brenna," Jared said, "I detailed Protectors to secure all the family and other high-value targets, but we can't find RB."

"What do you mean you can't find her?"

"She was here a few minutes ago. As soon as she heard about the attack, she came here and then disappeared. We're searching everywhere."

"Jared, where is 'here'?"

"The security command center. She hung around for a couple of minutes, but I don't know when she left. No one's seen her and we can't find her. I had people check, and no one has taken a vehicle out of the estate. Is Teleportation one of her Gifts?"

"No, she's not a teleport. Jared, is Brian in that building in Paris?"

"As far as we know, yes. I've tried to contact him and

failed. Rhiannon told me he was there before she disappeared. I think she was talking with him when the second bomb went off."

"Shit." Brenna thought furiously. "Jared, where is Lord O'Byrne?"

"In France, as far as I know. Devlin spoke with him a few minutes ago."

"Check the library," Brenna said, "or maybe my office—Lord O'Byrne's office. Call me if you find her."

Brenna hung up and sent a spear thread to Rhiannon but was blocked. Frustrated, she tried to contact Lord O'Byrne. She found him, but he blocked her. If either of them was standing in front of her, she probably had the power to force communication, but it would be difficult.

"Have Shia contact me if you need me for anything," Brenna said, and disappeared, leaving Collin staring at the air where his lover had stood an instant before.

"Where did she go?" Thomas asked.

"If I had to venture a guess," Collin said, shaking his head, "I'd guess Paris."

~~~

Rhiannon had been in the O'Byrne library reading a typed manuscript entitled *A History of Clan O'Byrne* by Maureen O'Neill O'Byrne. Rebecca had told her Maureen had written a similar history of Clan O'Donnell.

The general alert, broadcast by Devlin, telling everyone on the estate of a security lockdown, sent her flying to the basement command center. Seeing Jared, she approached him and asked, "What's happening?"

"A bomb went off at our offices in Paris," he answered. "I'm trying to figure out what the hell's going on."

Rhiannon sent a spear thread to Brian O'Byrne.
~~~

What's going on there? Are you all right?

Someone managed to get a bomb into our lobby. I don't know any ...

Brian?

Bloody hell! Another explosion just outside. Rhi, I have to go. I'll let you know when I find out something. Brian broke the connection.

"Jared, Brian said there was a second explosion."

Jared spun from the console he was watching. "How do ... Oh, you have the Gift. A second one? Damn." He raised his voice, "Someone get me Collin Doyle at O'Neill. And get hold of the O'Donnell offices in Paris and London. There's been a second bomb."

The command center turned into a beehive of activity. Rhiannon watched them for a minute. She didn't see anything that she could help with, so she slipped out of the room, hurrying through the halls to the library. On the way, she called Lord O'Byrne.

My Lord? There's been a bombing at our offices in Paris.

Yes, I've just been informed.

I need to get to Paris. May I trouble you for a ride? She tried to keep her panic out of her transmission.

I'm not sure that's a good idea, Lord O'Byrne answered.

I'm going to Paris. If I take a plane, it might be too late. But I'm going just the same.

Where are you?

She trotted into the library and shut the door, then sent an image of the empty space in front of her. Lord Fergus O'Byrne appeared seconds later.

"Do you have a landing spot in Paris?" he asked.

"Yes, my mother's flat in Montmartre," she said,

sending another image.

"I still don't think this is wise. What do you think you'll be able to do?"

"I'm not sure. I'll figure that out when I get there. I hate to sound egotistical, but there isn't anyone in Paris who can do what I can. Do you want me to ask Brenna for a ride?"

"Oh, hell no." He took her by the elbow and the world disappeared. She blinked her eyes and looked around at her mother's familiar home.

"Do come in," her mother said. "And to what do I owe this sudden visit?"

"I need your car keys," Rhiannon said.

"So you can jump into that mess in Le Marais? Not a chance," her mother responded, waving at the television set. The O'Byrne building filled the screen. The front of the building had a gaping hole where the front doors should be, and debris filled the street. Bodies lay on the front portico and in the street. A commentator was saying that there were reports of two explosions.

The camera panned the scene, showing gendarmes, police vehicles, ambulances, and television news crews. Occasional flashes of light could be seen through the windows of the building and the sound of gunfire could be heard from inside.

An explosion, with smoke and flying debris, suddenly erupted in front of the camera and the screen went black. At least half a minute passed, and a new image appeared on the screen—a studio shot of newscasters sitting at a desk.

"It appears there has been another explosion," the man on the screen said, then paused and seemed to be listening to something the audience couldn't hear. "I'm being told there have been two additional explosions," he said. "We seem to have lost communication with our camera crew.

We'll return to this story when we have more information."

"I need the damned keys," Rhiannon said, leaping across the room and grabbing her mother's bag.

"Morwyn," Fergus said, touching her mother's arm, "I'll go with her."

"No, you won't," Rhiannon said, holding the keys up in triumph. "Your arthritis will slow me down. Besides, I might need you to give me a ride out."

She drew her mother into a hug, and then hugged Fergus. "I'll be careful. I promise."

Morwyn snorted. "If you are, it will be the first time. Fergus, give her your coat."

Nodding, he took off the black jacket he was wearing. "Protector issue," he said. "Bullet proof. It's a little heavy, but it will also help you blend in." He nodded to the window where twilight was quickly fading into darkness. A bolt of lightning split the night.

She took the coat and rushed out into the rain. It seemed like an eternity since she'd heard from Brian, but her watch showed it had only been fifteen minutes since the first report of an explosion had reached Wicklow.

~~~

Broadcasting aversion at other drivers, Rhiannon drove as fast as she could and still keep the car on the rain-slicked roads. She found a radio station broadcasting from the scene of the attack. The latter two explosions had occurred away from the building, killing dozens and wounding many more. The gendarmes and news crews had taken the brunt of the casualties.

The radio said that all buildings within three hundred meters of the O'Byrne building were being evacuated, and the authorities were keeping everyone well back of the building. Along with the second set of explosions, several gunmen inside the building had sprayed the street with
~~~

automatic weapons fire, killing and wounding even more. The reporters on the radio traded speculations as to which group of terrorists was responsible.

She parked the car on a side street and began jogging toward the O'Byrne building. It was raining steadily, and she used Aerokinesis to create an umbrella. Soon, she reached the edge of the security zone the authorities had set up. Forcing down the panic rising inside her and blurring the minds of those around her, she worked her way past the gendarmes. The streets leading toward the building were almost deserted, with occasional groups of gendarmes. Many of them were wearing tactical assault gear, and their fear hammered against her.

Le Marais is one of the oldest parts of Paris, and the O'Byrne building had originally been a noble's palace. Built in the sixteenth century and six stories high, it covered a city block. Two wide boulevards bordered it at the front and back. On one side was a narrow street, barely wide enough for a car, and on the other side an alley that carried only foot traffic.

Slipping past more pockets of heavily armed gendarmes and Protectors, she came at last within sight of the building. Helicopters clattered overhead, shining spotlights on the scene. Gunfire could be heard inside and those strange flashes of light she had seen on the television sometimes lit up the interior. The gunfire and fireballs were oddly reassuring, telling her that the attackers were still meeting resistance. She reached out with her mind and found Brian O'Byrne.

Brian? Are you all right? she sent.

Yes, he answered, **but getting tired. I'm not sure how much longer we can hold out. We're badly outnumbered.**

What's going on? How many are there?

**Andrew hit us with about three hundred men. They're*

*killing anyone they find. About forty of us are holed up on the fifth floor and we've beaten them off twice already. Got to go, Rhi. It looks as though they're coming for us again.**

He broke the connection.

She slipped around the gendarmes' perimeter until she was on the side with the small alley. Broadcasting confusion to blur people's minds, she leaped up and raced into the alley. Halfway across the boulevard, she thought she heard someone call her name, and then attempt to contact her mind. She recognized the mental signature of an O'Byrne Protector, a friend of hers, but she ignored him.

Crouching in the dark alley, she reached out for the minds of the helicopter pilots. One by one, she told all three to fly away from the building and shine their spotlights in a different direction.

Expanding her air shield so that it completely surrounded her, she used her Telekinesis to push off from the ground. Rising into the air, she looked toward the mouth of the ally. A lone Protector stood there, watching her. A flash of lightning showed his face, the twin of the man across the street who had called to her.

She saw Davin shake his head. **Take me with you.**

I can't. You'll slow me down, she replied, and saw him slump against the wall in resignation.

As she rose past the parapet, she saw several gunmen on the roof. A bolt of lightning split the air, backlighting her for Andrew's men. She reached for the lightning, drew it into her, and channeled it toward the rooftop. A second explosion of thunder joined that from the lightning itself.

Half-blind, she pushed herself onto the rooftop. Hurriedly looking around, she found the bodies of the guards. All were dead, sprawled where the lightning had blasted them.

Rhiannon cautiously opened the door to descend into

the building. Everything inside was pitch black. She felt for minds ahead of her and found a couple of hundred people in the building.

Brian,* she sent, *are all of your people on the fifth floor?

I don't know. Probably. And everything is dark. I think Andrew killed the electricity at the main switch. Rhi, I'm not going to make it out of here. They're massed for another attack and there are only twenty of us left. I need to tell you something. I love you. I've always loved you. I kept pushing you away because I didn't think Father would approve. Same stupid reason I never killed Andrew. Rhi, the next time you fall in love, don't let him be a damn fool.

Brian, I'm here. In the building. Just hold on a few more minutes.

Goddess, no! Get out of here!

Just hold on. I'll be there.

Checking her air shield, she plunged down the stairs, broadcasting Neural Disruption ahead of her. At the bottom of the first flight of stairs, she tripped over something and flew into the opposite wall. Sitting up, she created a tiny fireball. A man's body lay at the bottom of the stairs.

Maintaining her light, she worked her way down to the fifth floor. The halls were full of the bodies of both sexes, and the walls showed scorch marks and bullet holes. Twice she touched living minds ahead of her and burned them out. Gunshots rang out ahead of her. The shooting went on for some time and then there was silence again.

Brian?

There was no answer. Reaching the area of Brian's office, she found more bodies—a lot more bodies, wearing both normal office clothing and black commando gear. She had to step over them, and sometimes on them, to make her way through.

Up ahead she could see light. From the way it moved, she assumed Andrew's men had electric torches, or flashlights as Rebecca called them. Entering the reception area of Brian's office, she found piles of bodies and a dozen men passing around a bottle of whiskey. Without a second thought, she killed them all.

Peeking around the edge of the doorway into Brian's office, she saw Andrew sitting in Brian's chair with another bottle of whiskey. Six men were with him and they were all laughing. Among the bodies, Brian lay on the floor, staring at her. His upper body was drenched in blood and there was a single bullet hole in his forehead.

~~~

Chapter 23

I like the dreams of the future better than the history of the past. - Thomas Jefferson

When Brenna teleported out of the command center, she reappeared in her room. Quickly stripping out of her clothes, she put on the bulletproof corset and the Protector clothes she had worn when she confronted Hugh.

Rebecca, I need a landing spot.

No, you're not coming to Paris.

Rhiannon is in Paris and she needs backup.

She asked you for backup? Rebecca's mental voice dripped with skepticism.

Of course not. Neither would you. That doesn't mean she doesn't need it.

I'll do it.

Neither of you is a teleport. I don't plan on assaulting Andrew's forces, just pulling her out of there.

Rebecca was silent for so long that Brenna checked if the link still was active.
~~~

Rebecca?

An image of an empty stretch of floor appeared in Brenna's mind, and she immediately teleported to it.

"I'm going with you," Rebecca said.

Brenna glanced at Carlos. He stood with his eyes closed, shaking his head, an agonized expression on his face.

"I'm not sure where, or if, I'm going," Brenna said. "Rhiannon is blocking me."

"Then how do you know she's in Paris?" Rebecca asked. "And how did she supposedly get here?"

"Fergus is blocking me, too."

Teleportation is one of the extremely rare Gifts. Brenna and both of her grandfathers had it, but only a few other teleports were known to the Irish Clans.

"Do you have any contacts with the Protectors on the scene?" Brenna asked. She gestured at the TV across the room. "I'd like to get a better idea as to what's going on there."

"I've been getting updates from Edwin," Rebecca said, referring to one of her friends among the O'Byrne Protectors. "I have him on speed dial." She held up her phone.

"Can you use my Distance Communication Gift to contact him?"

"Sure," Rebecca said, taking the invitation to slide into Brenna's mind and trigger that Gift. She reached out to Edwin.

Edwin, this is Brenna, Brenna sent. **The only visuals we have are from the damn TV cameras. Can you please let me see through your eyes and scan the scene?**

Certainly, Brenna, Edwin replied. He let her into his mind and obligingly turned his head side-to-side so she could see the crowd beyond the gendarmes' perimeter, the helicopters overhead, and the building across the boulevard.

Thank you, Brenna sent.

RB is here, Edwin told her. **I saw her in the ally next to the building. Davin followed her.**

Rebecca was a bit disoriented with two people in her head. In addition, she was seeing through Edwin's eyes at the O'Byrne building, as well as with her own eyes in the hotel room. As a result, her reactions were slower than usual. When Brenna's hair turned the exact shade of burnished copper as Rhiannon's, Rebecca realized she'd been scammed.

"Brenna! Nooo!"

Brenna disappeared.

Through Edwin's eyes, Rebecca saw a redheaded woman appear in front of the O'Byrne building. A bright flash of lightning split the night and the lights trained on the building dimmed.

"Rebecca," Carlos said, grabbing her by the arm and spinning her around, "the television."

For a brief moment, the TV showed a redheaded woman floating above the building and another, almost a twin, standing in front of it. The scene on the TV screen dimmed. The woman on the ground waved to the camera, then turned and raced toward the entrance. But what the voice on the television was saying riveted Rebecca's interest.

"We don't know where the helicopters are going, but it appears as though a woman is floating above the building," the reporter on the scene said. The camera panned up and zoomed in on Rhiannon floating in the air.

Through Edwin's eyes, a bolt of lightning lit the whole scene brighter than day. On the TV, with the camera pointing straight at the lightning, it was so bright that nothing but white registered. Then a second lightning bolt struck, hitting the roof. All the lights in the building went out.

Both through Edwin's eyes and the TV camera, the two women disappeared.

~~~

Brenna landed a bit roughly, stumbling over the rubble from the explosions. Righting herself, she looked back at where Edwin was standing and waved. She drew electricity from the surrounding area into her, seeing the lights trained on her dim. Then she sprinted for the entrance to the building.

A crash of thunder caused her involuntarily to look up. Rhiannon was silhouetted against the sky. A bolt of lightning leapt from her hand toward the building, and another deafening explosion of thunder echoed amongst the buildings. All the lights in the O'Byrne building went out.

Locking down her mental shields to the point she was practically invisible and covering herself with an air shield, she cautiously peered inside. It was totally dark. Sending her mind ahead, she felt her way toward a stairwell and started climbing.

She could feel other minds throughout the building, but the largest concentration was on one of the upper floors. Casting her mind ahead, she could tell the lights going out had caused a lot of confusion.

"Halt! Who are you?" a tall man said, shining his flashlight in Brenna's face.

"Your worst nightmare, asshole," Brenna responded, smashing his shields and those of the three men with him, and capturing their minds. None of them was very bright, but they had the layout of the building memorized and knew where the current fighting was. She drained their life
~~~

energy, stopped their hearts, and then picked her way past their bodies.

She encountered more men in the halls as she worked her way through the building and dealt with them the same way. Reaching the fourth floor, she felt the last of the O'Byrne defenders die. Leaning back against the wall, she took several deep breaths. The pain she felt made her want to just sit down and cry.

Shaking off her emotions, she pushed on, reaching the executive suites. Only one mind remained in front of her, so she lit a flame on her palm and held it ahead of her.

Rhiannon sat on the floor of Brian's office, cradling him in her lap and sobbing as if her heart would never mend. They were both drenched in blood, but his torn body gave Brenna hope that all the blood was his. His blank stare told her he was dead. Looking around, she saw a couple of dozen bodies. Andrew sat in the chair behind the desk with a single hole in the middle of his forehead.

Squatting next to Rhiannon, Brenna reached out with her Healing Gift and touched her cousin's face, reading her body. Rhiannon wasn't physically injured, but the emotional pain that flooded through the link sat Brenna back on her heels. Sudden tears sprang to her eyes and ran down her cheeks.

As gently as she could, Brenna entered Rhiannon's mind and laid a mild Comfort on her. The gut-wrenching sobbing slowed, and Rhiannon turned a tear-stained face toward her.

"He loved me, Brenna. He told me at the last. Goddess, it hurts so bad. It hurts so damned bad."

"We have to go, Rhiannon. We can't stay here," Brenna said.

She had to repeat herself before Rhiannon seemed to hear her. "Rhiannon, we have to get out of here. There are a hundred of Andrew's men still in the building, and the police are getting ready to storm the place."

"We can't leave him here," Rhiannon said. "We have to take him with us."

Brenna nodded. "Can you wrap him in an air shield and bring him? I can if you want me to."

Rhiannon shook her head. "I can do it."

"We have to hurry," Brenna said, rising to her feet and tugging on Rhiannon's arm.

Rhiannon still had Brian in her lap, her arms wrapped around him. Brenna reached out with Telekinesis and floated his body enough for Rhiannon to stand.

Rhiannon staggered, and Brenna fed her some of the energy she had drained from Andrew's men. Wrapping Brian's body in an air shield, Rhiannon lifted it with her Telekinesis. Brenna picked up two of the flashlights and the two women ventured out into the halls.

Can't we just teleport out? Rhiannon asked.

We can't leave the building the way it is. We can't let any of Andrew's men fall into the hands of the authorities, Brenna answered. **You know they won't go easy. They'll fight and there will be more casualties. Besides, this is my mess. I need to clean it up.**

So where are we going?

To the basement.

When they reached the third floor landing, a group of Andrew's men opened the door on the floor below them and started up the stairs. Brenna released the electrical energy she had been holding and followed it with a fireball. Bullets from a burst of automatic weapons fire rattled against the stairs beneath their feet, and she dropped another fireball. Screams of pain and horror echoed up to them.

Into the hall, Rhiannon sent. **We'll use different stairs.**

Brenna pushed the door open and let Rhiannon go past her, pulling her grisly burden behind her. Brenna loosed another fireball down the stairs and followed.

It seemed to take a long time to reach the basement, cautiously threading their way through the dark and trying to avoid the bodies they found on every floor. They came out into a large room near the front of the building.

"Now what?" Rhiannon asked.

"Do you think we can flood the building with Neural Disruption and keep it all in the building?" Brenna asked. Rhiannon was twelve years older and had more experience in using her Gifts.

"The whole building?"

"Yes. The floors won't stop it. I'm just worried about it bleeding out the walls and harming innocents."

Rhiannon thought for a moment.

"If we stand opposite each other at the outer walls," she said slowly, "and aim straight up, then gradually shift our aim toward the center, we should be able to cover the whole building. There shouldn't be any bleed out behind us."

Brenna nodded. "Sounds good to me." She handed Rhiannon a flashlight and headed down a hallway toward the other end of the basement.

I've reached the back wall, Brenna sent.

Okay. Just be sure of where you're aiming, Rhiannon answered. **It's better to be too narrow. If we miss anyone, we'll know it and we can do a second sweep.**

I've never killed this many people at once, Brenna said. **I won't even see their faces.**

Just think of the people they've killed tonight,

Rhiannon sent. **There are no innocents here, only cold-blooded murderers.* *

Brenna raised her hands into the air and prepared to trigger her Gift. Then a thought struck her.

Wait! Are there any helicopters above us?

Both women probed with their minds, seeking minds above the building.

No. No one is above the building. Now! Rhiannon sent.

Brenna discharged a full-strength stream of Neural Disruption and then slowly swept her hands forward until they pointed at the center of the ceiling.

Hold! Rhiannon sent. Both of them probed the building, but it was silent of any mental activity.

Brenna trotted back to where Rhiannon stood.

"Now what?" Rhiannon asked.

"We set the building on fire," Brenna answered, sending a sheet of flame at the ceiling. The walls were stone, but the floors were wood. She was pretty sure that setting the first floor ablaze would ignite the floors above.

Rhiannon added her own steady stream of flame, and the beams above them began to burn.

"Rhiannon, you need to dissolve the air shield," Brenna said, gesturing toward Brian.

"Why?"

"Because I need to touch both of you to transport us. If he's separated from me, I'll leave him behind."

Rhiannon lowered Brian's body to the floor and knelt by him. Tears began running down her cheeks again.

"I murdered Andrew," Rhiannon whispered. "I pinned him to the chair using Telekinesis, then I smashed his shields and captured his mind. I felt his terror as I pressed the pistol to his forehead and I enjoyed it. Goddess help me, I reveled in it."

Jared? Brenna sent.

Brenna! Where are you?

Is there anyone in my room? In Lord O'Byrne's room?

No.

Then look for me there.

Brenna knelt and put her hand on Brian's leg. Taking hold of Rhiannon's thigh with her other hand, she teleported.

~~~

Rebecca pelted out of the hotel room with Carlos hot on her heels. Two blocks to the Metro and then waiting for the next train strained her patience to the limit. When a train finally came, she climbed onto the first car and took control of the operator's mind. The train pulled out of the station and then raced through the next three stops without slowing. Carlos watched as passengers became increasingly anxious. After a while, he decided he needed to do something and used Empathic Projection to broadcast a calming feeling over the people in their car.

When they reached the station where they had to transfer trains, they sprinted to the platform they needed, blurring everyone's minds to their presence. Rebecca repeated her performance on the next driver.

Emerging from the Arts et Metiers station, they ran until they encountered streets blocked by gendarmes, ambulances and television news crews. It took them some time after that to reach the O'Byrne offices and find Edwin.

What's going on? Rebecca sent.

There was a lot of gunfire right after RB and her clone entered the building, but we haven't heard anything for the last five minutes, Edwin replied. **Your range is*
~~~

*better than mine. Can you contact anyone in there?**

Rebecca reached out with her mind, searching for the spark of living minds in the building. She found over a hundred men but only two women. She breathed a sigh of relief as she recognized them.

Edwin turned to her. "The gendarmes are getting ready to storm the building. I wonder if I can find a uniform that fits."

Looking up at his six-feet-seven-inch height, Rebecca doubted it.

Brenna, what's going on? Are you okay? she sent.

I'm a little busy right now, Brenna answered.

What are you doing?

Setting up a mass execution.

The gendarmes are getting ready to storm the building, Rebecca sent.

Have the Protectors influence them to wait fifteen minutes. Brenna broke the connection.

Rebecca looked at her watch. It was a little more than an hour since the first bomb had gone off.

"We need to give RB and Brenna time. Can we influence the gendarmes to wait fifteen minutes?"

Edwin nodded. "Taken care of." He gestured toward the gendarme command post fifty feet away.

"Casualties?" she asked Edwin.

"One hundred forty-two dead, thirteen wounded," he answered. "The norms took some casualties, too. Thirty-two dead and over a hundred wounded. That's assuming all of our people in the building are dead."

She shot him a look. "Why are you assuming that?"

"Because the last communication I received from Brian was that they were losing. Then he cut off and I can't reach him."

Edwin's face was stony, but the emotions pouring from him were so painful that Rebecca wanted to break into tears.

"You and Brian are close?" she asked.

"He was my half-brother. I felt him die. If RB doesn't kill Andrew, Davin and I will."

They waited. Twice they heard gunfire inside the building, and once a ball of fire shot down a hallway, lighting each of the windows facing them on the second floor as it passed.

And then a wave of psychic energy rolled out of the building, stunning every telepath within a half mile. Even the normal humans in the area seemed disoriented.

"Holy shit!" Rebecca exclaimed.

"What was that?" Carlos asked of no one in particular.

"Neural Disruption," Rebecca answered. Everyone turned to look at her. "That's the same kind of psychic backlash I felt when RB cut loose in Scotland," she explained. "Only this was a hell of a lot stronger."

"Brenna wasn't with her in Scotland," Carlos said.

Rebecca sent her mind into the building, searching. "There're only two minds left in there. Brenna and RB. Goddess, they killed them all."

A couple of minutes later, she pronounced, "They're gone. The building's empty."

"Where did they go?" Edwin asked.

"I have no idea. If Andrew wasn't inside, then I think he'll get a couple of unexpected visitors. If not, I have no idea. They could be anywhere in the world."

"Is that smoke?" Carlos asked, pointing at the open front doors. As they watched, the smoke became thicker, and then suddenly boiled out into the street. A red glow could be seen inside the building.

"Containment," Rebecca said. "Edwin, we need to delay the gendarmes more. And have your men delay any fire trucks that show up. Brenna's destroying the evidence. They set the building on fire before they teleported out."

They stood long into the night watching the building burn. By the morning, only the stone shell remained.

~~~

Chapter 24

And ever has it been known that love knows not its own depth until the hour of separation. - Khalil Gibran

Rhiannon constructed a burial mound such as the ancient clans used to bury their chieftains. A bronze plaque listing the dead of what was already being called the "Battle of Le Marais" was fixed next to the mound. Brian had been well liked, and almost every family in the O'Byrne Clan had been touched in some way by the losses. Lord and Lady O'Byrne and Brian's mother were devastated. Morrighan conducted the funeral ceremony, and afterward Brenna made a short speech.

The mood was somber for days, but eventually, as people went about their daily business, a feeling of normality began to return.

For Brenna, Rebecca and Rhiannon, the demands of cleaning up the dislocations at O'Neill and O'Byrne occupied their attentions. Brenna sent Rhiannon back to Russia. She would work on helping Irina and Galina consolidate their seats. Rebecca worked with Devlin and Thomas to integrate the command structures of the Protectors.

Brenna and Michael O'Byrne worked with Jeremy to integrate the O'Neill and O'Byrne accounting and financial systems.

Nigel Richardson, director of O'Donnell's European
~~~

regional office in London, took the lead in the containment and public relations efforts to downplay the battles in Scotland and Paris and the bombing in Wales. Every effort was made to sweep the incidents under the rug. With constant pressure on the police and news media, the wars faded from memory as new crises and stories arose around the world.

~~~

Standing with Collin's arm around her shoulders on top of a hill overlooking Dunany, the Irish Sea glistening in the sunlight in the distance, Brenna surveyed the area she had chosen for her headquarters. Her mother's horse farm, the original holdings she had inherited, lay before her to her left. It was much the way she had originally seen it, but the expansion of her mother's 'country cottage' currently underway would triple the size of the dwelling.

Closer to them, to the south of the farm, a massive project was underway. Three commercial office buildings in various stages of construction were there, with workmen and heavy machinery bustling about. The complex would hold the communication and computing center for all three Irish Clans. The original thirty acres of the estate had been supplemented by purchasing as much of the surrounding land as she could, adding another seven hundred acres. Negotiations to add even more were in progress.

Brenna had called a 'council of consolidation', or alternately 'a plan for the 21st century'. The Clan councils hadn't been invited. This was a high-level brainstorming session for those at the very top of the Clan structures. Her intention was for everyone to get to know each other, share their ideas, their plans, and their dreams.

Irina, Rhiannon, Jill and Galina had teleported in from Russia. Morrighan and Michael from O'Byrne were there, and Seamus and Callie had come in from the States, bringing Cindy and baby Samantha. Along with Collin,
~~~

Rebecca, and Carlos, they had met for two days already. Today, the group rode horses into the hills west of Dunany for a picnic.

"It's incredible to consider that we're talking about mapping a path for the next two hundred years," Brenna said. "A few years ago, I couldn't conceive of thinking that far ahead."

"Realizing that you'll live that long sort of changes your perspective, doesn't it?" Collin said with a grin.

"Yes. Realizing that you have this kind of responsibility does, too."

She looked back at her friends and her fellow Clan Chiefs, a few yards away, sitting on blankets or on some of the large rocks that dotted the hillside. Eating, drinking wine, chatting and laughing, they appeared to be a group of mostly young people out for a lark.

"Hey, you two," Rhiannon called. "Are you being anti-social? No going off on your own to play kissy-face when the rest of us are flying solo. I already had to tell Rebecca and Carlos to be more discreet about their public displays of affection."

Brenna turned with a smile and responded, "Rhi, you are turning into such a sour old lady. You need to get laid more."

Pulling Collin with her, she began walking the few yards back to the gathering. "How's that handsome man from O'Neill doing? Have you finally succumbed to his charms?"

Jill and Irina laughed. "She keeps insisting that they're just friends," Irina said. "It's an interesting relationship. He follows her around with big cow eyes, and she abuses him. Eventually, they get in a fight, he loses, then mopes around while she abuses him some more. Then when his back is turned, she stares at his ass and licks her lips. I think she gets some kind of perverted pleasure out of self-denial."

Rhiannon blushed scarlet. "That's not true," she protested. "He really is the most infuriating man I've ever met. Why would I want to get involved with him? All we ever do is fight."

"That's a good start," Morrighan said with a grin. "Making up can be so much fun. And if you fight a lot, that's a whole lot of opportunities to make up."

"My intelligence sources have included some pretty juicy gossip in some of their reports," Collin said. "Since Brenna has said our intelligence should be shared among all of our allied Clan Chiefs, would you like to hear the latest?"

The following silence, with every eye turned expectantly toward him, caused his grin to grow.

"I had a report out of Helsinki that a certain red-headed operative held extensive consultations with the O'Neill regional director at his home there. The consultations are reported to have taken almost three days, during which neither of them left the premises." He shrugged. "Not particularly noteworthy, except that he lives in a one-bedroom flat."

"You son of a bitch!" Rhiannon cried. "That's not fair!"

The group greeted this with gales of laughter.

"I also heard a rumor," he said, "that the Clan Chief in St. Petersburg was keeping company with an O'Donnell Protector, and that the relationship wasn't entirely professional. Galina, please, dispel that rumor. I would hate to think that the Russian ice queen was melting."

Galina turned a beaming smile on him. "I can neither confirm nor deny such a report. Russian inscrutability prevents me from commenting on unfounded rumors."

When everyone again laughed, Galina simply winked

at them.

"I've also heard that the Moscow Clan Chief is being particularly selfish with her favors," Rebecca said. "It truly is a scandal when a succubus starts acting monogamously. I'm sure it's simply slanderous gossip, but I fear her reputation is in serious jeopardy."

Laughing gaily, Irina said, "Sometimes a pretty boy can turn my head for a month or two. Give it some time. If I bring him to the Solstice Ball, then you can tease me."

"As long as we're sharing salacious rumors," Rhiannon said. "During my side trip to O'Byrne earlier this week, I stumbled across evidence of a succubus deliberately planning a pregnancy that will produce an s-gene carrier. In fact, the evidence is fairly strong that she's already pregnant."

Everyone turned to look at Morrighan. Her daughter had recently turned two. She had never revealed the father of her baby succubus, but Rhiannon and Rebecca were fairly sure she was in love with the team leader of her security team.

"Guilty as charged," she said with a smile. "Peter and I are going to have a baby, a boy. I'm about two months along."

"Is Peter a carrier?" Collin asked.

"Is that an attempt to identify Seana's father?" Morrighan asked in return. "For the last time, I'm standing by my story that I was visited in my dreams by an incubus. The dastardly creature impregnated me and abandoned me, a poor, despoiled woman, left alone in the world to raise her wee bairne by herself. Fortunately for me, Peter has taken great pity on me, and vowed to raise the little bastard as if she were his own." Batting her eyelashes, she grinned at Collin as if daring him to dispute her. "However, with my Lady Brenna's vow that a child's legitimacy shall be decided only by her matrilineal inheritance, I guess she's not a bastard after all, is she?"

"Nor you, or Rhiannon, or Rebecca," Brenna said. "Goddess, what a load of patriarchal crap. Half the damned so-called legitimate children probably couldn't pass a paternity test. At least we can prove whether a baby came out of a woman's womb."

That evening after dinner, the group sat in the living room of the cottage, some sipping cordials, and others coffee or tea. Seamus cleared his throat, and everyone turned to him.

"As much as I'm enjoying the pleasant company, there is something about this get-together that bothers me," he said. "It seems as though there's an undercurrent, an understanding or agreement that I haven't been informed of."

"I'm not sure what you mean," Brenna said. "I called the meeting to discuss our plans for the future. How we should set goals and coordinate our efforts going forward. There has been a lot of change over the past year."

"Yes," Seamus said, "but in my experience, and looking back through my inherited memories, there are aspects of this meeting that are unprecedented. Corwin and Fergus and I were always fairly good friends, but we never got together for a meeting like this without a small army of advisors hanging off our coattails. Here we have the leaders of five Clans, six if we include Carlos as heir to Vargas, and none of the Clan councils know about it."

Several people shifted uncomfortably in their seats, and numerous glances were exchanged.

"I think I can explain," Irina said. "I may be Gorbachev Clan Chief, but I swore fealty to O'Donnell years ago, and I have no intention of renouncing that fealty."

Seamus eyebrows rose in surprise.

"Brenna will be uniting the Irish Clans," Irina continued. "Galina and I have signed a pact, and it's a lot more than simply a contract, to unite our two Clans. In practice, if not yet formally, she plans to also swear fealty to O'Donnell."

Now Seamus sat up straight in his chair. Carefully setting his coffee on the table, he looked at Galina. "Is this true?"

She nodded. "Yes. I have to consolidate my control, and then Irina and I must successfully merge our Clans. But once that is done, I shall formally follow her lead and swear to O'Donnell. I don't know how long that will take, possibly decades. But the world is a far more dangerous place than it's ever been. The Clans can't continue to pretend we're still in a fragmented feudal world. For all of our survival, we must unite. And there is only one person all of us feel has the strength to lead us."

"Yes, there is only one logical person who can unite us and hold us together," Carlos quietly said. "I have discussed some of these issues with Michel de la Tour. We are friends, and since I moved to Paris, our friendship has strengthened. We have a lot in common. We had dinner with Karl Lindstrom one evening, and he seems to be thinking along the same lines."

"We don't agree with CBW's philosophy," Rebecca said, "but we can't deny that humans are dangerous. Without guidance, they could destroy themselves, and take us down with them. They're destroying the environment and continuing a state of constant warfare among themselves. You would think they would have gained some wisdom, but with all their technological advances and modern communication capabilities, they steadfastly continue to ignore the lessons of history."

Brenna said, "We can't continue to keep a hands-off stance toward human affairs. In two countries, we have the ability to influence the path of governments far more than we have in the past." She motioned toward Morrighan. "She would make a fine Irish President. Galina and Irina can move toward taking over the Russian government within the next two decades. Vargas has almost full control of Ecuador. Some of the lessons they've learned should help us."

Smiling at Cindy, Brenna continued, "We've decided that Cindy, Maggie, and Karen need to map out how to create a stronger presence in determining the direction of the U.S. government. Those fools in Washington may be the most dangerous madmen on the planet. We have the capabilities to covertly steer what humans do. We don't have to enslave them, or try to rule them, in order to establish some degree of rational thought among them. It's not a matter of power, but of survival."

"But we have to ensure we have an organized, coherent plan of action," Rhiannon said. "We have to agree on our goals and our methods. We have to have a firm understanding, not just a vague idea, of what we're doing and how we're doing it. That means everyone needs to agree as to who is in charge. And we need to agree as to the breadth and scope of her mandate, as well as its limits. We've been talking in generalities for a while. This meeting is to get everyone in the same room so that we all have our say, and everyone hears the same things."

She smiled fondly at Brenna. "Something I have come to understand, quite forcefully, is just how strong of a tendency toward being a tyrant she has. All of you know how headstrong she is, how stubborn. But at most, you can only read her mind, and see how her personality manifests. To truly understand another person's personality, to understand how they feel and see the world, you have to share their mind. And just as only she truly knows both the fragile, whimpering insecurity, and the overwhelming, indestructible arrogance—those are her words, not mine—that are the foundation of Rhiannon, only I know how much of a tyrannical, self-righteous bitch she really is. Just as only I know exactly how deeply the need to nurture and comfort and protect guides everything she does."

Standing, Rhiannon walked over to Brenna and sat on the arm of her chair. Throwing her arm around her cousin, she said, "But she's *our* self-righteous, tyrannical bitch, and we love her."

"So, you're planning on taking over the world, turning it into a matriarchy, and making Brenna queen?" Seamus said.

"That's a fairly good summation," Jill said.

"Any objections, Father?" Callie asked.

"Hell no," he said. "Count me in. Brenna, where's your Middleton's? You've been pinching my booze for years. Now that you have your own house, it's my turn."

###

If you enjoyed ***Succubus Ascendant***, we hope you'll take a few moments to leave a brief review on the site where you purchased your copy to share your experience with other readers. Potential readers depend on comments from people like you to help guide their purchasing decisions. Thank you for your time!

This is the final book in the story of Brenna and Rebecca O'Donnell. There may be other books set in this world, but none are planned at the current time.

Also look for ***Broken Dolls,*** a paranormal mystery/thriller with RB Kendrick, Private Investigator, set in the world of the Telepathic Clans.

~~~
~~~

The Telepathic Gifts

(Rare Gift)*

(# Part of Succubus Complex)

Gift: Telepathy

Common label: Telepathy

Read minds, project thoughts into the minds of others, shield their thoughts from others - telepaths have additional awareness and ability to understand their own minds and bodies and the minds and bodies of others. Telepaths can, for example, detect and eliminate pathogens, poisons, and other foreign substances in their own bodies. An example is the ability to detoxify alcohol. Telepaths mature and age very slowly. Average physical maturity occurs in the early 20s, but mental development isn't complete until the mid-30s. Complete development and command of their Talents is not complete until then. Natural life expectancy is 160 - 220 years. Mental acuity and Talent don't begin to decline until the person is in their last 10 - 15 years of life.

~~~

Gift: Charisma #

Common label: Charisma

Influence others, project an impression of a person so that others' perceptions of the person are enhanced. A very short-range projection, i.e. "wrapping" oneself in Charisma, can simulate the Succubus talent of Glamour. Part of the Succubus complex.

~~~

Gift: Empathy #

Common label: Empathy

Feel the emotions of others. The person with the

Talent can feel other people's anger, joy, fear, hope, anxiety, etc.

~~~

Gift: Bernard #

Common Label: Empathic Projection

Project emotions into the minds of others. Change the way people feel and manipulate their emotions.

~~~

*GIFT: O'Donnell **

COMMON LABEL: Domination (Strong dominance)

Ability to penetrate or destroy another telepath's shields and take control of their mind. This is a rare and extremely powerful talent. It cannot be blocked.

~~~

*GIFT: O'Neill **

COMMON LABEL: Super shielding

A complex talent that provides the telepath with stronger, deeper shields, with 17 shield levels in the mind rather than the normal 9. Shields can be extended to others, even without physical contact. Shields can be projected onto others without their permission, blocking them from using their talents. Shields can be so strong that the telepath can mask their telepathy from other telepaths, and can even become invisible to others - telepaths and norms. A defense against any mental attack except the talent of Domination. The only complete defense against Neural Disruption.

~~~

*GIFT: De la Tour **

COMMON LABEL: Telekinesis

Manipulation of physical objects, including animate objects.

~~~

*GIFT: Murphy **

COMMON LABEL: Teleportation

Instantaneous relocation of an object or person. Usually only the person with the talent is relocated, but some talents can take another person or object with them, and some can relocate other objects or persons.

~~~

GIFT: Kilpatrick

COMMON LABEL: Power Shielding/Shield Projection

Stronger than normal shielding with the ability to extend their shields to others with whom they have physical contact (the attributes of this Gift are part of those in the O'Neill Gift). May deflect or diminish an attack by Neural Disruption.

~~~

GIFT: Christopoulos

COMMON LABEL: Aerokinesis/Air Shielding

Manipulation of air molecules - an air shield will harden air into a transparent, solid shield that will block a physical object, such as a bullet or car. This is the only talent that can block attacks of Electrokinesis, Ogonekinesis, Pyrokinesis, and Cryokinesis. Diminishes and deflects Neural Disruption.

~~~

GIFT: O'Byrne

COMMON LABEL: Dominance (weak domination)

Ability to penetrate another telepath's shields and take control of their mind. This Gift is not as strong nor does it have the range and power of the O'Donnell Gift, and cannot penetrate the shields of one with the O'Neill Gift (the attributes of this Gift are part of those in the

O'Donnell Gift).

~~~

GIFT: Lindstrom

COMMON LABEL: Construction

Construction of mental constructs inside the mind of a person that create a strong illusion that the person is a different person, masking the underlying real personality, memories, etc. The person carrying the construct may or may not be aware of the overlying construct. Compulsions and other kinds of control can be built in if desired.

~~~

GIFT: Shamun

COMMON LABEL: Precognition/Clairvoyance

Awareness of an event prior to it happening - may range from a "feeling" to clear "visions" of the event - may occur immediately prior to the event, days to weeks prior, or in some it manifests as visions of far-future events.

~~~

GIFT: Lubomudrov

COMMON LABEL: Postcognition/Psychometry

Perceive information about events that have already occurred. Psychometry: is another form of postcognition. It enables a person to envision information about events that have already occurred by being in close contact with the area or object where the event took place.

~~~

GIFT: de Filippo

COMMON LABEL: Magnetokinesis

Manipulation of magnetic fields. An adept can erase a computer hard drive by removing it's magnetic charge or cause complex machinery, such as a car engine, a pistol or a lock, to freeze by magnetizing the parts so they can't move. By putting a super magnetic charge on a piece of metal could cause it to attract other objects.

~~~

GIFT: Sivakumar

COMMON LABEL: Pyrokinesis

Manipulation of fire, including starting fires, shielding from fire, and hurling fire.

~~~

GIFT: van Serooskerken

COMMON LABEL: Cryokinesis

Can manipulate the temperature of an object or person to immediately drop to -20C. When applied to a person can put them into immediate hypothermic shock. Can condense moisture from the air or other source into ice. Can thaw frozen objects within seconds. A person with the Gift can regulate the temperature of their immediate environment (several inches) to allow them to be cool in hot weather or warm in cold weather.

~~~

GIFT: Hakizimana

COMMON LABEL: Healing/Biokinesis

Healing and manipulation of a body to cure injury or disease. The method used is similar to micro-telekinesis, moving pieces of broken bones or sealing blood vessels, then using energy infusion to accelerate the bodies own healing mechanisms.

~~~

GIFT: Jalair

COMMON LABEL: Animal Telepathy

Telepathic communication with animals - this is more of an empathy-influence communication. An adept can usually feel the "thoughts" of primitive creatures, such as reptiles, fish or insects, but can truly communicate only with mammals.

~~~

GIFT: Krasevec

COMMON LABEL: Distance Communication

Telepathic communication over long distances - often hundreds of miles. This can't be blocked by physical means but strong electro-magnetic fields may interfere.

~~~

GIFT: Soul Reading or Truth Saying

The ability to see auras, essentially reflections of people's souls. Part of this Gift enables the adept to see what Gifts a telepath has. This is a late developing Gift, and as the telepath matures, evolves into the ability to determine if someone is telling the truth.

~~~

GIFT: Matter Merge

The ability of a person to change the speed with which the molecules in his/her body resonate to match that of a different form of matter. By matching resonance with a solid object, the telepath can move through the object.

~~~

GIFT: Soul Thief

Ability to take a soul from a person's body and implant it in another body. The adept can also use another telepath's Gifts and use any of the normal Talents that a telepath can use on themselves on others, such as pathogen scans.

~~~

GIFT: Rivera #

COMMON LABEL: Neural Disruption

Neural energy from the wielder is projected into the neural network of a victim, disrupting their neural network. Depending on the strength of the projection, can be used to shock/stun a victim, or can burn out the neural synapses,
~~~

causing permanent damage. At its most extreme completely burns out the mind of the victim. A weak talent must be in physical contact with the victim. A strong talent can strike several victims at once, and at a considerable distance. This type of attack cannot be blocked by mental shields except by one having the Super Shielding talent. It can be deflected or diminished by one with the Power Shielding talent. Without strong focus and direction, everyone in the vicinity of the wielder is at risk.

~~~

GIFT: Simsek #

COMMON LABEL: Electrokinesis

Channeling of electrical energy. The wielder can drain electrical circuits, store the electricity in their own neural network temporarily, and discharge the energy into another object or the air. Care must be taken by the wielder as too much electricity, such as trying to channel a lightning strike, may overload the wielder's own neural circuits. As a weapon, the channeler may be able to discharge the energy for a considerable range, both distance and breadth. Without strong focus and direction, everyone in the vicinity of the wielder is at risk. As a weapon cannot be blocked by mental shields.

~~~

GIFT: Petrescu #

COMMON LABEL: Orgonekinesis (life energy)

Projection of life energy into another person or animal. A person possessing the Talent always also possesses Energy Draining. Depending on the strength used by the wielder, this can be used to restore a person's life energy after being drained or wounded, or as a weapon. This type of attack cannot be blocked by mental shields except by one having the Super Shielding talent. It can be deflected or diminished by one with the Power

Shielding talent.

~~~

GIFT: Farooqui #

COMMON LABEL: Energy Draining (human or animal)

Drain a person's life energy from them. Similar to the drain a Succubus effects during sex. A weak talent must be in contact with a victim. A strong talent can drain several victims at once at a considerable distance. This type of attack cannot be blocked by mental shields except by one having the Super Shielding talent. It can be deflected or diminished by one with the Power Shielding talent.

~~~

GIFT: Kashani #

COMMON LABEL: Druid or Succubus

Found only in women (X-linked trait). The Druid Gift includes both mental Talents and physiological attributes. The genitalia have several internal and external differences from normal female genitalia. Specialized glands in the groin, breasts, underarms, and throat contain strong sexual pheromone attractants and the release of these chemicals as an invisible aerosol is under the wielder's control. Spectacular physical beauty is also considered part of the manifestation of this Gift. Other attributes include specialized modifications of Charisma (Glamour or the Glam), Empathic Projection (Influence) and Energy Draining (the Drain).

When a Druid has sex with a man, his climax causes an automatic reaction in the Druid, she drains his life energy by about 75%, which puts him into an immediate stupor until his energy levels can recharge. This cannot be blocked by mental shielding. Evidence exists that this is at least partially enhanced by a reaction to

chemicals in the man's semen, as wearing a condom cuts the energy drain to about 60%.

Notes on Kashani (Druid) Gift: Limited evidence indicates that certain other Talents are strongly tied to the Succubus gene, indicating an interrelated gene complex - full Neural disruption, Empathic Projection, Electrokinesis, Orgonekinesis, and Energy Draining have been found in all Druids tested. It also has been found that carriers of the S-gene, both men and women, manifest the same Gift/Talent complex as full Succubi, with the exception of the Succubus Gift.

Made in the USA
Coppell, TX
10 November 2019